RIVAL DESIRES

THE SCOTTISH BILLIONAIRES

M. S. PARKER

BELMONTE PUBLISHING, LLC

This book is a work of fiction. The names, characters, places and incidents are products of the writer's imagination or have been used fictitiously and are not to be construed as real. Any resemblance to persons, living or dead, actual events, locales or organizations is entirely coincidental. V1

Copyright © 2024 Belmonte Publishing LLC

Published by Belmonte Publishing LLC

ONE

Cory

"Another glass of champagne, sir?" the waiter asked, holding out a silver tray crowded with crystal flutes bubbling over with golden liquid.

"Don't mind if I do," I said, plucking one of the slender glasses from the tray.

"Cheers to overpriced booze and overdressed bar flies," I told my stepcousin and business partner, Fury, as I tipped my glass toward him.

His wolfish grin was visible even behind the black and gold masquerade mask covering half his face as he let out a barking laugh, the sound drowned out by the steady thump of club music dominating the ballroom.

"I'll definitely drink to that, cuz," he said. "Especially the bar fly part. Have you seen some of the hotties in this place tonight or what?"

He wasn't wrong. The Annual Silicon Valley Tech Charity Gala brought out all the usual suspects - models, actresses, and Instagram influencers hoping to bag themselves a billionaire tech nerd sugar daddy. Tonight's theme was "A Midsummer Night's Dream," and most of the women had really committed to a dramatic look, with wispy multi-colored gowns, wings, and flowers woven into intricate up-dos. Meanwhile, us dudes had almost universally gone the "Phantom of the Opera" route. Can't beat a classic black suit and a mask to hide our faces behind.

"Yeah, I've noticed," I said as I adjusted my simple black mask, the edges digging into my cheeks. "The question is, have they noticed you? Or can they not see past the mask covering up your ugly mug?"

"Har har," Fury said dryly, scanning the sea of partiers around us. "All I know is my dance card for the night is already filling up fast. That little redhead by the chocolate fountain has been eyeing me hard for the last ten minutes. And the brunette in the sparkly green dress over by the string quartet just slipped me her number while you were in the bathroom."

"Look at you, Mr. Popular." I shook my head, laughing. "Meanwhile, I'll be hanging out here seeing how many of these tiny crab puff things I can shove in my mouth before someone tries to talk shop with me."

"Oh, come on," Fury scoffed. "I've already seen at least three babes check you out since we arrived. You're Cory McCrae, the founding partner of Gracen and McCrae. You're telling me you can't snag any of these ladies for a dance or two?"

I shrugged, gulping down more champagne. It wasn't exactly a secret that the opposite sex made me slightly, uh...nervous. And parties like this were breeding grounds for anxiety. Too many strangers vying for my attention. Too many overly direct women who think that a guy like me - decent looking enough in a sort of standard business casual way, with what the finance magazines called an "impressive" career trajectory - should be prime bait.

Truth be told, I was only here because Fury had persuaded me to appear since we were trying to reel in new clients. At least the open bar made schmoozing with the Silicon Valley elite slightly more tolerable. Like right now, for instance, pleasantly buzzed on Taittinger and stuffed with mini quiches, this whole scene felt less like my own personal 9th Circle of Hell.

"Here, more liquid courage," Fury said, pressing another full champagne flute into my hand. "Now, chug that bad boy, and let's dive back into the mingling madness."

Before I could protest, he was disappearing into the writhing crowd of bodies gyrating under the neon strobe lights, making a beeline for a statuesque blonde swaying in a slit-up-to-there red gown. I watched him sidle up to the woman, saying something in her ear that made her tip back her head and laugh.

Yep, and just like that, my wingman had flown the coop.

Sighing, I scanned the crowds, giving my tie a nervous little half-Windsor adjustment. As I people-watched, a striking woman suddenly caught my eye from across the room. Or at least I assumed she was striking - all I could really see behind her filmy purple mask dotted with crystals was a pair of intense amber eyes lined in kohl.

I realized with a jolt she was staring straight at me.

Quickly looking away, I downed more champagne.

Smooth, McCrae. Real smooth. Nothing sexier than sudden awkward eye contact from across a crowded party.

Still, I couldn't resist sneaking another glance. This time, she didn't look away. And was that the hint of a smile playing about those pouty, purple-painted lips?

Before I knew it, I was floating towards her, this mysterious woman who had me in her thrall. There was just *something* about her, an irresistible allure that had my feet moving of their own accord. She was all luscious curves poured into a shimmery dress the color of a ripe grape, her cascade of dark curls bouncing across her bare, golden shoulders as she swayed to the music. I was a hapless sailor caught in the siren call of her rhythm.

Stop being fucking weird, Cory. I gave myself a mental slap, hanging back on the edge of the dance floor. Downing the last drops of liquid courage, I looked anywhere but at the mystery woman. The ice sculpture of Puck and Titania. The chocolate fountain I wanted to dive head-first into. The pair of bankers talking derivatives markets in the corner.

Still, I could feel her gaze still lingering on me, prickling my skin.

You're imagining things, dude. Get a grip. She's just people-watching like you. I loosened my tie, feeling suddenly suffocated. Too many bodies pressed close, clogging up the air. Too hot. Were those damn strobe lights actually getting brighter?

I had to get out of here.

Shoving my way past the throngs of people, I finally reached the gloriously empty outdoor terrace. I sucked in a huge gulp of crisp night air, instantly feeling the champagne haze in my brain dissipate. I loosened my painfully tight shoes and let my toes rest for a bit. Ahh, sweet relief.

My heart rate slowly returned to normal as the distant thump of music and party chatter from inside was drowned out by the soothing gurgle of a stone fountain. Floating lanterns bobbed lazily in the tiny pond, casting ripples of soft golden light that danced across the flagstones under my feet.

Leaning my elbows on the carved railing edging the terrace, I stared out over the perfectly manicured gardens below, getting lost in the sculpted hedges and flower beds, which during the day probably smelled amazing this time of the year with that jasmine vine and -

"Well, hello there, stranger."

I just about leaped out of my skin as a sultry feminine voice suddenly spoke behind me. Whirling around wildly, I found myself face-to-face with the mystery woman, the fountain light creating glints of amber fire in those cat-like eyes.

"Oh geez, I uh…hi," I stammered out oh-so-smoothly.

"I didn't mean to give you a heart attack," she said, her lips twitching beneath that purple mask. Was she actually having a laugh at my expense?

"No, no, it's all good. I just…didn't hear you coming," I babbled like an absolute buffoon.

Get a grip, Cory! I was rambling on like a nervous wreck, my palms turning into mini swimming pools, while this bombshell of a woman stood there cool as a cucumber.

She took a step closer, and I could feel my brain cells desperately trying to regroup as I continued to trip over my own words.

"It's just…you know…these shoes…" I gestured vaguely at my shiny wingtips. Wow, yes, tell her all about your boring footwear. What a great conversation starter. Gold star for you!

Rather than retreating from the blabbering dork in the mask (yours truly), she moved even closer, which was both thrilling and terrifying.

"Mmm, I spotted those classy shoes of yours earlier," she practically purred, sending a jolt of confusion through me.

Was this breathtaking woman actually flirting with me? My ears felt like they were on fire beneath the mask, and I could barely contain my bewilderment.

Snap out of it, Cory! This enchanting mystery woman has just given you an opening, and you're fumbling it like a rookie! Spit something out, you buffoon!

"Uh, about earlier," I stammered, finally finding my voice. "I, uh, I kind of noticed you checking me out a few times during the party."

Smooth, Romeo. Real smooth. She probably thinks I'm a creep now. But instead, she laughed lightly, the sound low and musical and incredibly sexy.

"Busted, I suppose. You got me there." She nonchalantly propped her impeccable hip against the railing, looking like she'd been born to lean on things with effortless grace. "How could I not spot you when you strolled in with your friend? Two good-looking guys, although no mask in the universe could hide how awkward you felt at this whole shindig."

My stomach took a strange little somersault. Geez, was it that noticeable? So much for my attempts to keep it chill and act like I fit right in, mingling with the Silicon Valley VIPs and stunners.

"Yeah, this isn't exactly my usual scene," I admitted with

an awkward little laugh. "My business partner made me come. Cozying up clients is usually his department."

"Well, aren't you just the dutiful partner?"

The way she looked at me from behind that mask was like she was staring straight through me, seeing things no one else could see. It was unnerving and thrilling.

Get it together, my brain screamed at me again. Say something clever, dammit!

I fumbled for a smooth reply. "What about you? Is schmoozing with the tech nerds in masks your usual idea of a fun Friday night?"

Okay, a semi-decent comeback. I considered it progress.

She laughed again. "I don't know if I'd call it fun necessarily. But it's not without its...perks."

She reached out and boldly adjusted my tie, smoothing it between nimble fingers. I froze at her sudden touch, my breath catching sharply in my chest. She smelled amazing. Like jasmine and cinnamon, some fancy perfume, I couldn't name but instantly loved.

"There. Much better," she said softly. Had she somehow drifted even closer? Mere inches separated us now. I stared into those hypnotic tiger eyes glowing behind her mask. Was I imagining the sudden electricity charging the night air between us?

I opened my mouth. Closed it again. Gulped. Tried one more time.

"Would you, uh..." Oh god. Was my voice actually cracking? I coughed, willing it an octave lower. "Would you maybe like to, you know...dance?"

I held my breath, watching her reaction. She went still, those amazing eyes searching mine for a long moment. My heart pounded so loud, surely, in the sudden silence, she could hear it, too.

A smile slowly spread across her face, and she leaned in close. Her fingers grazed my suddenly sweaty palm, and she breathed one simple word into my ear:

"Maybe..."

TWO

Rylee

I took a slow sip of champagne, savoring the bubbly sweetness as I surveyed the scene before me. The annual Silicon Valley Tech masquerade ball was in full swing. A classical quartet vibrated their strings smoothly on a small stage, but soon, their efforts were drowned out by the steady throb of club beats dominating the dancefloor.

Costumed partygoers laughed, schmoozed, and flirted in dizzying whirls of color. Gods, goddesses, and fantasy creatures from myths and legends came to life under the pulsing neon lights.

I smiled behind the bejeweled safety of my purple mask. I was shocked when the engraved invitation arrived on heavy cardstock in my mailbox last week. I - little Rylee Palmer, new in town from Sacramento - was invited to rub shoulders with the Silicon Valley elite at the social event of the season.

Apparently, the local business chapter was already taking our new firm more seriously than I'd realized. This masquerade ball was the perfect opportunity to do some subtle networking.

And, you know, maybe have a little fun for once. I smoothed the skirt of my shimmery amethyst gown. When was the last time I'd actually felt pretty? It had been ages since I dolled myself up, longer still since I'd flirted just for the thrill of it.

Tonight called for a fresh start on both fronts. I added a dash more lipstick, pressed my lips together, and strutted towards the crowd with newfound confidence.

Over the next hour, I charmed my way through businessmen who wanted to talk crypto, starry-eyed entrepreneurs pitching app ideas, and even a semi-famous retired athlete who asked me to breakfast. I deftly distanced myself from any morning-after expectations but didn't shy from coy smiles or light brushes of fingertips along muscular biceps.

Harmless fun. The anonymity provided by silky masks and the champagne buzz gave everyone pleasant, plausible deniability.

Throughout it all, though, I found my gaze returning again and again to one man. He stuck out sorely - tall and broad-shouldered in a classic black suit, his hair a tousled coppery mane. But the tense set of those shoulders intrigued me, the way he tugged at his tie like it was a noose strangling him. His companion seemed in his element, working the room with easy laughter. Yet Masked Ginger looked ready to crawl straight out of his skin.

I sensed a story there. And I wanted in on it.

I'd always had a knack for digging up dirt, figuring out what made folks tick and how to push their buttons. It was all part of the game.

So I watched him from across the room, curiosity well and truly piqued. Waited to see what he would do.

Our eyes locked with a bolt of lightning. He looked away quickly, but the connection had already snapped into place. I bit my lip to hide a smile, noting the endearing splash of pink coloring the tips of his ears.

Hook, line, and sinker. I just had to reel him in now.

Patience was key. I let him gather his courage, sensing the impending approach as surely as a shark scents blood diffusing through the water.

But I noticed he slipped outside the doors to the patio, and I followed him.

When I spoke, I must have surprised him as he jumped and turned. I gazed up into sea-glass eyes behind an inky black mask.

After a little small talk and flirting, he finally popped the question, "Would you maybe like to, you know...dance?" His voice cracked charmingly on the question, and my grin flashed wolfishly. Gotcha...

We flowed together on the dance floor, conversation clipped and jittery. He fumbled words, raked nervous hands through his hair, and grimaced at his own awkward jokes. I smoothed down his rumpled collar and rested a steadying hand on his shoulder. Slowly coaxed him out inch by inch onto the slippery ice of flirtation.

Asking for his name was on the tip of my tongue - I could see the shape of it waiting behind his teeth, too. But real names had no place here. Ours was a world spun from champagne bubbles, and snatches of song lyrics and secrets whispered in ears smelling of expensive perfume.

We swayed to the rhythm, his hands inching their way

down my waist, a shy cat on the prowl. My fingers traced a path up his neck, getting lost in that copper mane of his. With every new song, our lips drew closer, each touch igniting sparks that crackled in the air.

"Want to slip outside for a breath of air?" I finally murmured against his throat during a bass-heavy dip. He nodded wordlessly, Adam's apple bobbing.

The autumn wind smacked us in the face, a chilly wake up call as we left the ballroom's stuffy, humid embrace. I tossed my head back and gulped the crisp air like it was a top-shelf merlot. My enigmatic dance partner mimicked my actions with an exaggerated groan that had me biting back a laugh. For a moment, we stood there like two random strangers, silently bonding over our shared relief from the refreshing cold.

"God, I needed that." Raising his mask, he scrubbed both hands briskly over his face. "Much better out here."

"Mm-hmm." I slid a look at him, still hidden behind purple lace and crystals. "The company's improved too."

He flushed and reattached his mask. But instead of stammering, he boldly caught my hand, pressing a kiss to the knuckle.

"What do you say we lose these masks too?" Long fingers plucked at my lace. "I want to see if the face matches the silver tongue."

My breath caught at the unanticipated daring, an electric thrill chasing down my spine. There was more to this shy gentleman than met the eye. Peeling back those layers one by one filled me with unexpected longing.

Wordlessly, I removed his mask, then my own in turn. Eyes locked, the thousand unspoken rules governing this glittering make-believe world unfurled around us. We finally stood face to face, and the nameless Adonis smiled. His eyes sparked with appreciation, devouring the sight of my wild, dark hair cascading down my shoulders before recapturing my gaze.

"Well, hey there, gorgeous." His voice was a warm whiskey, meant just for me. "I gotta tell ya, I don't think I'm quite ready to let you disappear on me just yet."

His words oozed smoothly, but his fingers quivered ever so slightly as they reached to cradle my jaw with sweet gentleness.

I tipped my chin up, nudging my nose against his in a slow, easy nuzzle. His breath hitched, and I could feel the heat of his body through the crisp cotton of his shirt. My fingers lazily traced their way up his chest, reading the Braille of his muscles before curling possessively around his lapels. I was staking my claim and wasn't afraid to tell him.

"You think I'm just going to let you slip away after all this?" I murmured, punctuating it with a kiss to seal the deal.

He let out this cute little sound, all helpless-like, as his hands dove into my hair, deepening the kiss, leaving my lips buzzing and my head spinning.

When we finally came up for air, he rasped, "How 'bout a lift somewhere?"

I grinned. "Oh, you're offering rides now, huh?"

His cheeks went red again - man, I loved watching that polished exterior crack to reveal the fire beneath.

"Uh, yeah. I mean, my car. I can get it and drive you home. Or you know, wherever you need to go..." He stumbled over his words, once again looking unsure.

Home was a tiny studio apartment with books still in

boxes stacked waist-high and a mattress on the floor. I wasn't quite ready for those dreary dimensions of reality to intrude on guests.

"Mm, I know the perfect place." Catching his hand, I towed him towards the golden glow of the valet station.

Twenty minutes later, I had him pull his sleek BMW off into a secluded overlook. The city sparkled below like our own private galaxy. I leaned over, letting the skirt of my dress ride high on my parted thighs as I nipped delicately at his earlobe.

"Kiss me," I breathed, my voice a seductive whisper.

A low growl rumbled from his chest as he hauled me against him, his lips finding mine with a desperate hunger. His hands roamed up my thighs, hiking my dress up until his fingers found the lace edge of my panties. I writhed and bucked against him, my body burning with desire. He groaned into our kiss, his fingers digging into my flesh with an intensity that left me breathless, sure to leave a trail of bruises in their wake.

Even without knowing his name, the idea of him branding me had me buzzing with excitement. I couldn't resist giving his bottom lip a nibble, eliciting a growl that made my toes curl. Then, I pulled back just enough to ask the all-important question, "Got protection?" I breathed, my voice barely audible.

Grunting softly, he adjusted his grip on me, reaching for his wallet with one hand while holding me tight against him with the other. I could feel the heat radiating from his body as he fumbled for the condom, and it sent a shiver down my spine.

As soon as he handed it to me, I reached between us,

tracing my fingers along the length of his erection through his pants. My clit pulsated in sweet agony, craving to savor him fully with my lips. Regretfully, I knew that pleasure would have to wait.

A swift tug undid his pants, and my hand slipped inside his boxer briefs. My initial assessment had been a gross understatement; his cock was magnificently thick and long, graced with a delicious curve that left my mouth watering.

I gripped him firmly, caressing him leisurely from base to tip. A guttural groan escaped him, and I felt his fingers clutch my hips tighter.

"I want to make you come first," he said, his voice rough with desire. "And when I do, I want to be inside you."

I nodded, rolling the condom down over his shaft. He let out a strangled moan as I worked it over his length, and I felt a surge of power knowing that I was the one driving him wild.

I didn't waste any time, going up on my knees, I moved over him, smirking as he gripped my hips to keep me balanced. Our eyes locked, and I slowly lowered myself onto him, savoring the way his breath hitched as I sank down inch by glorious inch.

"Oh." My nails dug into his shoulder, and I bit my lip to keep from moaning too loudly. "Oh, fuck."

He squeezed his eyes shut, his grip on my hips tightening. "Yeah. Fuck. Definitely fuck."

I panted as I rocked back and forth, fighting my body to take him. I was wet, but we hadn't had any foreplay, and he was just so damn big. His head fell back as he continued to curse, and I begged him to tell me his name just so I could scream it. My experience with men was not extensive, but they'd all been above average.

This man was so far beyond average that it felt like he would split me in two by the time he bottomed out. My entire body was on fire, my muscles twitching and spasming as my pussy struggled to adjust to something this large inside me.

My original plan was to ride him until we both came, no lingering or drawing things out, but now, I didn't have any choice but to go completely still until I could finally breathe again.

"Fuck you feel amazing." He raised his head, his eyes blazing with desire. Curling his hand around the back of my neck, he pulled me in for a kiss.

Our lips moved together, and then the rest of our bodies caught on. His hips rose to meet me as I set a brutal pace, rising and dropping at a rate that made the line between pain and pleasure blur. We came together, mouths only parting long enough for us to gasp for air. I vaguely knew my hair was coming out of its updo, but I didn't care. All I cared about was the building pressure in me and the race to release.

Only when I slumped down on him, spent, did any semblance of coherent thought return. And the first thing that went through my head was simple.

Holy Fuck.

THREE

Cory

I tapped my fingers to an imaginary beat on the leather steering wheel, my gaze drifting yet again to the passenger seat as I sat through another red light. The echo of last night still lingered, a haunting silhouette of tousled curls, bare golden shoulders, and the enticing curve of a thigh peeking through the slit of a glittering dress.

I scrunched my eyes shut, attempting to exorcise the memory of her body molded against mine in the hushed privacy of my car. The way she confidently led my hand up her leg, her nails dancing lightly over my knuckles before—

A blaring horn snapped me out of my daydream. I muttered a curse under my breath and floored the gas just as the light blinked back to red. This was absurd. I couldn't shake the replay of every steamy moment from that enchanting masquerade ball. I couldn't stop obsessing over her.

The secretive woman without a name.

I'd spent the whole freakin' weekend racking my brain

for any clue about who she was. Did she drop a hint about her friends? Her job? But all those heated chats just swirled together in my head, boiling down to the rush of her fingers tracing my thigh and the flutter of her lips on my neck.

Useless. Even now, I could still feel the heat of desire crackling beneath my skin.

Way to go, McCrae. Pining over a woman like a lovesick puppy, and you didn't even snag her name. Or her number. Or anything!

I smacked my head against the headrest in sheer frustration. This was the first woman I'd really clicked with in god knows how long, and my bumbling self had totally botched any chance of seeing her again.

"Real smooth, Romeo," I mumbled.

Twenty minutes later, I swaggered through the sparkling lobby of Gracen & McCrae, "Good morning, Mr. McCrae" echoing behind me like a broken record. I tossed out crisp greetings, sidestepping small talk like a pro. The sooner I dove headfirst into work, the sooner I could drown my distraction in spreadsheets and game plans.

As I approached my office, I sensed a presence beside me. Glancing over, I did a double take. Jules, Fury's assistant, was keeping pace with me, her stride as smooth as melted butter.

"Jules," I said, trying to sound casual. "What's the deal?"

She shot me a sly grin, her eyes scanning me from head to toe. "Well, well, well, Mr. McCrae. You're looking mighty fine this morning. Glowing, even. Nice weekend?"

A flush crept up my neck, and I fought the urge to tug at my tie. Was I really that obvious? Did I have a neon sign above my head flashing "love-struck"?

"Ah, you know, just the usual," I replied with a careless shrug. "Fury's waiting for me, right?"

"Uh-huh, in his lair," she purred. "Don't let me hold you up."

With a wink, she sashayed away, leaving a trail of rose perfume behind her. I stood there, staring after her, slightly stunned. Since when did Jules Vortak bat her lashes at me? In five years, we'd exchanged maybe a dozen words not related to work. Now she was giving me the once-over.

My steamy rendezvous Saturday was etched all over my face for the world to see. Fury was going to have a field day with this.

After depositing my bag in my office, I stumbled upon my partner lounging behind his mammoth oak desk, feet perched nonchalantly on a precarious stack of files. He welcomed me with a rakish grin.

"Well, look who's doing the walk of shame this morning," Fury chortled.

I blinked, taken aback. "Uh, sorry, what?"

"You heard me." He cackled at my bewildered expression. "Jules just filled me in on how she caught you blushing like a schoolgirl with a crush in the hallway. Judging by the goofy look on your face, she figured you'd had one hell of a weekend. Is there anything you'd like to share with the class, McCrae?"

With a groan, I plonked myself down in the chair opposite him and raked both hands through my hair. So much for keeping my secret entanglement under wraps.

"Oh, come on, don't be like that," Fury cajoled. "I'm not asking for specifics here. Just tell me whether our little boy is finally becoming a man out there."

His grin morphed into a sly smirk, and a dark eyebrow arched with mischief. Despite my reddening cheeks, I chuckled.

"Alright, alright, you win. Something...went down this weekend."

Fury whistled low and swiveled his chair to face me. "Spill it."

Reluctantly, I shared the bare essentials: the liquid courage, the irresistible pull towards the mysterious woman in purple, the flirtatious banter on the terrace, the lost masks, and the enchanting night that ended tangled up with each other in my car.

"So, let me get this straight - you meet this drop-dead gorgeous woman, but you don't even get her number?" Fury clicked his tongue disapprovingly when I finished my tale. "Amateur hour, my friend."

In frustration, I threw up my hands. "I know, I know! Believe me, I've been beating myself up all weekend for not even getting her name."

"Well, hey, you finally took the leap! You gotta applaud those baby steps, buddy." He chuckled and gave me a solid whack on the back. "Look at you, getting some action!"

I rolled my eyes, a wry grin playing at the corners of my mouth. "Don't go popping the cork just yet. I've got a feeling she was a one-time wonder, a stroke of pure luck."

"Ah, don't sell yourself short! Maybe this is just the beginning, the end of your dry spell and the start of a romantic deluge, eh?" A sly grin spread across his face. "If you're in the market for some pointers on sealing the deal *and* getting her number, I'd be more than happy to share a few tricks of the trade—"

I raised a hand, cutting him off. "Nah, I think I'm good, thanks. Really." I cleared my throat, steering the conversation back to safer waters. "So, uh, about the charity ball, I take it you left quite the impression that night..."

He launched into the tale of his own escapade - some socialite heiress who apparently hadn't seen the light of day all weekend. I let his playboy banter wash over me, my thoughts drifting back to my own elusive enchantress. As much as I knew I should let her go, there was a part of me that mourned the lost opportunities, the chances that slipped through my fingers.

If only I'd been braver, bolder, and asked the right questions. But that had never been my forte with women. I thrived on strategy, data, solid numbers, and the comforting certainty of the business world.

Not the frightening unknowns of attraction and romance.

Fury's voice yanked me back to the present, steering our chat towards business ventures and recent acquisitions. I resolved, for the umpteenth time, not to let my brain waste any more energy mulling over the mysterious woman. After all, I had a company to run.

"And I've got that startup CEO you were schmoozing at the party last week," Fury added. "But more importantly, I've been looking into this new crew, Palmer Money Management, that's been nibbling at our toes - or rather, our client base."

I scrunched my eyebrows, drawing a blank at the name. "Who the heck are they?"

"That's the million-dollar question," Fury tapped his pen on the desk, his forehead creasing. "There's this big Randall Palmer Management outfit in Sacramento. I figured they just opened a branch here in Palo Alto. But I called in a few favors, and I've got it on good authority that Randall Palmer isn't connected."

"So, it's someone else, and they're already snatching up our clients?"

He nodded gravely. "You got it. My sources tell me it's run by some guy named Riley Palmer. Never heard of him. He appeared out of thin air and had already bagged a Facebook finance VP and an actress married to some Snapchat bigwig. Big fish, let me tell you. I heard a rumor they're trying to reel in Jessica Zhang's accounts, too. And you know we've been trying to land her for months."

I pressed my lips together in a tight line. I'd built my career on predicting the market's next significant moves, staying three steps ahead of any potential rivals. It was unnerving for a new firm to materialize overnight and already have enough clout to challenge our hard-won territory.

"Think this will mess with our quarterly numbers?" I asked, starting to fret.

Fury reassured me, "We should be alright for now. But if Palmer keeps this up, we might have to batten down the hatches."

"I guess we've got ourselves a bit of a challenge," I chuckled, rubbing my hands together. "We've got to polish up our image, make sure we're the shiniest apple in the barrel."

Fury shot me a grin, his eyes twinkling with mischief. "A little rivalry never hurt anyone, right?"

"You bet," I nodded, pushing myself up from the chair. "How 'bout we hash this out over lunch?"

He was already lost in a new task, but he gave a quick, absent-minded nod. "Sounds like a plan," he said.

With a newfound determination, I strode out of Fury's office, ready to zero in on this mysterious upstart who'd sprung up like a weed in the garden. Palmer Money Management, eh? Just who was this Riley Palmer character swiping our prized clients right from under our noses? It was time to roll up my sleeves and do some serious private eye work, uncover the dirt on him and his slick operation.

Ah, that enchanting woman from the ball, she'd have to remain a tantalizing memory, a wisp of perfume lingering in my thoughts.

FOUR

Rylee

I basked in the early sunshine as I stepped out of my apartment complex, the crisp morning air raising goosebumps on my exposed legs. The temptation to sprint back upstairs for a light jacket crossed my mind, but I dismissed it. The weather forecast had promised a balmy mid-70s by lunchtime, just right for the stroll I had in mind for my midday break.

Tugging on my hoodie zipper, I set off down the quiet street towards the office, a pleasant mile or so away - far enough to get my heart pumping, but not so far that I'd be a sweaty mess when I got there. I took a deep breath, letting the morning air fill my lungs, carrying a whisper of jasmine from someone's nearby garden. I rarely got to enjoy this time of day just before the world woke up and chaos took over - the calm before the caffeine-fueled storm.

My thoughts meandered back to Sacramento, the city I'd just left a month and a half ago. Moving to Palo Alto had been a rollercoaster of emotions - on the one hand, I felt like I'd busted out of jail, escaping the tense relationship with dear old dad Randall Palmer, the hotshot finance honcho. On the other hand, there was a twinge of homesickness for my old familiar stomping grounds. I always wondered how life might've played out if Mom hadn't left us so early. Would Dad have been less of a hard-nosed disciplinarian and more of a nurturing father if he hadn't been alone?

Shaking off the melancholy, I refocused on the present. Today was going to be a fantastic day. I had a mountain of work ahead at the new office, but I felt invigorated and hopeful. Building my own business from the ground up had been my dream for years, and now, it was finally happening.

"Good morning, Miss Palmer," the security guard said as I entered the lobby.

"Morning Warren! How was your weekend?" I asked.

"Oh, you know, same old," he said with a smile. "How about you? Did you get up to anything fun?"

"I may have had a few adventures," I said coyly, not wanting to give too much away. Warren just laughed.

"Well, you enjoy your day now," he said, holding the door open for me.

"Thanks, Warren, you too!"

I hummed softly as I rode up in the elevator. Despite being the opposite of a morning person, I felt energetic and ready to tackle the day ahead.

My assistant Mallory was already at her desk when I entered the office, a cup of coffee in one hand and my schedule in the other.

"Good morning, Rylee," she said as she greeted me. "I have your appointments for today all set. The 10 a.m.

appointment with Beau Canyon might be a tricky one, from what I hear."

I nodded, the name familiar. Beau Canyon was an up-and-coming social media influencer who had amassed a substantial following and wealth at a young age. But he was known to be entitled and difficult to work with. Well, I loved a challenge. "You bet," I replied to Mallory, grinning. "We'll bring Beau around, one way or another. It might require some fancy footwork, but I'm up for the challenge."

She gave me a knowing smile. "I have no doubt you'll win him over."

I glanced towards my office and noticed a figure sitting inside. "Who's that?" I asked, tilting my head in that direction.

"Ah, Sergio LaRicca. He's your first candidate for the associate position," Mallory explained. "He arrived a bit early, so I showed him to your office to wait. Just a heads up, he's quite the looker."

I chuckled. "Thanks for the warning," I said before heading into my office.

As I entered, the tall man with blue-black waves of hair and chiseled features rose to greet me. But it was his dazzling smile that nearly knocked me off my feet.

"Sergio LaRicca," he introduced himself in a silky baritone. "You must be Rylee Palmer. I have to say, I wasn't expecting someone so lovely."

I arched an eyebrow at the flirtatious tone but shook his hand firmly. "Please, have a seat," I said briskly, moving behind my desk. "Shall we get started?"

If Sergio was put off by my no-nonsense demeanor, he didn't show it. "Of course. Let me first say it's refreshing to meet a woman running her own firm. The finance world needs more female leadership."

"You're absolutely right," I replied with a chuckle, "and I've had my fair share of run-ins with the old boys' club. But I'm all about action, not just talk. You're already a step ahead if you can support a woman-led firm."

Sergio flashed a grin. "I consider myself pretty forward-thinking. To me, it's all about skill and talent, no matter if you're a guy or a lady."

For the next twenty minutes, I walked Sergio through the ins and outs of Palmer Money Management. I spilled the beans on our grand vision, the crew we catered to, and the bag of tricks we had up our sleeves. Sergio was all ears, lobbing thoughtful questions my way and looking downright dazzled by what we'd pulled off in such a short time.

"Money management's my bread and butter," Sergio piped up when I pressed him on what lured him into the gig. "Fresh out of Columbia, I dove headfirst into the New York scene. I racked up some solid years, but then..." He hesitated, his gaze drifting off into the distance.

"Don't leave me hanging," I nudged him, curiosity piqued.

He let out a sigh. "Let's just say there was a bit of a misunderstanding with a client who accused me of playing fast and loose with their cash. It turned out they were the ones with sticky fingers, not me. But by the time the dust settled, the damage was done. The vibe in the office was icy, and I could feel the cold shoulder from a mile away. So, I figured it was time to pack up and find greener pastures."

I gave him a once-over, taking in his unwavering gaze. "I respect your honesty," I said after a moment. "But let's get one thing straight. If you're going to jump on board with us, I expect nothing less than squeaky-clean ethics. We don't do shady business here."

Sergio bobbed his head in agreement. "You got it. My reputation is my brand in this game, and I'm dead serious about doing right by the client."

I had a gut feeling that he was the real deal. The guy had a knack for making things happen and an aura of confidence that was hard to ignore. We needed someone like him on our team to reel in the biggest fish in Silicon Valley.

"Well, Sergio, I gotta say, you've got some serious potential here. You've got that swagger and know-how we're after."

He flashed me a grin. "I'm more than happy to join forces."

I hopped up and offered him my hand. "You're our top pick. I'll contact you soon about the next moves."

We exchanged a firm handshake. As I walked him out, I felt a jolt of excitement at the thought of adding Sergio to our team. His charisma and chops could catapult Palmer Money Management into the big leagues. This was going to be a game-changer, and I had a hunch it would pay off. Especially when it came to winning over our female clients, his vibe could give us a leg up on Gracen & McCrae.

FIVE

Cory

Running a business isn't just about being good at what you do. Sometimes, it's about timing and a bit of luck. Having a unique service in a crowded field can really make a difference.

Fury and I were banking on that when we shifted gears to focus on money management. We had done our homework on the Palo Alto scene, making sure we had the right services at prices that would get attention. But what we didn't see coming was a new player crashing our party and poaching our clients left and right.

I might be laying it on a bit thick when I say they're 'poaching' our clients, but this unexpected allegiance swap has us running around trying to woo fresh faces. And that's where my little rendezvous with the legendary Bethany Chamberlain comes in. This lady's got more money than she can shake a stick at. She's one of those iconic former models who's on the prowl for a reliable money manager after her last one tried to make off with her fortune.

With Fury, our go-to smooth talker, already booked and busy, it fell on my shoulders to win over the illustrious Bethany Chamberlain. Now, Bethany was no-nonsense, not one to fall for sweet nothings, so I figured this would be a straight-to-the-point chat about her financial situation.

As I pulled up to Bethany's mansion, I noticed an eye-catching sports car parked in the driveway. It was not exactly the ride I'd expect from someone like her if you know what I mean. My curiosity was piqued, and I wondered about the owner of that flashy set of wheels.

As if on cue, a tall, suited-up, good-looking guy strolled out. What the hell? My intel didn't mention anything about Bethany having family or tight connections in the area, but I already had a hunch who he might be. This was not family or friends.

"Hiya," I greeted him, flashing a fake friendly smile. "I'm here to meet with Ms. Chamberlain."

He beamed back at me. "Ah, Gracen & McCrae, right?"

Well, shit. I bet this guy is Riley Palmer.

Taking a shot in the dark, I asked, "Are you with Palmer Money Management?"

He gave a slight bow, still wearing that grin. "That's the one," he confirmed before hopping into his car.

I stood there, watching his taillights disappear into the distance, as I tried to shake that nagging feeling in my gut. Maybe it was the annoyance of possibly losing to Riley Palmer or the fact that I felt like a fish out of water compared to my old finance strategy job.

Whatever it was, I had to let it go. I was here to win Bethany over to Gracen & McCrae and steer her clear of what I saw as a potential disaster.

Taking a deep breath, I pushed thoughts of that flashy car and its owner to the back of my mind and gave the door a firm knock. Bethany answered with a friendly smile that immediately put me at ease.

"Mr. McCrae, please come in," she said, ushering me into her home.

Bethany's mansion was the definition of low-key sophistication. She herself was rocking a chic pantsuit, the epitome of class without being too flashy. Even her diamonds were more about style than bling.

I had a hunch on how to approach this. "Can I get you a drink? Water, juice, tea?" she asked, all hospitable-like.

"No, thank you. I'm good," I replied.

She nodded, and it was time to get down to brass tacks. She sat in one of those swanky looking but probably not too comfortable armchairs, gesturing for me to do the same on its twin across from her.

"Thanks for considering us at Gracen & McCrae," I began, diving into our usual sales pitch. But after a minute, something told me it wasn't quite landing with her. It was time for Plan B, the personal touch. "At Gracen & McCrae, we don't just focus on bulking up your assets. We ensure your money works for you – supporting only the charities and projects *you* care about."

Her eyes lit up, and she leaned in closer. "That's really considerate," she said. "To be honest, until earlier with the other young man, I had no idea such a tailored service existed."

Well, damn! It sounded like Riley Palmer might've beat me to the punch on that one.

Still, I pushed on. "What are you looking to achieve with your finances?" I said, keeping my game face on.

Bethany looked amused as she answered, "It's nice being wooed by such dedicated professionals."

Her voice had a hopeful note, but I had this sinking feeling.

"However," she continued, "I've already decided to go with Palmer's firm."

Man, keeping my cool was tough. Riley fricking Palmer. "I understand. Thanks for your time," I said, leaving. "Just remember, Gracen & McCrae is here if you change your mind."

Bethany was all smiles as she walked me to the door, but it was just a polite brush-off. I wondered if Fury, with his silver tongue and Hollywood good looks, would have had better luck than me, the nerdy sidekick in this whole operation.

The drive back to the Gracen & McCrae offices was sour thanks to Riley Palmer. Losing Bethany Chamberlain to that dude was a serious gut punch. With her refined grace and old-money charm, Bethany was exactly the kind of client we needed to boost our rep. But Palmer had swooped in just as we were getting cozy.

I white-knuckled the steering wheel, my hands turning a ghostly shade. This constant game of one-upmanship was getting old really fast. Since Palmer had swaggered into town a few months ago in that flashy ride, it was like he'd made it his mission to make our lives a living hell. He was always one step ahead, snatching our top clients and generally being a pain in the ass. And now, he'd added Bethany to his list of victories. It was enough to make me want to pull my hair out.

It was damn infuriating. Humiliating, even. I should've given that pretty boy a piece of my mind, scratched up that damn car, something. Anything to wipe that smug grin off his perfect dimpled face...

Yikes, I blinked, trying to shake off the sudden flare of anger. Whoa, where'd that come from? I wasn't usually the spiteful type. I was the calm and collected twin who always kept a cool head.

Chill out, man.

By the time I got back to our swanky office with the killer view of the bay, I had managed to rein in my temper, but I could still feel the lingering frustration bubbling just beneath the surface. I couldn't let this keep happening. Our client base was shrinking, and the future of Gracen & McCrae was hanging in the balance.

Fury was there, giving me this quizzical look. "So, how'd it go?" he asked, eyebrows raised. I dropped into my chair and rubbed my eyes. He looked at me with concern. "That bad?"

"She's going with Palmer," I said, defeated.

Fury arched an eyebrow. "So, Bethany jumped ship to Palmer's camp. Color me shocked." He leaned back in his chair, his tone matter of fact. "Cuz, we gotta shake things up. Butting heads with Palmer is just not cutting it. He's been running laps around us, scooping up our best leads without breaking a sweat."

I winced at the brutal honesty of his words, but I couldn't deny it. "Yeah, you're right. We can't keep hemorrhaging our top-tier accounts like this. If we keep going down this road, we'll be left with nothing but crumbs."

"Exactly." Fury's expression turned dead serious. "And losing Bethany today? That was a wake-up call. It means the bleeding's spreading beyond just our current clients. Palmer's also sinking his claws into the fresh prospects we've cultivated for months."

I rubbed a hand roughly over my face, my stomach churning. Our very business was teetering on the razor's edge. If our clients kept jumping ship en masse, we'd be bankrupt within a year.

"Alright, so what's the grand plan?" I asked, cutting to the chase. "How do we stop this mass exodus before Gracen and McCrae sinks like the Titanic?"

Fury let out a sharp breath, his brow furrowed in deep thought. "Well, it's clear that going head-to-head with Palmer for the same accounts is a losing battle. We must get creative and switch up our strategy."

I leaned forward, hanging on to his every word. "I'm all ears. What's the brilliant idea?"

"We need to reel in those new accounts before the rest of the vultures even get a whiff of them," Fury said, a determined glint in his eyes.

"Hey, that actually sounds like a solid plan," I nodded. "But how the heck do we execute it?"

"The answer, my dear cousin, lies in your recently discovered charm and charisma," Fury grinned, slapping me on the back. "Time to work that magic of yours."

SIX

Rylee

I was still riding the sweet wave of a win, ready to pop some bubbly and celebrate. But when my go-to gal pal, Natalie, bailed on our Saturday night shenanigans for the umpteenth time, I once again was flying solo, having a party for one.

I couldn't really hold it against her, though. Ever since she dove headfirst into the wild world of second-grade teaching, it's been a non-stop parade of snotty noses and queasy tummies. The poor girl's been sicker than a dog lately, and it almost makes me reconsider the whole kiddos thing, seeing her hanging on by a thread.

With Natalie out of commission, my Saturday night plans nosedived from boogying on bar tops to a low-key night in with a pint of ice cream and the hum of the TV.

As I stood in the convenience store, a half-gallon of ice cream in my basket, I contemplated the wine aisle like it held the secret to eternal happiness. My choices were clear: either indulge in a bottle of vino or accept my fate as a hopeless romantic, swooning over chick flicks and ice cream. Talk about rock bottom. I mean, who needs wine when you've got whine, right? Yeah, I know, that joke's older than dirt. But there I was, waging this internal battle when a velvety-smooth voice broke the silence:

"I'd suggest pairing that chocolate ice cream with a rich, oaky Zinfandel."

Startled, I fumbled the bottles and spun around to find none other than the sexy masked stranger from the masquerade ball, now smirking at me with his mask-free face. His striking features and the glint of humor in his sea-glass eyes sent a shiver of recognition down my spine.

"Hey, I'm really sorry!" He raised both hands in a peace offering, obviously thinking my show of surprise was annoyance. "Didn't mean to startle you."

He can scare the daylights out of me anytime, I mused, heat rushing to my cheeks. But I quickly quashed that thought and managed a decent smile instead.

"Well, if it isn't my mysterious dance partner in the flesh," I said, aiming for nonchalance despite the adrenaline rush. I extended my free hand towards him.

"What a coincidence, huh?" he drawled, flashing a grin that made my heart race. "Great to see you again."

"Likewise," I replied, my voice husky as I shook his hand, feeling that familiar electric current sizzle through me once more.

"Stocking up on supplies?" he asked, his eyes twinkling.

"Just a few things," I murmured, suddenly aware that I was still clutching his hand, my fingers interlaced with his. "What brings you here?"

"Oh, just a few necessities," he said, glancing at his empty basket with a wicked smile. "Guess I forgot what they were."

"If you forgot, they can't be that important," I teased, my eyes locked on him.

He glanced at my ice cream and raised an eyebrow. "You might want to hurry before that melts," he said.

His smoldering gaze held me captive, leaving me breathless and weak in the knees.

"You know what? That ice cream's not looking so tasty anymore," I murmured, my voice low as I found myself mesmerized by the intensity in his eyes, now fixated on my lips. "I seem to have lost my appetite for anything edible."

"Strange, me too," he replied, his voice dropping to a low, husky rumble. "I've got a craving for something else entirely."

I hesitated for a moment, my heart pounding in my chest. "Fuck it," I muttered, a small smile playing on my lips. "Let's go do something."

"I'd like that." He grinned, his eyes lighting up with excitement. "Where do you want to go?"

My brain buzzed with options, weighing the pros and cons of finding a secluded spot. His pad or mine? No, either was too iffy, especially because I didn't even know his name. Normally, I'd be cautious, but this guy had my inner daredevil itching to break free. The pull towards him was weirdly enough, too strong to ignore. A hotel room flitted through my mind, but that would take time and might kill the vibe; I didn't want to risk ruining the moment with doubts or cold feet. We needed something impulsive, a little risky, even - a dash of danger to add some extra zing to the mix.

And then, like a bolt from the blue, the perfect plan popped into my head. "C'mon, follow me," I blurted out, shoving my half-filled shopping basket toward a cashier without glancing at her reaction. My gaze was locked on my hunky, sexy mystery man.

We practically sprinted out of the grocery store, our anticipation buzzing like a live wire. No need for words, I took the reins and led us to a nearby retail shop. I'd been there several times since moving here, so finding the fitting rooms was a cakewalk.

A minute later, I fumbled with the lock on the fitting room door, finally clicking it shut just as he followed me in. I spun around and flashed him a wink, instantly regretting it as I realized how utterly ridiculous I must've looked. Oh well, there's no time for second-guessing now.

He reached out, but instead of diving straight for the goods, he surprised me by playing with a lock of my hair. "A public dressing room? You're quite the adventurer, aren't you?" he quipped, his voice dipping into a seductive murmur. "I must admit, I *have* been fantasizing about seeing you undress," he confessed, his voice dropping to a sultry whisper.

Well, that confirmed it - we were both on the same wavelength, and it was heading straight for the gutter.

"Oh, my. It looks like I'm not the only one with a dirty mind," I said, playfully tugging at the hem of his shirt. "Have you ever wondered what it'd be like to have me peel off your clothes, one by one as I lick every inch on your body?" I asked, raising an eyebrow suggestively. "Because I've got to say, you feel pretty incredible, so I can only imagine how good you look."

Then, he did that impossibly sexy thing where he pulled his shirt off in one smooth motion, revealing a torso that was even more chiseled than I'd imagined. His breath caught as I traced my fingers over his abs, but when I ventured lower, following that enticing trail of hair down to the waistband of his pants, all that restrained power and strength I had sensed in him... just snapped.

His mouth collided with mine, just as hot and electric as it was the first time. One hand tangled in my hair, while the other grabbed my ass, making me moan. No doubt, this guy could seriously rock my world if I let him have an entire night with me.

"Please tell me you have a condom," he panted, pulling away from me for a second. "I didn't replace the one we used the other night."

I gave a quick nod, still catching my breath. I rummaged through my purse and pulled out one of the condoms I'd stashed there a while back. When I looked up, he was down to just his boxer briefs, which left little to the imagination.

I passed him the condom and wriggled out of my jeans, taking my panties with them. Once they were off, I unhooked my bra and let it join the pile.

"Damn," he murmured. His voice was deep and gruff, sending a shiver down my spine. But before I could even register it, he was all over me again, his mouth demanding and insistent on mine. His hands were rough and eager as they explored my body, squeezing and caressing my breasts, his fingers teasing my nipples until they were hard and sensitive.

I bit his bottom lip gently, breaking our kiss for a moment.

"I need you inside me."

I spun around, and spread my legs, planting my hands on the mirror. I had a split second to worry about the palm prints

I was leaving behind for the store employees, but then a hand was on my ass, curling around my hip. His other hand went straight for the gold, and a single finger slid into me.

"Goddamn, you're soaked," he said, his lips brushing against my shoulder blade. "Did I do that?"

I nodded, my eyes squeezed shut as he worked his finger in and out of me. "Please," I moaned, begging for more.

And then, without warning, I felt the blunt head of his cock nudging at my entrance. I tilted my hips, eager to feel him stretch me once again. He didn't disappoint, pushing his way inside with a slow, deliberate pace that had me biting my lip to keep from crying out. My leg muscles were quivering when he was fully seated, and I wondered if they'd hold me up through this.

As if he could read my mind, he wrapped an arm around my waist, holding me steady as he pulled out almost all the way before driving back in. Each thrust pushed me up on my toes, filling me to the brim. I wasn't sure how much more I could take, but my body seemed to rise to the challenge, accepting every inch as if it was meant to be there.

I opened my eyes, finding him in the mirror's reflection and holding his gaze. The sound of someone nearby snapped us both back to reality, and he picked up the pace, slamming into me with a force that stole my breath away. The pressure inside me built, and I felt his rhythm falter, but I wasn't quite there yet. I was about to take matters into my own hands when he leaned closer and whispered in my ear, "Be a good girl and come for me."

His teeth gave my earlobe just the right nip, and that was all it took. I was a goner. I slapped a hand over my mouth to muffle the whoops of delight as pleasure surged through me, but my handsome partner didn't bother hiding anything. He let out a groan that I felt rumble. His arm around me tightened, and we stayed there, locked together in the most intimate of dances, for what felt like forever.

With great reluctance, we pried ourselves apart and started the process of getting dressed. He couldn't tear his gaze away from me. "What kind of dark magic are you working that I can't seem to resist you, even in a lingerie store in the middle of the day?" His eyes twinkled with mischief. "I don't even know your name yet, and I'm already planning on parading down the street with messy hair just to have you alone again. Let me introduce myself. Hi, I'm Cory."

A delightful rush washed over me, and I just had to swipe one more delectable kiss while standing on my tippy toes. "Rylee," I said with a cheeky grin, giving his luscious lower lip a playful nibble. "Rylee Palmer, your very own enchantress extraordinaire."

He returned my smile in that teasing moment, but then he froze as my name sank in. As I leaned back, I saw a whirlwind of emotions flit across his face - disbelief, consternation, and shock, all flashing by in a heartbeat in those mesmerizing sea-glass eyes. His hands weighed heavily on my shoulders, and I could practically hear the proverbial penny drop from where I stood.

"Palmer," he echoed slowly after an awkward pause. "As in, Rylee Palmer, CEO of Palmer Money Management?"

I scooted back, slipping out of his hold, and hugged myself tight. I felt utterly exposed under the unforgiving glare of the dressing room lights and his piercing gaze. The passionate haze had dissipated, leaving me with a clearer view. Details I'd previously missed now jumped out at me –

his impeccably styled haircut, the glint of an absurdly pricey watch peeking out from under his shirt cuff. Subtle yet unmistakable signs of wealth, success, and familiarity.

My playful prince morphed right before my eyes into someone entirely different. Someone I recognized all too well, unfortunately. I'd spent countless hours strategizing how to outmaneuver and outshine the competition he represented.

"You're Cory McCrae," I blurted out as the lightbulb flickered on. His handsome mug shifted into a grimace, and I could practically see the gears turning in his head. "As in, Gracen and McCrae."

We stood there for what felt like an eternity, locked in a staring contest that could have frozen hell over, and the air between us turned frosty. "Well, shit. Of all the rotten luck..."

Cory—the guy who'd just taken me to the moon and back, with his smoldering eyes and irresistible charm—looked like a deer caught in headlights. He half-raised a hand as if to reach out to me but then thought better of it. The tension radiating off him was obvious.

"Rylee, I...maybe we should talk about this...?" he stammered, his voice barely audible over the deafening silence.

But my tongue was twisty, like a pretzel, leaving me mute. In a frantic scramble, I snatched up my clothes, grabbed my purse from the bench, and made a beeline for another dressing room. The door hinges squeaked in protest as I barreled past him, doing my best to dodge his eyes like they were landmines.

Tears bubbled up in my eyes, blurring my view and streaming down my face. I didn't even bother trying to rein them in as I threw on my clothes and hightailed it out of there, eager to put some miles between me and Cory. The chilly, harsh reality of those four tiny letters left me feeling like a fish out of water.

Cory, as in Cory McCrae. The McCrae of Gracen & McCrae.

Oh, for the love of God. This was going to be one fucking mess.

SEVEN

CORY

Rylee flashed me a grin as she introduced herself, and for a moment, time stood still as my brain struggled to catch up with who she was - Rylee Palmer, our new rival who'd been swiping clients left and right. Then, before we could talk, she was gone, leaving me alone in the dressing room with only her business card as evidence. It must've slipped out of her purse during her hasty exit.

There I stood, gaping at her card like a clueless pup, rubbing my head in total confusion. Fury and I had hit a brick wall trying to find any scrap of info on Rylee Palmer - no photos, no breadcrumbs. Clearly, we'd been way off base with the spelling. We'd been looking for "Riley" instead of "Rylee." And that dude, I thought, was Rylee Palmer? He must've been one of her new associates.

I was sure her initial shock was nothing but a well-rehearsed act. As my rival, she had to know who I was. Fury and I aren't exactly living in the shadows. Stanford grads; still hanging around Palo Alto plastering our faces all over our company's website and whatnot. There was no chance she wouldn't recognize me, right? And the way she kept her identity on the down-low, insisting on keeping our encounters incognito and mysterious, it was all just a sneaky setup.

She was fucking with me in the most literal sense possible. She wanted to throw a wrench in my focus and then waltz in and swipe our clients.

Ugh, I fell for it, hook, line, and sinker! One too many glasses of bubbly at some fancy-schmancy gala, and she pounced like a hawk on a defenseless bunny. One thing led to another, and before I knew it, we were going at it like rabbits in my car. Then, wouldn't ya know it, I run into her at the grocery store, and I think, "Hey, maybe the universe is giving me a sign." I could chat her up without my usual jitters taking over. For a fleeting moment, I thought she saw the real me - the man behind the awkward shyness - and liked me.

How stupid does one have to be not to see that, obviously? I was just her mark.

THE REST OF MY WEEKEND? Let's just say it was about as much fun as having a root canal.

My past flings had always been simple, no-strings-attached deals. We would have some fun and games; then we'd wave goodbye, forget about it, and never look back. Okay, maybe not completely forget about it, but you get the idea. But Rylee, she was something else. She was like a breath of fresh air...until the moment I realized who she actually was.

So, there I was on Monday, driving to work with my jaw

clenched tighter than a pit bull with a new chew toy. It was a dead giveaway that I was more wrapped up in this Rylee mess than I cared to admit. To loosen those knots a bit, I made a pit stop at a cozy café, snagging a couple of buttery croissants and two cups of piping hot coffee. If I was going to drop this bombshell on Fury, I figured it was best to show up with some peace offerings - namely, his favorite breakfast treat.

Ugh, I was dreading that chat with Fury. He was going to go all Hulk-smash on me, no doubt. He was that overprotective big brother type who transformed into a green rage monster at the faintest whiff of trouble for his friends.

But this wasn't just about me. Our company was on the line here. Fury needed the 411 on Rylee's sneaky moves. If she had the nerve to play me not once but twice, who knows what other shenanigans she was cooking up for her business deals?

I sauntered into our building, breakfast and coffee in hand, giving a friendly nod to the security guy. It was still early, but I knew Fury would be nestled in his office, especially on a Monday. The guy's a creature of habit.

Fury looked genuinely surprised as I stood in his doorway with my peace offering. I couldn't blame him; I wasn't exactly known for being the office's morning pastry fairy.

"You? Bringing me breakfast?" he asked, leaning back in his chair, eyes narrowed in curiosity. "Something's up. What gives?"

"I figured it's either this or whiskey," I said, dropping the bag on the table. "And booze in the morning isn't a great look."

His expression morphed from curious to full-on worried in a flash. "Alright, lay it on me."

"Remember that swanky masquerade ball where I, shockingly, found myself tangled up with some mysterious lady?"

"Sure, I do. And hey, I'm stoked for you, cuz. You deserved a little fun."

I tossed Rylee's business card his way. "Well, your happiness might change when you discover that the 'mystery woman' was Rylee Palmer herself. And FYI, we hooked up twice."

Fury's coffee cup froze mid-air like time had suddenly hiccupped while he examined the card. "Wait, what? Rylee Palmer is a woman, and you slept with her twice?"

"Yeah, and I'm pretty sure she did it just to screw with us."

EIGHT

Rylee

I dashed out of the store, my cheeks wet and teary. The shock of discovering that the new guy in my life (or whatever he was) was Cory McCrae, my rival, felt like getting hit by a truckload of bricks. It was so fucked up I couldn't find the words to describe it. My head was spinning with a whirlwind of feelings, and I was way beyond just being upset – I was completely steamed, feeling like fate had played a cruel trick on me.

I picked up the pace, practically sprinting to my car, brushing off the puzzled looks from the other folks on the sidewalk. How on earth had this happened? How did I let down my guard and let myself get duped like this? The anger coursed through me, and I balled my fists, my nails biting into my palms. All I wanted was to get the hell out of there, find a quiet spot, and try to make sense of this whole freaking mess.

I flung myself into the driver's seat and slammed the car door. My fists pounded the steering wheel like a wild drummer, the sting barely registering through the haze of my fury.

Each thud echoed my frustration, and I kept going until my knuckles screamed for mercy, and my tears had no choice but to take a breather.

I leaned back against the seat, shut my eyes, and sucked in a deep breath, trying to tame my heart. Inhale, exhale, I chanted silently, focusing on the rhythm of my breathing, hoping it would lasso my emotions and drag them back under control.

Once my breaths leveled out and my heartbeat slowed to something resembling normal, I reluctantly faced the music. I needed a game plan, a strategy for dealing with this colossal curveball life had thrown my way. It was time to put on my big-girl pants and figure out this mess.

Before I could peel out of there, my phone started buzzing in my bag. I peeked at the screen, and my heart dropped when I saw Dad's name flashing. For a second, I thought about letting it go to voicemail and making a run for it, but that old sense of duty kicked in, and I groaned as I swiped to answer.

"Hey, Dad," I said, sounding as neutral as Switzerland.

"Rylee, how's my little girl doing?" His voice was about as warm and fuzzy as a robot's. "I've been hearing good things about your business in Palo Alto. Word on the street is you're making quite the splash."

Now, that was weird. Was he keeping tabs on me or something? Shouldn't his hands be full wrangling those billionaire bigwig clients of his instead of snooping around my little company?

"I'm doing fine, Dad," I said, keeping my voice even. "And yes, business is going well. Thanks for asking."

"I've been chatting you up to my partners," he said, "and

let me tell ya, their ears perked right up when they heard about your gig. We think it could be a slam dunk for both sides if we teamed up."

I clenched my jaw, barely holding back the fiery retort that wanted to escape. Oh, I knew exactly what kind of "partnership" my old man had up his sleeve. He'd waltz in and take control; before I knew it, my clients would be his.

"Thanks, but no thanks," I managed to say, my tone as tight as a drum. "My business is doing A-OK without any help."

"Ah, Rylee, you know I've got your best interests at heart," he said, oozing manipulation like a cheap used car salesman. "Just imagine how much the firm could grow if I lent a hand. It's a lot for just you to handle, right?"

My fists clenched, nails digging into my palms, and I fought the urge to let out a frustrated scream. Oh, I knew Daddy all too well. I was sure he really meant it was too much for a *woman* to handle.

"I gotta go, Dad," I said and flung my phone onto the passenger seat. The screen lit up briefly before fading to black, cutting off the call. My dad's voice still echoed in my head, a cacophony of expectations and manipulations. But I refused to let him control me any longer. He may have wanted a son to take over his empire, but he got me instead, and I was determined to prove that I was just as capable, if not more so.

I took a deep breath, inhaling the scent of leather and gasoline that filled the car. It was a familiar smell, one that always made me feel grounded.

I could do this.

AS I SWAGGERED into the office on Monday morning, my heels clicked away confidently on the polished concrete floor. The glass door shut behind me with a snappy "click" that practically screamed, "Brace yourselves, folks, it's game time."

I was packing an assortment of pastries from the poshest French bakery just around the corner because even the toughest financial associates enjoyed a little flaky delight with their high-pressure meetings.

After placing the elegant treats in the minimalist conference room, I sent a quick, firm email to my team: "Mandatory strategy meeting in ten minutes. Conference room. Urgent."

My employees soon trickled in, chatting in hushed voices and exchanging uneasy glances as they helped themselves to pastries and coffee. They settled into their usual spots around the imposing glass table.

I inhaled deeply and scanned the room, taking in my team's faces, etched with a mix of anxiety and curiosity about this urgent meeting, as I straightened my shoulders and prepared to deliver the news that would shake up their Monday morning.

"Alright, folks," I began, "I know this is out of the blue, but I've been cooking up a new plan."

A few eyebrows raised, and whispers erupted around the table. Most of them looked hesitant. But not Sergio. My newest recruit leaned forward, his gaze locked on mine, a fierce determination in his eyes. "We're changing strategy?"

I could see the fire in his eyes. He was already on board no matter what.

"Well, kind of," I said, drawing out the word with a grin. "Our goal is still to reel in new clients everywhere we can, but now we've got our sights set on a juicy target. We're going to snatch up every single account we can from Gracen & McCrae, our so-called 'friends' down the street."

The room went silent, then Sergio's eyebrow quirked up, almost like he relished the challenge. The others? Not so much.

"Good call," Sergio declared, slapping the table for emphasis. "Let's shake things up and show those old-school assholes what we're made of."

A smirk danced across my lips. Sergio might be a little over the top, but this was exactly the kind of enthusiasm I'd been fishing for.

Sergio hung back as the team dispersed while discussing strategies in hushed tones. He flashed me a roguish smile. "You know, we should toast to our new mission. What do you say we grab a drink tonight?"

I hesitated, biting my lip. I had a strict policy against mixing business and pleasure. But there was something about Sergio's confidence that made it hard to resist.

I raised a hand, shaking my head. "Sorry, Sergio. You know the rules. I can't cross that line."

His smile faltered, but he quickly recovered, giving me a nod. "Right, right. I understand. Just thought I'd ask."

Alone in the conference room, the earlier exhilaration seeped out of me, leaving behind a deflated sense of longing. I slumped into a chair, its plush leather cushion doing little to comfort my restless body. My thoughts drifted to Cory McCrae, his chiseled physique, and that generously proportioned package that had left me breathless. I could still feel my hand wrapped around it, the heat of his skin searing my palm. A shiver ran down my spine, and I bit my lip, savoring the illicit memory.

"Get a fucking grip, Rylee," I muttered, trying to shake off the distraction. I sighed, rubbing my temples as if I could massage away the desire that pooled in my belly. Maybe I did need that drink after all. Anything to dull the edge of my frustration, to quiet the insistent voice in my head.

NINE

Cory

When I told Fury about Rylee Palmer, I knew we'd be working overtime. It wasn't just about keeping Gracen & McCrae's new investment management strategy on the straight and narrow; it was also about giving Rylee a taste of her own medicine.

But man, trying to push those thoughts of the mind-blowing sex we had to the back of my brain? It was like trying to stuff a beach ball into a shoebox. No matter how hard I pushed, the memories kept bouncing back, reminding me of just how incredible it felt to have her body pressed against mine. It was infuriating, really. I mean, here I was, attempting to concentrate on business and revenge, and all my brain wanted to do was replay our two juicy encounters on an endless loop. Talk about a fucking distraction. Literally.

I sighed and rubbed my temples.

Stupid, stupid brain.

A rap on my door jolted me back to reality. Warner, my trusty sidekick, peeked his head in. Despite being thirty-one, he had that youthful vibe going on with his baby face. But don't let that fool you. He was the best assistant I'd ever had.

"Fury's summoning you," Warner informed me, his face expressing his disapproval of Fury's tone. Typical Fury turning into a bit of a tough cookie when he's set his sights on something.

"Appreciate it," I replied, hopping up from my seat. "Reschedule my morning appointments to the afternoon, would ya? Just in case Fury's got a lot brewing."

"Sure thing. Text me if you want lunch ordered in," he said, returning to his desk.

I barged into Fury's office. There was no need for a knock since he was already expecting me. I plopped down in a chair, ready for action.

"Hang on." Fury kept his eyes glued to his screen until I'd been warming the seat for a solid thirty seconds.

I bit back an eye roll and waited.

"I've got it," he finally declared.

"Got what?" I prodded, intrigued.

"I found our golden ticket," he said, puffing up his chest with pride. "Nadine Seaworth."

"Uh, Nadine, who now?" I asked, furrowing my brow.

He spun his monitor my way. "Meet Nadine Seaworth, the latest mega-rich widow," Fury announced, leaning back with a self-satisfied smirk. "Word from her hairdresser is she's shopping around for a new money manager. If we score her, it'll be a major coup after the whole Palmer debacle."

"Sounds promising," I agreed. "But when did you start chatting up hairdressers for insider gossip?"

"Well, I kind of bumped into her at a party," he admitted

with a sly grin. "Let's just say, besides good intel, she's got some serious moves between the sheets."

"Too much information," I said, chuckling. "Why am I the one hearing all this? Once you've got Nadine on board, just shoot me her files, and I'll take care of the paperwork."

"Nope," he shot back. "You're not just doing the paperwork this time. I want you to be the one to reel her in."

I blinked, dumbfounded. "Wait, are you serious? You want me to seal the deal with a loaded widow?"

Fury's grin stretched even wider. "You got it."

I just shook my head, "No fucking way, man. We agreed I'd stick to the background stuff. You're the one with the million-dollar smile and charm."

"I remember," Fury said, almost too casually. "But we're in a bind here. We can get in before anyone else, but if we don't meet Nadine on Monday, she's heading straight to Palmer."

"I get that, but what's the deal with you on Monday? Do you have a hot date or something?" I asked, raising an eyebrow.

"Nah, man. Heading to Colorado. Not sure when I'll be back," Fury replied, looking a little uneasy.

"You really think throwing me into the lion's den with this wealthy widow is a good idea? I mean, come on," I could feel a knot form in my stomach.

Fury's expression turned serious. "You're selling yourself short, man. You just need a little more confidence when it comes to the ladies. Plus, I can give you some tips on how to handle Nadine."

I scoffed. "I appreciate the offer and vote of confidence,

but is now the time to test my skills? Our whole business is on the line here, Fury."

He just gave me a faint smile. "We don't have much of a choice. Nadine will get the wrong idea if we send anyone else but a partner. She might think we're trying to brush her off with one of our associates because she's a woman."

I released a deep sigh, raking my fingers through my unruly hair. "Fine, I'll give it a shot. But if I screw this up, I'm blaming you."

Fury flashed me a grin as he nodded. "Fantastic, partner. Trust me, I would be all over this if I could."

"So, what's the big deal in Colorado that you can't reschedule?" I asked, furrowing my brow. "Everything okay with Rose?"

Rose, Fury's twenty-five-year-old sister, being the youngest, has always been a concern for him. Fury wouldn't bolt at the last minute unless it was something significant. I swear, sometimes, he and his brother Blaze acted more like parents than her brothers.

Fury dismissed my question. "She's fine. It's not something you need to worry about."

I wasn't entirely convinced, but Fury would be there for Rose. "If she needs anything, just say the word. I'm here to help."

"I know," he replied. "But this is something I have to take care of. I'll let you know if things change."

He'd better. Rose was practically like a little sister to me, too.

Fury got down to brass tacks. "Alright, can you manage Nadine Seaworth while I'm gone? I can't exactly juggle keeping you knuckleheads in check and looking out for Rose at the same time."

Oh, the classic guilt trip. It never failed with me. "Alright, alright. I already told you yes. Hand over whatever dirt you've got on Nadine. I might not have your suave moves, but I can ace a pop quiz like nobody's business."

Fury pushed a file across his desk with a knowing smirk. "That you can, my friend."

I grabbed the folder, eager to dive into it in the comfort of my office, where I could scribble to my heart's desire. At least I wasn't crushing on Nadine. That would've been a whole other can of worms. She wasn't someone I fantasized about having earth-shattering sex with in my car. Or in a dressing room where I could catch a glimpse of her naked and...

Whoa, boy.

"You've got this, Cory," Fury encouraged me. "I wouldn't pass the baton if I didn't think you could run the race."

"Yeah, I hear you," I replied, not entirely sold but trying to sound like I was.

"Just stick to your strengths, like numbers and strategy. That's your wheelhouse."

"As long as you're not going to suggest I picture her naked, I'll be alright," I said, half-joking.

Fury let loose a belly laugh. "Oh, hell no. You remember what happened when Blaze tried to play wingman for you back in junior high, right?"

How could I ever forget that disaster? I was trying to work up the nerve to ask Jessica Maverick to the dance, and Blaze's brilliant plan was to have me picture her in the buff. I was so freaking nervous that I puked all over her shoes instead.

"Cory, you're a pro," Fury said, all serious now. "Treat her like any other client. We don't need you turning on the charm. Just show her how sharp that brain of yours is. Convince her she needs someone like *you* managing her finances."

It sounded like a solid plan. "Alright, I can handle that," I said, heading for the door. "Got a lot to study for."

My cousin already had his eyes on the screen, no doubt scouting the gossip pages for potential leads.

Back in my office, Warner's eyebrows shot up when he saw me, but he caught on quickly when I told him to clear my schedule.

As soon as I was alone, I scribbled a to-do list on a sticky note.

Go through Nadine Seaworth's file with a fine-tooth comb.

Schedule a meeting for Monday.

Learn everything there is to know about her.

Spend the weekend cooking up the perfect pitch.

It should be a piece of cake, right? But then again, baking a cake isn't always a walk in the park.

"Pull yourself together, McCrae," I mumbled. "No room for mistakes this time."

This was my chance to make things right. Failure wasn't in the cards. I'd show Nadine Seaworth what I was made of and swoop her in before Rylee Palmer could even get a whiff.

It was time to roll up my sleeves and get to work.

TEN

Rylee

My team had been pulling all-nighters for a solid week, cooking up some killer game plans to lure in a few clients from Gracen & McCrae. Their hard work seriously paid off - we didn't just land one, but two sparkling new accounts! I was stoked about their determination, but let's be real, these wins were just the appetizer. Cory was about to find out, big time, that he'd made a huge mistake fucking with my world in every sense of the word.

Now, don't get me wrong, I was hell-bent on making sure he knew that no one could knock his socks off like I could. I wanted to play mind games with him and throw him off his game, both in the boardroom and outside of it.

But let's be honest, just thinking about him - those piercing eyes, that sharp jawline, the memories of his touch - had me feeling more keyed up than ever. I couldn't deny his magnetic pull on me, no matter how hard I tried.

The pressure was getting to me. My shoulders were so

tight I thought I'd get a crick in my neck. I had to force myself to slow down, take a few deep breaths, and just chill out.

I was just about to give up when, lo and behold, something on a social media feed snagged my attention. It was a post about Nadine Seaworth, a well-off widow who was revamping her financial situation, including the charities she backed.

The piece was mostly about her philanthropy, but my curiosity pricked up at the mention of her investment portfolio. Seaworth was on the prowl for a new financial guru. And who better than a bright, innovative company like mine? The only catch was figuring out how to wedge my foot in the door.

Most people would probably go for a traditional business proposal or try to charm her with flattery. But not me. I'd always had a knack for getting inside people's heads. Maybe it's my way of pushing back against all the logical, number-crunching stuff my dad was so hell-bent on instilling in me. You know, the stuff guys are supposed to "get," while women are relegated to the "emotional" stuff.

But hey, my offbeat strategy has served me well so far, right?

I told Mallory to wipe my schedule clean, giving me some breathing room to dive headfirst into Nadine Seaworth's world. I was on a quest to uncover enough intel to reel her in. If Nadine was all about girl power, I'd tempt her with the idea of a woman taking charge of her finances. If experience was her thing, I'd send in my most seasoned pro. And if Gracen & McCrae happened to be her type, I'd find a third way to make her see us in a whole new light.

By the time lunch rolled around, I had a semi-devious plan brewing. It was not completely above board, but at least it was within the bounds of legality and ethics. And let's be real, it was a walk in the park compared to Cory's stunts.

Nadine Seaworth, a widow in her late fifties, had been on her own for over twenty years, ever since her hubby bit the dust when her kid, Bennett, was just a wee ten-year-old. Now, Bennett was in his early thirties and seemed to be protective of his mother.

I guess losing a parent at that age would do that to you. My gaze kept sliding back to the photo on my desk - the last snapshot of me and Mom, taken before she departed from this world. I was twenty-three, a decade older than Bennett when he lost his dad, but I didn't think our age difference would affect how we processed the tragedy. Nah, that distinction belonged solely to my pops, Randall Palmer, and his unending disappointment that his late-in-life surprise package turned out to be a girl. A daughter, not the son he'd always dreamed of.

"You would've understood," I murmured to my mom's photo. "You would have understood why I'm here in Palo Alto and what I'm trying to build."

And why Cory's betrayal had hit me so hard.

With a deep breath, I refocused. Bennett was my ticket in. I would score a meeting with him for Monday. Persuade him that Palmer Money Management was the right call for his mother. With his seal of approval, I'd have the perfect angle to pitch Nadine.

That's how I'd show Gracen & McCrae they'd picked the wrong person to underestimate.

MY WEEKEND WAS a whirlwind of research, with Bennett and Nadine Seaworth taking center stage.

Bennett's reputation as a ladies' man didn't ruffle my feathers - I've got a strict "no client/employee relationship mixed with pleasure" policy. But his being a client's son? That was a bit of a sticky wicket. And let's not forget that Nadine wasn't technically my client...at least, not yet.

So, I decided to indulge in a dress that danced on the line between professional and flirty. It wasn't exactly "let's paint the town red" material, but this sunflower-patterned number was decidedly more fun than my usual work wear. After perfecting my makeup and sliding into a pair of heels that were as classy as they were comfy, I was ready to roll.

I rehearsed my strategy as I made my way to the brunch spot. I had to dazzle Bennett without selling my soul, even if the lines got fuzzy around the edges. But the real prize was outshining Gracen & McCrae.

The moment I waltzed in, I spotted Bennett – unmistakable since the images I'd found of him online were wedged into my brain. The guy towered over six feet, all lean and sharp in a suit that made him look beefier than his internet snapshots. His hair was styled to a T, nailing that sweet balance between youthful and distinguished. Yet, the frosty blue of his eyes, true to the pictures, hinted his dodgy reputation might just be rooted in reality.

Awesome. I sure knew how to pick them.

Okay, so he wasn't exactly the dreamboat I'd hoped for, but hey, he wasn't a total loss, either. I wasn't on the prowl for Cupid's arrow anyway. This guy was just my ticket to Mama Seaworth.

As I strolled up to the table, I plastered on a welcoming

smile and thanked the hostess. I braced myself when Bennett gave me a quick up-and-down glance before we exchanged handshakes. His touch was icy cold, yet his grip struck that perfect balance between firm and not too much. I somehow managed to keep from wiping my hand on my dress once he let go.

Maintaining my cheerful facade, I plopped down in the chair across from him. "Glad we could finally meet in person, Mr. Seaworth," I chirped.

"Oh, no need for formalities. Just call me Bennett," he said, waving down a server.

After we placed our orders, Bennett and I killed time with some easy-breezy chatter while we waited for our food. He seemed nice enough, but this tiny prickle at the back of my neck wouldn't go away. I tried to brush it off, figuring I was just being a bit jumpy after that whole Sacramento incident with the indecent proposal.

I was starting to see trouble in every corner, like a sailor who'd weathered a storm and saw danger in every wave. I had to stop assuming the worst and give people a chance - at least until they really stepped out of line. That's what the voice in my head, which sounded an awful lot like my dear old dad, kept hammering into me.

"Sorry to interrupt, Bennett," I blurted out, slicing through his tale about a trip to Europe.

His grin faltered, still clinging to his face but not quite making it to his eyes. "Everything alright?" he asked, sounding a tad concerned.

"Yep, just need to make a pit stop at the bathroom," I replied, earning a slightly condescending look from Bennett. I suppressed an eye roll - just barely - as Dad's voice chimed in my head, reprimanding me for derailing Bennett's story with potty talk. The more I heard my old man's voice, the clearer it became what a kiss-ass he was.

I was returning to my seat when I careened around a corner like a bull in a china shop and smacked right into someone. Of course, it had to be Cory. Like fresh-cut grass and a hint of sandalwood, his signature scent sent a jolt through my gut.

Great. Just freakin' great.

"What's your deal, showing up here?" Cory's voice was sharp as he caught me from falling.

I busied myself by smoothing out my dress to avoid eye contact. "My reasons for being here are none of your concern, same as I'm not interrogating you about yours."

"You've got to be fucking kidding me," he muttered, eyes locked on something behind me.

I peeked over my shoulder, and my heart took a little dip. Yep, he was gawking at my table, where Bennett was deep in conversation with Nadine Seaworth – his dear old mom.

"You're meeting with Nadine Seaworth here?" I asked, the pieces falling into place.

"And you're here with her son." It wasn't even a question from him. "You think getting cozy with him will sway his mother to your side."

I could tell he was biting back something harsher. "Parent-child relationships matter, especially regarding financial decisions," I said coolly. "I'm sure he's got a say in how his mom's wealth is managed." I walked past Cory, not wanting to linger. "I trust you won't be sitting near us."

"Trust me, Ms. Palmer," he replied, icy as ever. "I have no interest in being anywhere near you."

His words should've bounced off, but they didn't. They stung, even though he had played me first. But I wasn't about to let it show. I was better than that, stronger.

I forced myself to relax as I returned to Bennett, acting like I didn't see Cory escorting Mrs. Seaworth to their table. Chatting up Bennett was like pulling teeth, but I kept at it. I had to knock his socks off so he'd suggest my firm to his mom.

The Seaworths knew nothing about the silent war Cory and I were waging, but I couldn't let Cory win. Hell, no! I'd spent my entire life proving myself to guys like him, showing them that just because I wasn't born with a Y chromosome, it didn't mean I couldn't compete. I've got what it takes to make it in this cutthroat business, and neither Cory nor my dad could make me think otherwise.

Even if being near Cory made my heart do somersaults and my body tingle in all the wrong places.

ELEVEN

Cory

The whole twenty-minute drive back to the office after that brunch was me muttering curses under my breath. Didn't help much, though. Once I got back, I locked myself in my office, replaying the meeting with Nadine repeatedly, trying my best not to think about Rylee.

But, of course, that just soured my mood even more. With Fury out of town, I was kind of stuck in my own head, not really wanting to bother him since he was busy with whatever was going down with Rose. I kept picturing Rylee chatting up Nadine's son. After the stunt she pulled with me, I wouldn't put it past her to try some sneaky moves to sway him.

And honestly, I was at a loss on how to counter that.

That's usually Fury's arena, dealing with people. He would've had a field day if Rylee bumped into him. He would've used it somehow. Me? I just managed to stay civil and then went back to telling Mrs. Seaworth how we could help her out. All while pretending Rylee wasn't right there, probably turning on the charm with Nadine's son.

I hunkered in my office the entire afternoon, only exchanging pleasantries with the security guard on my way out. I flashed him a smile, nodded, and even mustered a "Have a good night."

The drive back to my apartment complex was about as thrilling as watching paint dry, and it didn't do much to soothe my jangled nerves or make me feel any less cruddy.

Once I finally got to the lobby of my apartment building, I figured a stiff drink and a good book might be my only hope for unwinding. The elevator seemed to be stuck on the top floor, so I decided to take the stairs instead - three long flights of them. I hadn't been to the gym in a hot minute, so it was better than nothing, right?

I was huffing and puffing my way up the second-floor landing when the stairwell door swung open, and Becky, my downstairs neighbor, popped out. In her mid-twenties, with light auburn curls pulled into a ponytail, she was quite attractive and nice. From the moment I moved into this building, she'd made it a point to greet me with a friendly "hello." She'd dropped by a few times, delivering misplaced mail or some extra muffins she'd baked. Today, she was as cheerful as ever.

"Hey there," I said, stepping aside to let her pass.

Her green eyes sparkled when she saw me. "Cory! Feels like weeks since I last saw you. How's everything?"

It was two days ago, but who's counting? "Busy," I replied, shifting my weight uncomfortably. "The usual work stuff."

Her grin stretched even wider. "That's fantastic! Your job

must be a real rollercoaster, handling those high-profile clients and their deep pockets. I can't even imagine how you keep your cool with all that pressure! A guy like you needs someone to help unwind at the end of the day, you know?"

I wondered if I'd ever let slip what Gracen & McCrae was all about. Probably not, but it wasn't exactly a state secret either. A quick Google search would've given her the lowdown in no time.

"What I do is a piece of cake compared to your high-stakes dealings," she said, her eyes lighting up with enthusiasm. "Opening my own little designer boutique is a dream come true, but let's be real, I'm not exactly curing cancer with my handcrafted accessories. Still, someone's got to keep the fashion world spinning, right? Might as well be me!"

Ah, yes, the boutique. She'd dropped not-so-subtle hints about it before. She'd also mentioned that her dad was paying for her swanky pad and probably helping kickstart her business too.

I'm not judging, but let me tell you, my family, loaded as they are, never threw a dime at Gracen & McCrae. Nah, that was all Fury and me pulling all-nighters and grinding it out.

Becky paused as if waiting for me to spout some Yoda-level wisdom or something. I was drawing a total blank, though, silently praying she'd move aside so I could finally make my way upstairs to my cozy little hideaway. But I couldn't just muscle past her – that'd be a serious breach of neighborly etiquette.

So there I was, stuck on the second-floor landing, huffing and puffing with the world's perkiest neighbor standing in my way.

Just peachy.

"Hey, you know what they say about all work and no play, right?" Becky chirped, closing the gap between us. "We've got to make room for some fun in there! Me? I'm all about swimming. In fact, I'm heading to the pool this very minute. Do you want to join the party?"

Mustering my best friendly grin, I replied, "Thanks, but I've got a to-do list longer than Rapunzel's hair. Plus, I'm fresh out of swimming trunks."

She leaned in, practically whispering in my ear. "Little secret between you and me: swim trunks are totally optional around here. Some guys just dive right in wearing their boxers."

Cue the deer-in-headlights look. What's the appropriate response to that? Fury would've had a witty retort at the ready, but me? I just stood there, looking like a lost puppy.

"Well, it's been a pretty exhausting day," I eventually blurted out. "I think I'll just eat and crash tonight."

Becky's smile wavered for a moment before rebounding with renewed vigor. "Alright, but if you have a change of heart, I'll be at the pool. Feel free to join me, whatever you're wearing."

She flashed me a cheeky wink and moved aside, letting me scurry up the stairs. Turns out, stairwells could be a hotbed of social interaction. Who knew?

As I finally entered my apartment, I closed the door and savored the blessed silence. I would've given my left pinky for it to be the weekend. Even if I had to trudge into the office, at least I could've enjoyed some sweet solitude with everybody off.

But with Fury still MIA, the entire responsibility-laden world was squarely on my shoulders.

I beelined for the kitchen, desperately craving a drink- hell, maybe even two. Or three- whatever it took to dull the edge of this rollercoaster day.

TWELVE

RYLEE

I was itching for a breather - a wild night filled with giggles and cocktails. Natalie was the perfect sidekick for this kind of escapade. She finally managed to dodge the sniffles for a week, and there she was, sitting right next to me. If she hadn't chosen to sculpt second-graders minds, she could have easily been a supermodel strutting down the catwalk. With her effortlessly cool blond curls and captivating hazel eyes speckled with green, she was a total head-turner. Hanging out with her sometimes made me feel like a drab wallflower, but Nat? She was oblivious to her own knockout looks and would brush off compliments like they were no big deal.

"You smile a lot," I blurted out after polishing off my second margarita.

Natalie raised an eyebrow. "Well, I've got plenty to be happy about."

I gazed into my now-empty glass. "That must be nice. I wouldn't mind having a few more reasons to smile."

"You've had a rough year," Nat reminded me. "But your new business is taking off, right?"

I glanced at my glass, contemplating the merits of scraping the last drop with my finger.

"Things are looking up," I confirmed. "Hired some new staff, landed a few accounts. If only those jackasses at Gracen & McCrae hadn't messed with my groove."

"Another finance firm?"

I nodded, signaling the bartender. Since I was taking a cab home, there was no need to hold back on the drinks.

"Those Gracen & McCrae cousins are sneaky if you ask me. Especially one of them."

"Sneaky in what way?"

I took a gulp of my newly served margarita. "Remember that hunk I told you about from the masquerade ball?"

"The one you haven't stopped talking about for the last week?" Nat sipped her drink, a knowing smile playing on her lips. "How could I possibly forget?"

I let out a deep sigh. "Ran into him again."

Her eyes widened, curiosity piqued. "Did you two...you know?"

Her teacher-like tone kicked in. She carefully avoided sex words, which I usually found endearing. But now, with a few drinks in me, it was downright hilarious.

"Played hide the salami? Had a rumble in the jungle? Partook in some horizontal tango?"

"Oh, for the love of God, just stop!" Nat begged, her cheeks flushing.

I grinned mischievously. "I've got a million of 'em. Tangoed between the sheets? Waltzed in the wild?"

"Enough, or I'm confiscating your drink," she warned, reaching for my glass.

I pulled it back. "Fine. Yes, we bumped into each other again. At the grocery store—"

"Please don't tell me you did it by the bananas."

"Nope." I sighed dramatically. "In a dressing room next door."

"You're kidding."

"Oh, we did," I confirmed. "And then he drops that *he's* Cory McCrae."

"Holy..." Nat's eyes bulged. "McCrae, as in..."

"Yep." I downed another gulp. "The McCrae of Gracen & McCrae. The bastard."

Nat's eyes lit up as the puzzle pieces fell into place, a grin spreading across her face.

"So, you think this Cory guy recognized you from the get-go?" she asked, leaning forward in her seat.

I rolled my eyes. "Please, I don't believe in coincidences like that. The first time, maybe it was just chance. But again? At a grocery store, of all places? Too fucking convenient if you ask me."

Nat's eyes narrowed as she considered this. "Well, if he made the moves both times, I can see why you'd think he was up to something."

I shrugged, taking another sip of my drink. "It was more like a mutual seduction, to be honest."

Nat laughed. "Mutual seduction? Really, Ry? I know you better than that. You don't sit around waiting for things to happen."

I raised an eyebrow, not about to apologize for being a woman who knows what she wants. "Okay, fine. I'll admit it.

I wanted to have sex with him. Both times. But that doesn't mean he wasn't being manipulative with those stupid dimples and that smirk of his."

Nat shook her head, a smile playing at the corners of her mouth. "Damn, girl. You've got it bad."

"Got what?" I glared at her. "Got the hots for Cory McCrae? Pfft." I made a dismissive gesture. "He irritates me."

"Yeah, exactly," Nat smirked. "He gets under your skin."

I rolled my eyes. "He annoys me."

She shrugged. "Same difference."

Shaking my head, I jabbed a finger in her direction. "Nope, there's a world of difference. He's a walking headache- aggravating, irritating, frustrating, infuriating."

"You sound like you just swallowed a thesaurus." She laughed. "I love how your vocabulary expands when you're drunk."

"I'm not drunk," I insisted. "I'm tipsy. Slightly buzzed. Vaguely intoxicated."

"You're doing it again," she pointed out. "Thesaurus."

"You're a thesaurus," I retorted, aware that my insult wasn't much of an insult. But it provided a great distraction from my friend's newfound obsession with *fucking* Cory McCrae.

I frowned. No, not fucking Cory McCrae. I didn't want her to do that. No one should be fucking him. Even though he was really good at it. I mean, the man knew what he was doing. It was unfair, actually. Guys who would seduce a competitor to mess with her shouldn't be that hot and sexy and good in bed. They should come with a warning sign or be downright ugly and stinky.

I sighed, thinking back to how amazing Cory smelled.

That cologne he wore at the ball was just...perfect. And then running into him at the store and again at the restaurant – oh crap, I hadn't spilled that part to Nat yet.

"He's been tailing me," I blurted out. "Or trying to get a scoop on my business moves. Trying to snag a client I'm after."

Nat's eyebrows shot up. "How do you figure?"

I leaned in, going for the dramatic reveal. "I was at this brunch meeting, right? With a potential client's son. And guess who was there with the client herself? Cory McCrae, all decked out in this smexy suit."

"Smexy?" she echoed.

"Smoldering and sexy. It's a thing," I insisted. At her skeptical look, I defended, "What? It's a legit word."

She laughed, eyeing my almost empty glass. "I think it's time to cut you off. You're inventing words now."

"Hey, all words are made up," I shot back. "Thor said that."

Nat shook her head, grinning. "You need more hobbies than quoting comic book characters."

"I prefer to think I'm quoting Chris Hemsworth."

She signaled the bartender for water. "Okay, Hemsworth fan, tell me you ate something earlier."

I rolled my eyes. "Yes, Mom. Had dinner."

"Geez," Nat said, half-teasing, half-serious. "This guy really gets to you. You definitely have a thing for him."

"I fucking despise him!" I protested a little too loudly.

"Alright, alright," she soothed. "You hate him, but you're definitely into him."

"Fuck no," I said, grabbing the water. "He's hot, though. Those dimples, remember?"

"You mentioned them," Nat said with a chuckle. "And don't forget the other, um, attributes," she added.

Her blushing face was a sight, and I started laughing. "You can't say 'cock,' can you?"

"Shut up."

"What about 'dick'? Or you could be completely teacher-y and just go with the anatomical term 'penis.'"

"You're such a jerk," Nat said.

"At least *I* can say penis."

Nat crossed her arms, giving me a pointed look. "At least *I'm* not mooning over my business rival."

"That's it," I declared, downing the water in one go. The bottle crumpled awkwardly, ruining my attempt at a dramatic gesture. "I'm gonna show you what 'mooning over someone' really looks like."

Nat's skeptical eyebrow raise told me she probably thought I'd gone off the deep end, but there was no stopping me now. I swiveled around, scanning the sea of people, and zeroed in on the first half-decent-looking bloke who seemed to be flying solo.

"Just watch me show how little I give a damn about Mr. Smexy," I proclaimed, marching towards the guy. "And for the record, 'smexy' is here to stay."

As I closed the distance between us, I sized up the dude; shaggy sandy blond hair, dark eyes that gave nothing away, and a physique that practically screamed, "I used to be the star quarterback."

I tapped his shoulder, and while there was no earth-shattering spark like with Cory, that wasn't the point. This was about making a statement.

"Wanna dance?" I asked, flashing him my best come-hither look.

He gave me the once-over and apparently liked what he saw. We navigated through the throng of people, and he found us a little spot to call our own. I draped my arms around his neck, moving to the rhythm, doing my darndest to focus on the current dance partner, not the last one.

I hoped Nat was getting an eyeful, seeing just how much I was absolutely, positively *not* thinking about Cory McCrae. Not one bit.

THIRTEEN

Cory

Saturday was my own personal oasis, holed up in my apartment and dodging humans like the plague. But by Sunday, there was no running from reality. Fury had rolled back into town and was hungry to get up to speed on everything, so we agreed to have lunch at my humble abode.

Fury made his entrance just as the food came. As we scooped up noodles, we shot the breeze about the usual suspects - the weather and his flights to and from Colorado. But I couldn't resist bringing up Rose once we plopped down at the table.

"She'll be alright," Fury reassured me. "Just had to help with a few things, but she's holding it together."

"So, no need for a full-blown family ambush to scare the living daylights out of some poor schmuck at her ranch?" I said, trying to inject a little levity into the situation.

He let out a hearty chuckle. "Nah, nothing like that. Just needed a good old heart-to-heart."

I extended my usual invitation. "If she needs anything, you know I'm here for her."

Fury nodded, and then he hit me with a curveball. "I really appreciate you taking the reins while I was gone. It's good to know our company is in safe hands with family I can count on."

Getting acknowledgment from a Gracen guy is like hitting the emotional jackpot. They're not exactly known for their touchy-feely side. But Fury went beyond mere words; he recognized our solid partnership.

Considering my recent blunders, I decided not to read too much into it.

"So, I bet you're dying to know how the Nadine Seaworth lunch went?" I asked, shifting the conversation. Fury nodded, and I launched into the story. "It was a hot mess from the start. We'd barely walked into the restaurant when Nadine spotted her son Bennett already there."

"Wait, you didn't invite Bennett, did you?" Fury asked, looking surprised.

"Nah, no way." I shook my head. "I figured it'd be wiser to meet with Nadine one-on-one and show her we respect her as our client, not just an extension of her son."

Fury quirked an eyebrow. "Nice strategy. Guess she'd had it with her previous team treating her like a second fiddle to her son."

I bobbed my head in agreement. "You got that right. Fed up to the gills with folks thinking Bennett's the one running the show."

Fury snorted. "So much for Bennett squashing that notion, showing up uninvited to the meeting."

I heaved a sigh. "But here's the kicker: it's more complicated than that. Bennett didn't just materialize out of thin air. Rylee Palmer invited him for a meeting."

Mentioning her name made my jaw clench. I had to remind myself to unwind my face.

Fury's expression was unreadable. "The Rylee you hooked up with? Twice?"

I glared at him. "Yeah, that Rylee. The one who *played* me all along. Twice."

He shrugged, all nonchalant. "Just making sure. So, Palmer's setting her sights on Nadine Seaworth now? Using Bennett as her pawn? Damn, she's sneaky."

I bobbed my head up and down, emphatic. "Oh, that's her go-to strategy, alright. She's cozying up to Bennett, the golden son of a loaded client. She used me like a puppet to keep me distracted and glean some insights, and now she's pulling the same stunt with him."

Fury leaned back in his chair, rubbing his chin thoughtfully. "You sure this isn't just one of those bizarre coincidences?"

I waved off his idea with a dismissive hand. "It's a clear pattern, Fury. She's playing the long game, treating these relationships like a chessboard. She got one over on me and is now trying to pull the same move on Bennett."

He squinted at me, his expression dubious. "You really think that's her whole schtick? Using her 'attributes' to get ahead?"

Frustration bubbled up, spilling over. "Yep, that's exactly what I think. And her little dance with Bennett just confirms it. She's up to her old tricks."

Fury raised a skeptical eyebrow. "It's just strange, don't you think? We haven't heard a peep about Palmer pulling these shenanigans. I mean, she's new in town, but she's been keeping a low profile. You'd think someone would've spilled the beans by now."

I grimaced. "Trust me, buddy, as the guy who got taken for a ride, it's not exactly the kind of thing you share during coffee breaks. I only said something because I was worried about her next play against our company."

Fury nodded, looking thoughtful as he pushed away his empty plate. "I get it, but still, not everybody is like you. I mean, she's young and attractive, right? Some of those old-timers would probably be bragging about it."

His words pricked like a cactus, making me bristle. The thought of Rylee with other men stirred up a storm of emotions I'd rather avoid.

I tossed my crumpled napkin on my empty plate. "No point in dwelling on it," I said, standing to tidy the table. "Mrs. Seaworth's playing her cards close to her chest. She hasn't made up her mind yet. But I'm gearing up for a showdown for her account. Been working my butt off since Monday, crunching numbers and whipping up spreadsheets. It's all on your desk, ready for your big meeting with her."

Fury knitted his brow, "Why am I meeting Mrs. Seaworth? You've already got a foot in the door."

I gave him a look that could kill. If I weren't elbow-deep in dishes, I would've flipped him the bird.

He chuckled, "I'm just yanking your chain. I planned to step in unless you two were really hitting it off."

"Yeah, right," I muttered.

"Could've happened. You scrub up good," he teased, flashing a grin. "When you actually put in the effort, that is."

"You know what's bugging me about Rylee?" I interjected, eager to steer the conversation in a different direction. "It's not just that she's easy on the eyes, but she's got some serious brains too. Starting her own company? That takes some serious smarts. Or is she just the pretty face of it all? I seem to recall reading something about her dad's firm in Sacramento being a big deal."

This whole thing had been bugging me. If Rylee's flirtations were just a ploy to score accounts without delivering the goods, we would've heard some grumbling by now. But nobody was saying they were losing money. It was still early days, but she seemed to know her stuff.

And that annoyed me to no end. It meant she didn't need to play those games to succeed. But I couldn't entertain Fury's suggestion that Rylee might not be playing those games at all.

"You know, for someone who doesn't like her, you sure do talk about her a lot," Fury said, flashing a grin.

"I'm talking about her because she's fucking with our business," I retorted as I snagged the dish towel to dry a plate.

Fury shrugged nonchalantly. "Maybe, maybe not."

I was about to lay into him with my rebuttal when a knock on my door cut me off. I tossed the towel at Fury and headed out of the kitchen.

I swung the door wide open, wishing I could hit the rewind button the moment I did. There was Becky, beaming brighter than the sun and holding a batch of cookies like she was the queen of baked goods. I just stood there, stunned, trying to wrap my head around her nerve and the fact that she'd brought sweets.

"Well, hey there," she chimed as if finding me at home was the most unexpected thing in the world.

She didn't waste a second before her eyes landed on Fury. "Oh, I didn't realize you had company, Cory," she said, trying to act all casual.

I'd been hoping to dodge any uncomfortable moments, but Fury had other ideas. "I wouldn't exactly call myself 'just company,'" he said and stood, a smirk playing on his lips. "Cory and I are family."

Becky gave me a look, and with a sigh, I nodded. Explaining our tangled family tree was more of a hassle than it was worth.

"Fury Gracen," he introduced himself, offering a handshake to Becky. Still beaming, Becky set the cookie jar on the table and shook his hand. "Becky Scheinberg. I'm always right under Cory."

Fury choked back a laugh that he tried to pass off as a cough, and I shot him a glare that could kill. My scowl only seemed to amuse him more. Not wanting him to embarrass Becky by pointing out her unintentional double entendre, I moved to the table where she'd placed the cookies.

"Here, let me find a box for these," I said, trying to keep things from going sideways.

"No worries, just keep the jar," Becky replied with a dismissive wave. "I know where to find you if I need it back."

I grabbed the cookies and hurried off to clear some space on the counter.

"So, you're just downstairs?" Fury asked, clearly intrigued.

"Yep, apartment 202. Right beneath this one," Becky confirmed, tapping her foot on the floor. "Thankfully, the soundproofing's top-notch, or I'd be privy to all Cory's wild parties."

Fury snickered. "Wild parties? You've got to be kidding me. Are we talking about the same Cory?"

Becky let out a full-bellied laugh. "I see what you're saying. The other day, I tried talking him into a swim, but no dice. All work, no play with this guy."

Fury shot me a sly wink. "Swimming, huh? I haven't seen Cory dive in since we were both ankle-biters."

Becky suddenly lit up. "Oh, wait a second, Fury Gracen. As in Gracen & McCrae? That's you?"

"Yep, that's me, in the flesh," Fury confirmed, leaning nonchalantly against the counter. "So, Becky, spill the beans. What's your story?"

I was thankful for Fury taking charge of the chit-chat, but I was starting to feel like a third wheel in my own home. His knack for charming the ladies was nothing short of astonishing. I figured it was time for me to jump in and steer the conversation towards a wrap-up. "Alright, Fury, we've got a towering mountain of work waiting for us tomorrow, so I think it's time we call it a night. And Becky, we don't want to keep you any longer."

Becky and Fury swiveled their heads to look at me, with Becky being the first to speak up. "To tell you the truth, I didn't have much planned today apart from baking those cookies. I wanted to make sure you got them while they were still warm and gooey, just out of the oven."

"Yeah, we do have to wade through some work stuff," Fury chimed in, flashing me a knowing smirk. "Isn't that right, Cory?"

"You got it, essential work stuff," I echoed, grateful for the lifeline.

Becky's expression turned tender. "Oh, I didn't mean to crash your workday. I'm really sorry."

"No worries at all, seriously, thanks for the cookies," I reassured her, gently nudging her to leave.

The moment the door snapped shut, I heaved a massive sigh of relief. Meandering back to the kitchen, I spotted Fury with his arm plunged elbow-deep in the cookie jar.

"You're aware she baked those for me, right?" I said, half-joking.

Fury merely chortled, waving a cookie in the air. "She's totally smitten with you, Cory."

I rolled my eyes, chuckling it off. "Nah, she's just being neighborly."

He shrugged, gobbling down the cookie. "Keep telling yourself that, pal. You're not exactly the world's best signal reader."

Rylee's face flickered in my mind, but I swiftly banished it. It wasn't like that with Becky. She was just being...well, friendly. I was positive.

I attempted to reassure Fury, but he didn't push it, whether he bought it or not.

Thank God for the tiny blessings.

The last thing I needed was more complications with women.

FOURTEEN

RYLEE

With a flick of my makeup brush, I nailed my winged eyeliner, and my phone went off on the bathroom counter. Glancing at the screen, I saw Natalie's name flashing up. "Hey, Nat," I said, multitasking like a pro as I applied powder and balanced the phone between my ear and shoulder.

"Hey, babe! How's it hanging in hot-stuff land? Are you still fantasizing about that dreamy finance guy?"

I rolled my eyes, Nat's playful tone ringing clear through the receiver. "Seriously, Nat, I do not have a crush on Cory McCrae!" I protested, rummaging through my closet for an outfit.

Natalie just chuckled. "Uh huh, sure. That's why you didn't make a move on Mr. Quarterback star the other night?"

I let out an exasperated sigh. "His girlfriend magically appeared and dragged him out of there. What was I supposed to do, start a catfight over him?"

"Mmmhmm, right," Nat replied, not buying my story for

a second. "Come on, Rylee. You're still head over heels for your rival, no matter how much you try to deny it."

I grabbed a silky burgundy blouse and held it up to myself in the mirror. "The only thing I'm obsessing over is landing Nadine Seaworth as a client. I've got another lunch meeting with her son Bennett today to try and make that happen."

"Uh-huh. Well, have fun buttering up the rich and famous. But do me a favor—if you run into lover boy Cory, try not to jump his bones in front of the clients."

I scoffed. "You're hilarious. I'll catch you later."

We said our goodbyes, and I tossed the phone onto the bed in exasperation. I was *not* still thinking about Cory McCrae. I wasn't! I had more important things to focus on, like impressing Bennett Seaworth and stealing his mother's business away from Gracen & McCrae.

Despite that odd run-in with Cory during the meeting with Bennett, I was holding up well and feeling optimistic about my progress with Bennett. Sure, he wasn't the life of the party, but honestly, I wasn't there to make new BFFs. I had a mission to accomplish and an unresolved issue with Cory to deal with.

I hardly believed it when Bennett called to schedule another lunch date after he already promised to put in a good word with his mom. So there I was, dolled up and heading to some ritzy restaurant, praying I wouldn't run into Cory McCrae again. Was it too much to ask the universe never to cross paths with that arrogant jerk? A girl could dream! Still, I had to stay focused on impressing Bennett. I was feeling pretty darn optimistic, with a ninety-five percent confidence level.

When I saw where Bennett wanted to meet, my good mood tanked. Evvia? Some hoity-toity Greek place I'd only heard whispers about. It's not that I was a super picky eater or anything, but let's just say my mom would beg to differ.

Taking a deep breath, I swaggered into Evvia like I owned the place, or at least like I belonged there. Bennett was nowhere in sight, but luckily, our reservation awaited me. I sat at the table, trying to ignore how the crisp white tablecloth seemed to glare at me, daring me to spill something. I flagged down a server, who glided over with an air of practiced elegance and ordered a glass of water with a slice of lemon. You know, to really class up the joint.

As I waited for Bennett, I scanned the menu, my eyes widening at the prices. Yikes! I could practically hear my bank account crying out in protest. But hey, this was all in the name of impressing Bennett and landing his mom's business, right? I could justify the cost if it meant securing a major client.

I squinted at the descriptions, trying to decipher the fancy-schmancy language. What the heck was "konzato keftedes" anyway? And "horta vrasta"? It all sounded so...Greek to me. I sighed, resigning myself to the fact that I'd probably end up pointing at something random and hoping for the best. At least the water with lemon was a safe bet.

Ten minutes late, Bennett sauntered in, all smiles and swagger. "Wow, you're looking fabulous this afternoon," he commented, dropping into his chair like he owned the place.

"Thanks," I replied, setting down the menu with a soft thud. "Just sticking with water for now."

"Oh, come on, we can do better than that!" Before I could blink, he flagged down the server and ordered a bottle of red wine. Classic Bennett, always taking charge without a second thought.

I put on a polite grin, biting my tongue to keep from commenting on his presumptuous move. There was no need to create a scene over something as minor as him ordering for me, right?

As the server poured each of us a glass of the deep red liquid, I mustered up another fake smile. Bennett raised his glass in a toast, a mischievous glint in his eyes.

"To new business ventures," he said, his voice smooth and confident. I clinked my glass against his, taking a small sip of the wine. It was delicious, but I couldn't let myself get distracted by it. I was here for a reason, and it wasn't to get tipsy on expensive wine, but man, Bennett was really feeling himself, leaning back with that smug look on his face. "Gotta say, Rylee, color me impressed. Not many gals can keep up with a guy like me," he boasted.

I cocked an eyebrow at that. "Oh really now?"

He nodded, eyeing me up and down in a way that made my skin crawl. "You're different from those other girls chasing after my family's money. You've got your own thing going on."

I laughed, playing along. "Well, hey, I've never been one to sit around twiddling my thumbs. I like making things happen for myself."

Bennett leaned in, dropping his voice to a low murmur. "I dig that. I like a woman with ambition. It's sexy."

I rolled my eyes, trying not to gag at his words. "Yes, well, I'm very driven when it comes to my work," I said evenly. "Your mom seems to be doing alright for herself, but she could be doing even better with the right advisor."

Bennett chuckled. "Straight to the point, aren't you? I like that too." He reached across the table, brushing his fingers over the back of my hand. "How about we enjoy our lunch first and discuss business later? I'd love to get to know you better...personally."

I gently pulled my hand back, trying not to show irritation. "Look, Bennett, I appreciate the compliments and the wine, but we really need to focus on why we're here. Can we please just talk about that?"

Bennett let out a dramatic sigh and leaned back in his chair once more. "Alright, alright, you win. Let's talk shop for a bit."

I stopped myself from another eye roll and instead jumped into my pitch, doing my best to convince Bennett of the advantages of teaming up with Palmer Money Management. He appeared attentive, occasionally nodding and asking a question or two. But I could sense his mind wandering off, his gaze frequently straying towards the other women in the restaurant.

After what felt like forever, I finished my pitch and took a deep breath. "So, what's your take on it?"

Bennett took his sweet time sipping his wine, his eyes locked on mine. "Well, Rylee, you're quite the impressive woman. I think my mom would be lucky to have you managing her money. But..."

My heart sank as he let the word hang in the air. "But what?" I asked, trying to keep my voice steady.

A sly grin spread across his face. "But I want a little something more from you first."

I felt my stomach turn. "Excuse me?"

He leaned in closer, his breath hot on my face. "I can get

my mom to sign with your firm," he said, his voice low and smug. "But you gotta give me a reason."

My skin crawled at the insinuation, but I kept my cool. "I appreciate your support, Bennett. I think I've given you plenty of reasons already."

Bennett's face tightened, clearly not getting the hint. "You know, I can be very persuasive with my mom. Especially if someone's...close to me."

Oh boy, here we go again. Every guy I meet these days is a Grade-A jerk. I was doing my best not to let my frustration show, trying to keep my fists from clenching under the table.

"Whoa there, buddy. I appreciate the offer, but I'm gonna have to pass," I said, keeping things light and breezy but still firm. "Right now, I'm all about my career and not so much about the romantic entanglements."

Bennett leaned back in his chair, trying to play it cool, but it was clear that he wasn't used to hearing the word "no." My pre-meeting research had suggested he was the type who usually got his way. Shocker, right?

But then, like a true master of manipulation, he switched up his tactics, flashing his best charming smile. It was like watching a bad actor in a soap opera.

"So, there's this shindig on Friday," he said, barely pausing for breath. "I need a plus one, just to keep up appearances."

Really? He wanted me as his eye candy? *Ugh*.

I hesitated, but then he dropped a bombshell.

"Cory McCrae's escorting my mom to that very same event."

"Alright, damn it, you've got yourself a date," I blurted

out without missing a beat. "But don't get any ideas, mister. This is strictly business, got it?"

"Of course," he replied, maybe just a touch too eager.

As we wrapped up, I couldn't shake the feeling I'd just been checkmated in a game of chess where every move was a calculated risk. Bennett's invitation seemed simple enough, but it felt like a pawn sacrifice in this high-stakes match. And let's not even get started on Cory's involvement - that just added fuel to the fire.

FIFTEEN

Cory

The next time Fury sprang a charity event on me, I would lay down the law - no more snooty parties where people were more interested in showing off their riches than the actual cause.

We hadn't even planned on attending this particular shindig. But Fury caught wind it was a cause close to Nadine Seaworth's heart, and it'd give us a chance to schmooze with her in a more laid-back setting. Since Fury hadn't had a chance to meet with her one-on-one, I had to tag along and make the formal intros.

I was getting annoyed with my cousin as I gave my tie a final check before heading down to meet him in the waiting car. Fury gave me a curt nod as I hopped in but didn't say a word about my suit or the fact that I couldn't stop fidgeting with my cufflinks. Without the disguise of a masquerade, I felt even more on edge than usual, and Fury knew me well enough to pick up on it.

Stepping into the party, heads swiveled in our direction -

par for the course, really. I was more than happy to hang back and let Fury take the lead, allowing clients to set their sights on him before they noticed me fidgeting.

Catching a glimpse of Nadine, Fury leaned in and whispered, "Let's mingle a bit before approaching her."

That sounded like a plan to me. With Nadine, we had to strike that delicate balance, making her feel like she'd be a valuable addition to Gracen & McCrae without coming off as desperate.

Flipping the switch on my 'charming businessman' persona, I trailed after Fury toward a group huddled near the bar. Some of them were already our clients, but the rest were untapped resources waiting to be discovered. Talking shop with them was a breeze - they weren't the usual high-society ladies, so my typical awkwardness took a backseat.

Gearing up for the main event, I inhaled deeply and prepared to dazzle Nadine Seaworth with my irresistible charms. It was time to break out the big guns.

As I approached her, I gently took her hand, just the way she liked it - a nice touch instead of a boring old handshake.

"Mrs. Seaworth," I began, ever the respectful one.

"Oh, please, dear, call me Nadine," she replied with a kind smile, squeezing my hand.

"Of course, Nadine," I played along, falling into our usual familiar routine.

As I Introduced Fury, I watched him work his magic on her with that signature Gracen grin. "Nice to finally meet you in person," he said, as smooth as ever.

"I've heard about the charm," Nadine chuckled, her cheeks flushing slightly as she looked at me. "No offense, of course."

"None taken." I shrugged it off and let them chat while I scanned the crowd. Not really in the mood for small talk, I avoided eye contact with anyone who might drag me into a conversation.

And then, there she was. Rylee Palmer. The same elegant updo, a stunning blue dress that hugged her curves - hard to miss. But just as our eyes met, she quickly looked away. A pang of something - maybe regret or irritation - washed over me. But when I saw Bennett Seaworth standing beside her, nearly touching her, a different feeling crept in - annoyance, teetering on the edge of anger.

It was like deja vu - another social event, Rylee in a captivating dress, laughing – charming everyone in sight. I could already picture the rest of the night: a dance, a suggestive whisper, a proposal for a secret rendezvous. The same script she'd used on me.

As I watched them, part of me felt foolish for ever thinking there was more to our relationship than her calculated moves. But another part - the part that remembered her touch, her laughter - couldn't completely shake off the idea that maybe, just maybe, there was something genuine hidden beneath all that deception.

Damn.

I stormed over to the bar, leaving Nadine and Fury in my dust, and ordered a shot of whiskey. It scorched my throat but barely made a dent in the emotional hurricane swirling inside me. Rylee flirting with Bennett Seaworth was all I could think about, and it was like a punch to the gut. The whiskey churned in my stomach, making me feel queasy. It appeared that she was using the same script on him that she'd used on me, leaving a sour taste in my mouth.

I ordered another, but Fury slid up next to me, raising an eyebrow before I could down it. "You sure that's a good idea?" he asked, nodding at the shot glass in my hand.

He had a point. The last thing I needed was to lose control, especially here. With a sigh, I pushed the glass towards him, and he downed it in one smooth motion. "You think Nadine will go for our pitch?" I asked, trying to steer my thoughts toward business.

Fury shrugged, his casual gesture belying the importance of the situation. "I hope so. We need the Seaworth account," he said. But for me, beating Rylee to this account had become more than just business. It was personal.

As we worked the room, playing our parts perfectly, I couldn't focus. My mind kept wandering back to Rylee, wondering what she was up to. So, I retreated to a quiet place for a moment's peace, and that's when she appeared, coming around the corner with a look of surprise on her face.

"Rylee," I said, trying my best to keep the venom out of my voice. "Fancy meeting you here."

She stopped dead in her tracks, recognition dawning in her eyes. "Cory," she replied as if we were old pals. "Are you here to avoid the drama, too?"

I stepped closer, my frustration bubbling up like a volcano. "It's more like trying to avoid you," I quipped, trying to sound casual.

A hint of surprise flickered across her face. "Avoiding me? You're not here to try and win over Nadine, are you?" she asked, her voice teasing.

"No way!" I shot back, my heart rate picking up. "Just being professional, unlike some people."

Rylee's eyebrows furrowed, skepticism written all over

her face. "Professional? Really? Because from where I was standing, it looked like you two were getting pretty cozy."

I clenched my jaw, irritation simmering. "Cozy? I'm just doing my job, Rylee. Maybe that's something you should try."

She crossed her arms, her lips pressing into a thin line. "So, seducing someone at a masquerade ball is just part of the job?"

Heat flushed my face as memories of our encounter in my car came flooding back. "That was different, and you know it."

"Different?" she scoffed. "Please. We're both playing the same game, McCrae. Don't act like you're above it."

I stepped closer, my frustration reaching a boiling point. "Playing the game? Is that what you call sleeping with someone to get information?"

Rylee's expression wavered for a moment before she regained her composure. "I don't need to sleep with anyone to get what I want. I'm good at what I do."

I gave a humorless laugh. "Right. So, what's your excuse for Bennett Seaworth? Are you just networking?"

Her eyes blazed with anger. "You don't know shit about it."

"I know enough," I shot back. "I know you're using him, just like you tried with me."

"Use you?" Her laugh was bitter. "You think you're so important that I was using you? I had no idea who you were that night."

I shook my head, disbelief clouding my thoughts. "So, it's just a coincidence you're after the same account as me?"

Rylee stepped back, her gaze icy. "Believe whatever you

want, McCrae. But don't kid yourself into thinking you're the center of my world."

The tension between us was a heavy fog. Part of me wanted to believe her, to think there was something genuine beneath all the games. But every word she spoke felt like another layer of deception.

"Alright, enough's enough," I blurted out, breaking the silence. "You need to back off, Rylee. And that includes Nadine Seaworth."

She cocked an eyebrow, challenging me. "Or what? You gonna throw down?"

"Oh, you don't wanna find out how good I am at this game," I warned her, trying to sound tough.

She poked me in the chest, and I swear, it was like she'd shocked me. "Don't try to play the big shot with me, Cory McCrae," she said, her voice low and serious. "We both know the score here."

Before I knew what was happening, I grabbed her hand and pulled her close. She looked surprised for a second before our lips met, and damn, she tasted like everything I'd been craving. As we pressed against each other, my hand found its way to her hair, and it was softer than I could've imagined, like finding a long-lost treasure.

Next thing I knew, I had her pinned against the wall, our hearts beating in sync. I could feel her responding, her lips parting as my tongue met hers, and she let out this little sound that sent electricity through me. Without realizing it, I let my hand wander, feeling the goosebumps rise on her arm as I moved up to cup her breast. Even through her clothes, it fits perfectly in my hand, and I couldn't resist the urge to brush my thumb over her nipple.

But just as things were heating up, we heard footsteps nearby. We sprang apart, both of us trying to catch our breath and get our bearings. Rylee's eyes were wide, and I could see the same desire in them that I felt pulsing through me.

The moment I let go, reality hit me like a ton of bricks. What the hell was I doing? This wasn't right. Our intentions were all twisted up in a mess of desire and competition, and we were just using each other. I couldn't let it happen again.

Before I could apologize or explain, she took off.

What the actual fuck just happened? My heart was racing, and I needed a cold shower, stat. Instead, I leaned against the wall, trying to get my shit together.

Eventually, I pulled myself together and headed back to the party, determined to talk to her about that kiss and our crazy pull. But she was nowhere to be found. There was no glass slipper, no breadcrumbs – nothing.

I told myself it was for the best. This whole situation was a disaster, and she clearly didn't give a damn about me. It was all just a game to her.

But deep down, I knew even I couldn't buy my own bullshit.

SIXTEEN

Rylee

My cheeks were on fire as I practically sprinted away from Cory. The flush wasn't just from embarrassment; it was because every cell in my body had ignited the second his lips met mine. And now, those same cells were screaming at me to do something completely insane, like drag him into a storage closet and fuck him senseless.

But therein lies the problem. While I couldn't get him out of my mind, he clearly saw me as some kind of villain, even though, ironically, he was the one who had seduced me under false pretenses.

The more I thought about it, the more I questioned my interpretation of what had happened between us. Was I getting it all wrong?

I pushed it away. Deep thinking was the last thing I wanted right now. I had to escape before Cory came back to avoid the awkward dance of evading him for the rest of the night.

I spotted Bennett right where I'd left him and made a beeline for him.

"Let's leave," I said quietly as I reached his side, then added, "Please," with as much politeness as I could muster.

The smile that spread across his lips sent a shiver of revulsion up my spine, but I brushed off the urge to comment on it. Getting out of there was what mattered.

"If you'll excuse me, gentlemen," he announced to his group in a smug tone. "It seems my date can't wait for me to take her home."

Again, I suppressed my anger at his implication and grabbed his arm more forcefully than I intended. "Now, Bennett."

As we headed for the exit, Bennett went full caveman. He wrapped his arm around my waist and leaned in so close I could almost taste the bourbon on his breath. "Your place or mine, sweet cheeks?" he asked with all the charm of a wet sock.

I sighed, taking a step back. "Drop it, Bennett. I have no desire to be your flavor of the week."

His face twisted into a sneer belonging to a cheap horror movie villain. "You're one ungrateful little piece of work, you know that?" he spat out, venom lacing his words.

For a moment, I thought I must have misheard him. But then my temper went from zero to sixty in record time. "Excuse me?" I asked, my voice deceptively calm.

"You must be slow," he snarled, eyes narrowing. "I showed up to help you out with Mom's account. You owe me now."

I gritted my teeth, barely holding back the urge to tell him where he could stick it. "Newsflash, Bennett," I said, my voice dripping with sarcasm. "I'm not some damsel in distress who needs help, and I sure as hell don't owe you anything. If you think I will jump into bed with you to seal a business deal, you've got another thing coming."

"Then I guess you won't mind if I recommend Gracen & McCrae to my mom instead," he said, his eyes narrowing.

I somehow kept my chill, not wanting to hand Bennett the satisfaction of watching me freak out. But man, his threat stung. Losing the Seaworth account was already bad news, but losing it to Gracen & McCrae? That was like adding insult to injury.

"Knock yourself out, Bennett," I said, doing my best to sound as chill as a cucumber even though I felt more like a pressure cooker about to blow. "Tell your mom whatever floats your boat. But let me repeat one thing to make it crystal clear to you, Bennett." I stepped within an inch of him. "I don't owe you, or anyone else, squat. And there's no way in hell I'm going to let you manipulate or blackmail me into sleeping with you."

His face scrunched up like he'd bitten a lemon, and for a second, I thought his head might just pop off like a cartoon character. Instead, he released an exasperated huff and stomped away, mumbling something under his breath that I couldn't quite make out.

Left alone after the showdown with Bennett, I sucked in a deep breath, inhaling calming vibes. I needed a new game plan and fast. This Seaworth gig was a biggie, no doubt about it - bigger than all our other accounts put together. But heck, was I really going to sell my soul or trample on my self-respect just to land it? No way. I gave my head a good shake, trying to rid myself of the slimy feeling that the whole scenario left me with. Time to regroup, recharge, and cook up a Plan B that didn't involve me playing pawn to Bennett's warped little sexual fantasy.

I made my way to the door, already brainstorming. As I stepped outside, the cool night air hit me like a refreshing slap in the face. Tonight's events were just another twist in the crazy theme park that is the world of finance.

I slid into the cab's backseat, and the city lights blurred together as I stewed over the whole Bennett and Cory mess. It was like a cringe-worthy throwback to the worst bits of my Sacramento days, but with an extra dash of rival desires tossed in for good measure.

Sacramento was the absolute pits.

Fresh out of UCLA with my shiny new degree in finance and economics, I landed a job at a money management company in Sacramento Town. It was smooth sailing at first - I was killing it day by day, and not a soul could find fault with my work. But after a couple of years, things went south with a new client.

This guy was a total creep from the get-go. Just sleazy comments and weird stares that made my skin crawl. Part of me wanted to say something, but another part kept thinking I should suck it up. That whole "this is how it is for women in business" shtick, like maybe if I couldn't handle the harassment, I didn't deserve to be there. It was like my dad's voice in my head.

I tolerated the jerk's remarks for a year, then, about eight months back, he went too far. I was alone with him in my office, and when I walked past him to get a file, he straight up grabbed my ass. I whipped around to give him hell, and the creep actually tried to shove his nasty hand up my skirt. Unbelievable.

I booted that asshole out of my office faster than you can say "harassment lawsuit," and then hightailed it to my boss's office to spill the beans. But, plot twist - the creep had the audacity to follow me and spin some yarn about me flirting with him. My boss promised he'd handle it, but what happened next was a real punch to the gut. The company wanted to act all concerned about harassment on the outside, but they didn't want to lose a big-time client. So, they basically strong-armed me into keeping quiet with an offer. Ultimately, the only viable option I had was to snatch a hefty severance check and skedaddle – so that's exactly what I did.

When my dad caught wind of this, he hit the roof. But not at the client – at *me*. I should've expected it from someone who still thinks "Mad Men" is a how-to guide for life. Anyway, my dad went off on a rant, telling me I was blowing things out of proportion, making mountains out of molehills, or whatever other cliché he could think of. He even had the audacity to tell me that the money management scene was a huge old boys' club, and I shouldn't hold my breath waiting for them to change their tune just because the times were a-changin'.

That brutal wake-up call hit me like a bomb. Making it big in this game wasn't just about being a rockstar at your job or grinding day and night. Oh no, it meant growing a spine of steel and the guts to stand up for yourself, no matter what surprises life threw your way. My pops had always been a tough old bird, but now I realized he'd been training me in his messed-up way for the shark-infested waters of finance.

As the cab dropped me off and I handed over the cash, a

sneaky little doubt tiptoed into my brain. Was I really calling the shots here or just running away from the ghosts of my past? Bennett's offer and snarky remarks had hit a nerve, and Cory's accusations had twisted the knife even deeper.

I shook off the doubts and stepped out into the crisp night air. Nope, I'm not going to second-guess myself- not now, not ever. Bennett was just another speed bump in this crazy journey, a tiny glitch in the grand cosmic plan. And Cory? He was a curveball I hadn't seen coming, but something I could totally handle.

Yet, deep down, a teensy voice whispered doubts, planting seeds of uncertainty. Had I really come as far as I thought, or was I still that same young woman, unsure and searching for her spot in a world that sometimes felt too rough and ruthless?

SEVENTEEN

Cory

As I headed back to the party, I was filled with a turmoil of feelings swirling around. That spontaneous lip-lock with Rylee had me in a twist. How was I constantly letting my guard down, especially around her? She was the rival, the one using every sly move in the book to one-up us in the dog-eat-dog business world.

Rylee's pull on me was like gravity - I could not resist. Those stolen moments must have zapped me with electrifying mojo, frying my senses in the process.

I stumbled back to Fury and Nadine, but my face was basically a billboard for the chaos happening inside my head. My tie felt like it was strangling me with each frantic heartbeat, forever reminding me of that kiss with Rylee.

Fury sized me up with a single glance, and I swear, the dude's got some kind of superpower when it comes to reading me. His eyes zeroed in on my disarray as if I'd been pushed through a hedge backward.

"Are you alright, man?" Fury's voice dropped to a whisper, his gaze scanning me. This was not the moment for a deep dive into my Rylee predicament.

"Yeah, yeah, I'm good," I mumbled, trying to channel a chilled-out Zen master. "I just need a blast of fresh air."

Fury responded with a slight nod, as if he knew there was more to the story but was willing to let it slide. "Alright, why don't you head on home, Cory? I'll keep Nadine entertained."

Thankful for the escape plan, I bobbed my head in agreement and shot Nadine a quick "catch you later" spiel.

"No problem, Mr. McCrae," she replied, her smile polite and genuine. "You have a good night."

Heading for the exit, a massive wave of "what the heck" smacked me right in the face. Seriously, what was I thinking, planting one on Rylee like that? Talk about a major brain fart. In the high-stakes world of finance, every move was like a chess match, and I'd just made a rookie mistake. I couldn't let my hormones play chess master and mess with my game plan. Scoring Nadine's account was a must, and I couldn't afford any more slip-ups. Time to get my head back in the game before I totally tanked this thing.

The crisp night air welcomed me as I stumbled out, but it barely put a dent in the wildfire of feelings raging inside me. Had I just gift-wrapped Rylee a victory? Ugh, I was such a loser. I kept my fingers crossed that Fury could swoop in and save the day.

BY THE TIME I got home, I was so over it all. I stepped in the elevator, hoping to dodge Becky this time around. But no such luck. The second I pressed the button, I heard her calling my name, asking me to hold the doors. There was no way I could ignore her without looking like a total jerk, so I grudgingly obliged.

As we rode up in the elevator, I tried my best to tune out Becky's chatter. Don't get me wrong, she wasn't annoying or anything; it's just that after the whole Rylee debacle, her bubbly talk was like white noise to my frazzled brain. I was about to slip into a coma when I noticed she hadn't bailed on her floor.

Well, this was weird. I gave Becky a polite smile. "Looks like you missed your floor back there."

"Nah," she said, her voice taking in an unfamiliar tone. "I actually wanted to talk with you about something,"

Before I could even utter another word, she pressed the STOP button on the elevator panel. My heart skipped a beat, but not in a good way. I had a bad feeling about this.

She whirled around, her eyes sparkling with a newfound boldness. "So, your buddy Fury let slip something interesting the other day," she said, hands on her hips. "Like you're a bit clueless when it comes to catching on."

"Catching on?" I echoed, utterly confused.

She moved closer, invading the tiny space. "You know, like when someone's digging you."

Stuck in this mental and physical corner, my brain scrambled for something to say- anything to end this conversation.

And then, BAM! Becky flung her arms around my neck and pressed herself against me. "Like this," she murmured, her breath warm on my cheek.

My body turned rigid as a board. This was so not what I had signed up for. I delicately pried her arms off me, trying not to hurt her feelings. "Whoa, Becky, hold up. This really isn't my scene."

Her posture slumped, and the glow in her gaze vanished as she narrowed her eyes. "Oh, I see. So, you're into...guys then?"

"No, no, no, not at all!" I quickly corrected her, my words tumbling out in a rush. "I like girls, it's just that I'm not looking for anything serious now."

I jammed my floor button with more force than necessary, desperate to flee the awkwardness that now hung heavy in the air. The rest of the ride was as silent as a library, the only sound being the soft murmur of the elevator machinery.

I practically bolted out as soon as the doors slid open to my floor, my brain still doing somersaults.

Stepping into my apartment, I gently closed the door behind me, relishing the peace and quiet. I stripped off my clothes, each piece dropping to the floor with a satisfying thud as if shedding the weight of the night's tangled mess. I was eager to scrub away not just the physical grime but also the mental muddle Rylee and now Becky had left me in.

I cranked the shower dial all the way up, letting the scalding hot water pummel me. The steam billowed up, fogging the mirror and creating a cozy cocoon around me. I hoped the heat would wash away any lingering traces and cleanse the whirlwind of confusion and irritation.

But as I closed my eyes under the relentless spray, Rylee's image was there, imprinted on the inside of my eyelids. The memory of Rylee's kiss haunted me, a mixture of anger and desire, a cocktail too potent to ignore. It was as if the water, rather than washing her away, was somehow etching her deeper into my senses.

I could see every line that made up her features. The brilliance of her eyes. The curve of her lips.

And then the rest of my senses caught up, bringing the memories of the silkiness of her hair when I'd buried my hand in it, the scent of her arousal, the taste of her mouth.

Cursing, I felt my blood rushing south, my cock stiffening. I tried turning my thoughts elsewhere, seeking something unpleasant.

No matter how much I tried, though, I stayed hard. Achingly, impossibly hard.

And I could only think of one way to take care of it.

Damnit.

With a defeated groan, I wrapped my hand around my aching length. I could almost imagine it was her hand on me, stroking me, her fingers tracing the veins beneath my skin. I moved my fist up and down, letting the water from the shower be my lubrication. My skin burned beneath my palm, and I welcomed the bite of pain, a harsh reminder of my inability to forget her.

It was her body, the sounds she'd made, the way she'd felt gripping my cock in that hot, wet embrace of hers that had me cursing as I sought release. Even with the anger that still simmered between us, I couldn't suppress the primal need to see her spread out beneath me, panting and begging.

My hand moved faster, my breaths coming in short, ragged gasps as my mind swirled with images of Rylee. The way she'd looked at me at the event, the heat in her eyes after I kissed her, how I wanted to claim her as mine. I imagined her naked, her skin slick with sweat, as I fucked her until she screamed my name. Her nails dug into my back, leaving red trails of desire and possession. "Cory," she moaned, her voice a siren's call that only fueled my lust. Her heated core clenched around me like a vice grip, milking me with every deep thrust. I could almost feel the way her wetness coated us both, our bodies slick with sweat and the evidence of our mounting arousal.

"Oh God, Rylee," I groaned aloud, the walls of the shower stall doing little to muffle my cries of pleasure. My hips bucked uncontrollably against my hand as I pictured her arching her back in ecstasy, her breasts bouncing enticingly with each hard thrust. The image was so vivid that it felt like she was right there with me.

Her hands were everywhere: gripping my ass, clawing at my back, guiding me deeper inside her molten heat. "Yes," she purred in my ear, "harder...harder." And God help me, but I obliged. My strokes became more frantic as I neared the edge of release. The water pounded down on me relentlessly as I imagined us fucking against the tiled wall of the shower stall. That sent me over the edge. I came with a guttural groan, spilling myself all over my fist. My breathing was ragged as I watched the evidence of my release being swept down the drain.

If only the same could be done with the lingering shame of my obsession.

THE NEXT DAY, I was at the office glued to my desk chair, gazing blankly at the jumble of numbers on my computer screen. My brain had been on autopilot for the last fifteen minutes, not registering a single figure. Instead, it replayed that kiss with Rylee like a broken record stuck in an endless loop. Each replay ended with a baffling blend of frustration and an unwelcome flicker of something else- something I didn't want to admit, even to myself.

Craving a distraction from the mental merry-go-round, I popped out of my chair and went to Fury's office. Maybe he had some task to yank my thoughts back on track. As I entered, he glanced up from his paperwork, a smirk tugging at the corners of his mouth.

"Rough day so far?" he asked, leaning back in his chair.

"You could say that," I confessed, sinking into the chair opposite him. "My focus is MIA."

Fury's eyes scanned mine for a moment before he spoke. "Well, I've got an update that might help. Last night's meeting with Nadine went better than we anticipated."

That piqued my interest. "Oh yeah?"

He grinned. "After you left, Nadine got a call from Bennett. He's recommending our firm to handle her estate, not Rylee's."

"Really? That's interesting." A frown creased my brow. This new piece of info didn't jive with the story I'd cooked up in my mind about Rylee. If Bennett wasn't recommending her, something must have happened between them.

"To celebrate this bit of good news with Nadine," Fury continued, "I was thinking we should go check out that new club on Friday. I heard it's awesome. You down?"

"A club? You're kidding, right?" I retorted, my mind still whirling from the unexpected turn of events.

"Come on, don't be such a party pooper," Fury cajoled, nudging my arm playfully. "Let's shake off the dust and cut loose for a change."

"Yeah, alright, why not?" I laughed. "Let's relive our twenties and make some bad decisions."

I strolled back to my cubbyhole, plopped into my chair, and half-heartedly attempted to get some work done. But dang, Rylee's laugh, the memory of her lips, just kept crashing my concentration party. Bennett's choice to bypass her had tossed a curveball at my assumptions, leaving me with many questions.

So, maybe, just maybe, I'd been barking up the wrong tree this whole time, and Rylee wasn't the manipulating rival I'd made her out to be.

EIGHTEEN

Rylee

I'd never been much of a drinker, but recently, I'd been craving alcohol every time Friday came around. Sure, launching a new startup is enough to drive anyone to the bottle, but that's not why I was here with Natalie, nursing my third glass of vino at this cozy little restaurant. I tried my hardest not to think about why I was more tense than a banjo string.

Natalie flicked a golden curl from her face, eyes twinkling with mischief. "You remember senior year, right? When you went full-on rebel and dyed your hair to match that wild purple prom dress?" Her grin was all tease, practically painting that chaotic day in vivid colors.

I sighed, the memory rushing back with all its mortifying glory. "How could I possibly forget? I looked like I'd stuck my head in a grape jelly jar."

Nat let out a laugh that was pure sunshine. "When you strutted down those stairs, Sean Ellis's face was priceless! He was expecting Cinderella but got a purple-haired punk rocker instead."

The memory coaxed a reluctant smile from me. "He was so horrified he barely spoke two words to me all night. But, strangely enough, it felt incredibly liberating to stand out in that sea of normality."

She raised her wine glass, her smile brightening. "Here's to standing out and make an entrance they'll never forget!"

I clinked my glass against hers, the sound echoing crisply in the cozy place. "To unforgettable entrances, indeed. Though, I have a feeling Sean Ellis might beg to differ."

Natalie's laughter rang out again, her joy infectious. "Oh, I bet he's still regaling people with the tale of his prom date with the audacious rebel."

As our laughter faded, I took a deep, fortifying breath, gearing up for a confession. I had to spill the beans about my latest Cory encounter.

"So, speaking of disasters..." I began, my voice trailing off as I nervously nibbled on my lip. I couldn't shake the memories – the earlier steamy encounters before I even knew who he was. It had been over a week, and I was still reeling from those intense moments with Cory. And now a kiss? Somehow, that kiss was more intimate than the sex.

Natalie raised an eyebrow. "Uh oh, I recognize that look. What's the scoop, Palmer?"

I sighed, lowering my voice. "I might have...kind of...locked lips with Cory again at an event."

"Cory McCrae?" Natalie's eyes widened in disbelief. "The Cory, who's your sworn enemy?"

"It just sort of happened!" I protested. "One minute, we were bickering, and the next..."

Natalie leaned in a pensive expression on her face. "Honey, you've got to get McCrae out of your head. He's messing with you." She took a deep breath. "You need to get laid with someone *not* affiliated with Gracen and McCrae."

"Nat, seriously," I said, feeling my cheeks redden. "That's not going to fix anything."

She shrugged. "Maybe not, but it'll help you forget about McCrae for a while. And who knows, you might even enjoy yourself."

I was about to say something when our waiter sauntered over, and Natalie turned on the charm. "My friend thinks you're cute. You up for anything later?" she asked, flashing him a smile that could light up a room.

The waiter chuckled, rubbing the back of his neck. "Aw, thanks, but I'm off the market. I just got engaged, and we expect a little bundle of joy soon."

"Well, congratulations!" Natalie said. "That's fantastic news!"

The waiter thanked her and scurried off to another table, leaving me to roll my eyes at Natalie. "Enough with the matchmaking. We're here to let loose and have a blast, not plan dates."

"You're right," Natalie said. "It's girls' night. I heard about this new club downtown. Let's go scope it out!"

I polished off my wine. "Now you're speaking my language. After you, my dear!" Natalie was spot on. A night of clubbing was just what the doctor ordered to clear my head and forget all about Cory McCrae.

Natalie pushed back from the table, her head tilting back as the last drops of wine disappeared into the depths of her smile. "Alright, I'm making it official. Tonight's mission is to find two tall, dark, and handsome strangers to sweep us off our feet."

A twenty-minute cab ride later, we stumbled past the line into the lively place, greeted by the pulsating bass and a warm, inviting glow.

It didn't take Natalie long to zero in on a pair of dudes facing the bar. "Bingo," she declared, "our dream dates for tonight."

Raising an eyebrow, I playfully ribbed her. "How can you tell they're good looking just from their backsides? Maybe they're an item? Could be they're a couple, Nat."

Natalie rolled her eyes knowingly and motioned towards them. "Have faith, they're not together. And even if they were, who says we can't enjoy the view?"

Chuckling, I gave the guys a once-over. Damn, those jeans were made to flaunt their assets. Not that I was on the prowl or anything, but hey, a little eye candy never hurts.

As I took in their broad shoulders and muscular arms, they both spun around, catching me off guard.

"Bloody hell," I muttered under my breath.

There he was - Cory freaking McCrae. And the other guy had to be his business partner, Fury.

Natalie's sly smirk morphed into full-blown curiosity when she caught my whispered slip-up. "What's the deal?" she urged, eyebrows shooting up expectantly.

"Figures," I confessed, watching her reaction. "We were ogling Cory McCrae and, I'm guessing, his partner in crime, Fury Gracen."

Her eyes went wide as saucers. "Wait, you're saying this hottie is Cory McCrae? No wonder he's been on your mind. And his partner? He's no slouch, either. Damn!" Then, she got all excited. "This is it, Rylee! Your chance to talk to Cory face-to-face. No more playing guessing games or making assumptions - just ask him what's up."

I sighed, shaking my head at Natalie. "No way, I'm not going over there. I don't need to talk to him."

"Really? Because it seems to me like there's some unresolved tension between you two."

I gave her an exasperated look. "The only tension is the massive headache I get whenever he's around. I'm here to have a good time with you, not rehash old stuff with McCrae."

"Old stuff?" Natalie laughed. "This happened last week!"

"Exactly, ancient history." I waved my hand dismissively. "Now, are we getting drinks or what?"

With no time to waste, I marched right up to the bar, flashing the bartender a bright smile. "Two rounds of Tequila shots, please," I said, hoping the booze would take the edge off my nerves. The last thing I needed was to butt heads with Cory tonight.

As the bartender slid the shots towards me, I felt a looming presence at my side. Ugh, speak of the devil. I stiffened, bracing myself for a fight.

"Well, well, look who it is," Cory's voice dripped with fake casualness. I eyed him warily.

"Just out for a good time with a friend," I replied curtly. I snatched the shots and moved to leave, but Cory's gentle grip on my arm stopped me.

"Rylee, hold on a sec." His voice softened. "Can we talk?"

My heart raced, but I met his gaze evenly. "I'd rather not, Cory."

He opened his mouth to respond, but Natalie popped up beside me before he could speak. "Great, you got the shots!" she exclaimed, plucking them from my hands with ease. She turned to Cory with a dazzling smile. "Hi there, you must be Cory. I'm Natalie, Rylee's friend."

Cory looked taken aback by her friendliness. "Oh, um, hi," he stammered.

"We should get these shots back to our table," Natalie said cheerily. "Enjoy your night!" Before Cory could utter a word, she nudged me with her arm and led me away.

I let out a breath. "Thank you," I murmured. "You're a lifesaver."

Natalie grinned. "That's what friends are for. Now, let's do these shots and hit the dance floor!"

The tequila burned a fiery trail down my throat, igniting a warmth in my belly. I reveled in the slight dizziness and the looseness of my limbs. It was liberating, intoxicating. As the music pulsed through the bar, I felt myself swaying to the beat. My friend grabbed my hand, pulling me onto the dance floor. I didn't resist; I just let the music take over.

It was a whirlwind of bodies, a thrumming sea of motion. Lights flashed and strobed across the room, creating an otherworldly spectacle. We danced for what felt like hours, our laughter mingling with the rhythm. The bass thumped in my chest, and I closed my eyes, losing myself in the moment. Blinking my eyes open, I found Nat swaying to the rhythm with none other than Fury himself. They grooved in perfect harmony, their bodies tangled up in a dance that could've been plucked right from some dirty dancing romance flick. A twinge of envy zipped through me, but I quickly brushed it off. Tonight was Nat's time to shine too, and she deserved a good time. Plus, it wasn't every day I saw my BFF cutting loose like that.

I spun around again before realizing I needed a break—a moment to clear my head from the intoxicating swirl of sights and sounds. "Nat!" I called out over the din, though she was clearly preoccupied. "I'm heading to the restroom!"

She threw me a thumbs-up without missing a step in her dance with Fury. With a smile tugging at my lips at their obvious chemistry, I waved my way through the crowd, feeling the bassline vibrate beneath my feet. As I stepped into the dimly lit hallway leading to the restrooms, I felt a moment of relief. The cool AC air on my sweaty skin was a welcome change from the sticky heat of the dance floor.

As I splashed the refreshing water on my face, I pondered making a hasty exit. The last thing I needed was another entanglement with Cory. Who knew what would happen if I lingered any longer? Better to play it safe, right?

But as I sauntered out of the stall to tell Nat that I was leaving, I caught a note of a familiar voice. My heart skipped a beat, and I froze in my tracks. Cory was just around the corner, chatting away on his phone. I held my breath, weighing my options. I certainly didn't want to bump into him again. But I couldn't just stand there either. So, I took a deep breath and braced myself, planning to slip past him as swiftly and silently as a cat on the prowl.

As I tiptoed forward, my foot snagged on something, and I stumbled. I let out a gasp as I tumbled, my hands flailing wildly. But before I hit the floor, a strong arm caught me, yanking me up. My gaze landed on Cory, staring down at me, his eyes as wide as saucers. He quickly released me, stepping back. "Rylee," he murmured, his voice low. "Are you alright?"

My cheeks flushed crimson. "Yeah, I'm good," I mumbled, trying to brush myself off. "Just tripped, clumsy me."

Cory looked at me for a moment, his face unreadable. Then, without so much as a peep, he spun on his heel and disappeared into the club.

I let out a shaky sigh and leaned against the wall, my heart still racing. I couldn't quite figure out what had just happened, but one thing was clear as day - that guy couldn't stand me.

After a minute, I mustered the courage to push through the door and dive back into the club's sensory overload. The thumping bass hit me like a wave, enveloping me in its trance-like embrace.

I scanned the crowd, my eyes darting back and forth in search of Nat's golden curls. But the sea of bodies seemed to swallow her whole, and panic surged through me momentarily. I told myself that she'd probably just gotten caught up in the crowd. I'd find her soon enough.

Just as I was ready to dive back into the throng of dancers, I heard a familiar voice behind me. My heart sank. So much for avoiding Cory.

"Looking for someone?" His voice was close, too close. I could feel the heat radiating off his body, sending a shiver down my spine. I closed my eyes for a moment to compose myself.

"Yeah, actually," I replied, my voice steady. "I'm trying to find Nat. Have you seen her?"

Cory chuckled, and I felt a pang of irritation. "You mean your friend who's currently outside getting to know my business partner?"

I whirled around, my eyes narrowing. "What do you mean?"

He shrugged, a smirk playing at the corners of his mouth. "They went outside for some fresh air. I guess they hit it off."

I sighed in relief, followed by a huff of frustration. "Great, just what I needed. Thanks for the heads up."

Cory raised an eyebrow. "You're welcome? I guess?"

I rolled my eyes, turning to leave. But before I could take a step, Cory's hand was on my arm, holding me back. "Wait. Please."

I turned to face him, my eyes flashing. "What is it, Cory? I'm really not in the mood for whatever game you're playing tonight."

He hesitated, his grip on my arm loosening. "I...I just wanted to talk. Away from the crowd, you know?"

I studied him for a moment, trying to discern his motives. But his expression was unreadable, his eyes guarded. Finally, I sighed, resigning myself to this unavoidable encounter. "Fine. But make it quick."

Cory led me through the bar, weaving our way through the crowd until we reached a quiet corner. He leaned against the wall, his arms crossed over his chest. I stood facing him, my hands on my hips, waiting for him to speak.

"Look, Rylee," he began, his voice low. "I know this whole rivalry thing is weird, and it complicated things between us, but I think we should try to clear the air."

I raised an eyebrow. "Clear the air? You mean like talk about how you accused me of using underhanded tactics to steal your clients?"

Cory winced. "I...I may have overreacted. I was just trying to protect my business, you know?"

I scoffed. "By spreading rumors about me? By trying to sabotage my meetings with potential clients?"

He held up his hands in defense. "I never spread rumors about you. And as for the meetings...I just wanted to make sure they knew all the facts before making a decision."

I shook my head, disbelief coursing through me. "You really expect me to believe that?"

Cory sighed, running a hand through his hair. "Look, I know I screwed up. But can't we just...move past this? For the sake of our businesses, if nothing else?"

I stared at him, trying to gauge his sincerity. Was he willing to let bygones be bygones, or was this just another ploy to get the upper hand?

Finally, I sighed, my shoulders slumping in defeat. "Fine. We'll try to...coexist. But don't expect me to roll out the red carpet for you, Cory."

He nodded, a small smile playing at the corners of his mouth. "Fair enough. I can live with that."

We stood there for a moment, the tension between us slowly dissipating. It was a fragile truce, but it was something. A start, at least.

"I should probably check on Nat," I said, breaking the silence that had settled over us. "I'm heading out, but she might want to stay with Fury."

Cory chuckled, pushing himself off the wall with a casual grace that made me roll my eyes. "I'll walk you out. Just in case you need help finding your friend."

I caught sight of Nat outside, amid a passionate lip-lock with Fury. She glanced up as we got closer, her eyes sparkling with amusement and recognition. "Well, look who finally decided to come look for me! I was starting to think you'd forgotten about me."

A chuckle escaped me. "It seems like I'm not the one doing the abandoning, am I?" I playfully nudged her shoulder. "Anyway, I'm heading out. You good here?"

Nat nodded, snaking her arm through Fury's with a content smile. "Yeah, I'm good. Thanks for looking out for me."

I shot Nat a grin, feeling all warm and fuzzy inside. "You know I've got your back, girl. Stay safe." I turned my attention to Fury, giving him a look that could freeze lava. "And you better treat my bestie right or face the wrath of...well, me."

Fury chuckled, "Yes, ma'am, I promise."

Cory stood there, smiling like a Cheshire cat. I spun around and made a beeline for the street before I did something I'd end up regretting.

A cautious sense of hope bubbled up inside me as I waved down a cab. Maybe, just maybe, this shaky truce would stick. At least, that's what I was telling myself, crossing my fingers behind my back.

NINETEEN

Cory

I was slouched over my desk, squinting at the quarterly reports like they were some sort of confusing, all-you-can-eat buffet, when Warner, my trusty assistant, burst into my office. His face was beet red, and his eyes were wide. "Boss," he sputtered, "I just got an earful from BiosynTech's CFO. They're threatening to yank their investment by week's end if our returns don't magically improve immediately."

"Seriously?" My stomach clenched. "Our analysts gave BiosynTech the green light in their last forecast." My words echoed my bewilderment as I frantically tried to piece together this sudden plot twist.

I anxiously scoured the reports once more, my heart plummeting as I caught a glimpse of a discrepancy that could spell out a major blunder. If word got out, our reputation would be toast faster than a marshmallow in a campfire.

My heart pounding like a drum, I leaped into action. "Set up an emergency meeting with the account manager and finance team, pronto," I commanded, my voice oozing with the urgency that was coursing through my veins. "We need to double-check if this is a genuine error and cook up a damage control plan before BiosynTech decides to walk out on us."

Warner gave a firm nod, his face a blend of grit and resolve, before dashing out of the room. I ran my fingers through my hair, my nerves buzzing. This was a disaster. A full-blown, five-alarm catastrophe.

I stormed into Fury's office to hash out this colossal mess and devise a game plan. But Fury was MIA, and his secretary, Jules, was the only one holding down the fort, clacking away at her keyboard.

"Hey Jules, do you know where Fury disappeared to?" I asked, trying to sound calm.

She looked up a mischievous glint in her emerald eyes. "Appointment, he said. He didn't say where."

Was that look meant for me? I brushed it off and wondered if this had something to do with Rose but dismissed the thought just as quickly. "When's he due back?"

Jules shrugged nonchalantly, "No idea, but he mentioned he'd be reachable by phone if anything urgent popped up."

Weighing my options, I debated whether to call Fury or tackle this mess myself. With BiosynTech breathing down our necks, time was of the essence, and I was already running late for the meeting.

"I gotta bolt; there's an emergency meeting I can't miss," I said, pivoting away from Jules. I could still feel her gaze on me.

"Sounds serious," she commented, her voice laced with curiosity. "Anything I can assist with?"

I shook my head. "Nah, I've got it under control."

Jules leaned back in her chair, a sly smile playing on her

lips. "Well, if you need anything, you know where to find me."

As I walked away, I couldn't shake the feeling that the look she gave me and her words, held a hidden message. The playful lilt in her voice made me wonder if she was flirting with me, but I didn't have the luxury of dwelling on it. A meeting awaited my presence, and tardiness was not an option.

The emergency meeting trudged along, each department head taking their turn to present analyses and projections as we collectively tried to resolve the discrepancy in Biosyn-Tech's portfolio.

The account manager was wrapping up his latest findings when my phone buzzed with a text from Rylee. Since I couldn't answer her in the middle of the meeting, I half-heartedly tried to ignore it, but her name danced across my mind like a Vegas marquee. Our unfinished business hung heavy between us, a tangle of unspoken words and unresolved tension. I needed to see her, to try and make sense of the whirlwind of emotions she'd stirred up in me.

Those sizzling flashbacks of Rylee and me came roaring in, making it damn near impossible to concentrate on the monotonous meeting. I could practically hear her moans from that unforgettable night at the gala, a melody that had me grinning ear-to-ear like a lovesick puppy. And let's not even go there with that sultry, mischievous gleam in her eyes when we snuck into the dressing room, ripping each other's clothes off in a feverish whirlwind. That electrifying, risqué escapade still had the power to send my heart racing.

Just as I was getting lost in another X-rated daydream, our lead financial analyst snapped me back to reality. "There," she said, jabbing her finger at a formula. "This should have been done every quarter, not just once a year. Once we fix that, the numbers should match up." A wave of relief swept over me as the team nodded in agreement. At least the mistake was something we could fix.

With a sigh and a loose tie, I escaped to my office, collapsing into my chair like a marathon runner at the finish line. As I leaned back and shut my eyes, there she was again - Rylee, taking center stage in my mind. I couldn't help but replay those steamy moments, her breathy moans and trembling body etched into my memory.

I uttered a groan, trying to adjust myself discreetly in my chair. This was going to be a challenge, but hey, I had to try. Buckle up; it's going to be a long day.

Just then, there was a knock on my door. I quickly sat up and composed myself. "Come in," I called out, hoping my voice didn't sound too strained.

The door opened, and Warner walked in, with a stack of papers "Hey, boss," he said, a triumphant gleam in his eye. "The finance team verified the miscalculation. We should be able to present a revised report to BiosynTech by tomorrow."

I nodded, my pulse quickening. "Excellent. Draft an email outlining the error and our proposed resolution. I want full transparency on this."

As he turned to leave, my phone buzzed again, the screen lighting up with Rylee's name. I hesitated, my thumb hovering over the message.

I mustered the courage and suggested we grab a drink after work at The Tipsy Tap, a quaint little watering hole nestled in the heart of Palo Alto. With its dim lighting, dark wood accents, and snug velvet booths, it seemed like the ideal spot to have an honest conversation. She was on board, and I took a deep breath, mentally preparing myself for the chat later.

As the clock inched its way towards 4 PM, I had muscled through a good chunk of my workload. I decided to slip out a tad early and get a head start on the evening. But no sooner had I made up my mind, than Jules came rapping on my door frame with those darn reports from Fury that needed my approval. Fifteen minutes later, I was running behind schedule when I finally threw on my jacket, the plush fabric whispering against my fingertips, and made a beeline for the exit. A cool breeze welcomed me as I stepped outside, sending a heady mix of jitters and exhilaration coursing through my veins. The electric hum of Palo Alto was in full swing as I navigated my way through the crowd to the cozy little pub, the mouthwatering scent of street food wafting through the air, mingling with the faint hint of exhaust.

Stepping up to The Tipsy Tap, my heart beat against my ribs like it was revving up for a reunion with Rylee. I gave the heavy wooden door a shove and was hit with a wave of ambiance equal parts booze and pheromones. The joint buzzed like a hive of chatter and clinking glasses, all bathed in the soft glow of mood lighting.

I squinted through the dimness as I hunted for Rylee. The post-work crowd was thick, making it a challenge to spot her. But then, as if the universe decided to cut me a break, there she was. Nestled in a corner table, her back to the door, she was nursing a martini.

My breath got all caught up as flashbacks of our steamy moment came rushing back. I had to give myself a mental slap to stay focused on the mission: patching up our work relationship and, who knows, maybe even checking out this crazy chemistry between us.

I slid into the chair across from her, trying not to notice how plump and round her hips were under that snazzy pantsuit. "Hey," I blurted out, sounding out of breath. "Sorry I'm late. I got stuck with paperwork." I raked my fingers through my hair, feeling like a nervous wreck.

She peeked up at me, her amber eyes blazing with a combo of resistance and...could that be interest? "Alright, Cory," she said, "I figured you got something you wanted to tell me, so let's hear it. I want all the cards on the table."

TWENTY

Rylee

I took a slow sip of my martini, already my second since I got here, savoring the burn as I regarded Cory across the table. A part of me still wanted to claw his eyes out, but another part was intrigued.

Cory cleared his throat, looking uncharacteristically nervous. "Look, I know things got heated between us. But I think we may have both jumped to some wrong conclusions."

I cocked an eyebrow, waiting. This ought to be good.

"I accused you of using dishonest tactics with the Seaworth account. That was wrong of me. You're clearly a principled person."

Now, it was my turn to shift uncomfortably. I hadn't expected him to lead with an apology.

"And our intimate encounters..." Cory paused, a slight flush creeping up his neck. "I haven't been able to stop thinking about them."

My pulse quickened at the memory of our trysts. As much as I hated to admit it, neither had I.

Cory met my gaze, his eyes filled with a mixture of vulnerability and determination. "I know this might sound crazy, but I think we have a real connection, Rylee. One that's worth exploring without the nonsense of this rivalry getting in the way."

I considered his words, weighing the pros and cons of pursuing a relationship with my professional nemesis. Could we move past the messy circumstances of our first few encounters? Did I even want to?

"Hey, how 'bout another round for the lady?" The bartender's smooth voice cut through my mental fog as he set down Cory's drink, his gaze locked on me like a laser beam.

The buzz from my martinis made my head pleasantly fuzzy, and Cory's unwavering stare wasn't helping matters. So, I found myself giving the bartender a nod.

"Why not?" I said, returning his smile. His answering wink sent a little shiver down my spine as he picked up my empty glass and sauntered off.

A low rumble from Cory's direction drew my gaze. His eyes narrowed as he watched the bartender walk away. I bit back a sigh and resisted the urge to nudge him with my foot.

"What's your deal?" I asked, raising an eyebrow.

"That guy's supposed to be slinging drinks, not flirting with the ladies," Cory grumbled, scowling into his glass.

"Oh, please," I said, gently leaning in. "You mean to tell me no cute bartender has ever batted their eyes at you or flashed a winning smile?"

Cory's face turned beet red, and he quickly looked away, fidgeting with his napkin. "That's not the point," he mumbled. "They're supposed to be professional at work."

I laughed at Cory's expression. "Oh, right, Mr. Perfect," I teased, waggling my eyebrows at him. "You've never turned on the charm for a client or a business contact, have you?"

The server returned with my fresh drink and scooched it in my direction on the table. Cory finally looked at me, a troubled expression clouding his pale green eyes. "That's the second time you've accused me of doing something unethical," he said, his voice barely above a whisper.

I rolled my eyes and took a sip of my drink. "Yeah, well, if the shoe fits, Cinderella," I replied, feeling the warmth of the liquor spread through my body.

He tilted his head as if seeing a different side of me. "As much as I'd like to discuss *that* comparison, I'm not getting side-tracked this time. Be straight with me and tell me what the hell you're havering on about."

I frowned at him. "What did you just say?" I asked, my words slurring slightly.

He made an impatient gesture with his hand. "My dad's Scottish, and I still have a couple of phrases floating around in my head," he explained. "Don't change the subject. Just tell me what you're talking about."

I let out a big sigh and leaned back in the seat. It was time to get it all out in the open. Maybe if I confronted him about it and got him to apologize, I could play nice and move on. And if he didn't apologize, well, I could spend the rest of the night stewing in righteous anger, and Nat couldn't say a damn thing about it. Either way, it was a win-win.

"Alright, I'll spill the beans," I said. "I'm talking about how you went all James Bond on me at that swanky gala just to get into my head. And then, to top it all off, you pulled a repeat performance at the grocery store, flashing your killer dimples. I mean, come on! I'm your arch-nemesis in the business world, and you knew it all along while I was clueless. Talk about playing dirty pool!"

His eyebrows shot up so fast I thought they might disappear into his hairline. The shock on his face was so obvious that I felt a flicker of doubt for a second. "Wait, that's exactly what I thought you did to me," he said, sounding surprised.

Now, it was my turn to be taken aback. "What? No way, I didn't do that," I said firmly, shaking my head.

"Well, neither did I," he insisted, crossing his arms over his chest.

For a moment, we just sat there, staring at each other in disbelief. It was like we were both actors in some bizarre comedy of errors.

Suddenly, so many things made sense. The way he'd sounded insulted when I'd suggested he'd been inappropriate with Nadine Seaworth. The fact that he'd seemed pissed at me like I'd done something wrong.

"Shit," I muttered, closing my eyes and sighing. "This really was a coincidence. We've been wasting so much time and energy being annoyed at each other when it was all just a huge misunderstanding."

"Fury's never gonna let this one slide," Cory grumbled, his voice a low rumble that sent a shiver down my spine.

I blinked my eyes open, looking him straight in the eye. "Alright, spill it. You fessed up to your cousin about us?"

Cory had the good grace to look a bit sheepish, a faint blush creeping up his cheeks. "Look, I'm sorry, but I had to. I thought you were playing us."

I raised an eyebrow at him. "So, you didn't tell him about

our first time at the masquerade since you didn't know we were competitors then?"

He scrubbed at the back of his neck, gaze darting away like a guilty puppy. "Alright, I might've let slip a tiny detail or two about that," he confessed. His eyes swung back to me, pinning me down. "Look, I don't normally do the whole one-night-stand-and-vanish thing, you know." He heaved a sigh. "Now, back to the grind. You're not gonna sit there and tell me you haven't been trying to swipe our clients because of that mix-up?"

I released a sigh, the tension draining out of me. "Yeah, I'll back off on that front. But the Seaworth's account is still fair game."

"Agreed," he said, a slow smile spreading across his face.

I took a deliberate sip, letting the vodka linger on my tongue before swallowing. My gaze flicked to Cory, watching as his eyes traced the curve of my mouth. Once I was certain he was entranced, I slowly ran my tongue over my lips and leaned in, his alluring scent enveloping me. God, he smelled irresistible.

"Did you know," I purred, aiming for a tantalizing tone, "that martinis are loaded with calories?"

His voice was gravelly. "Is that right?" I noticed the hand resting on his thigh clenched, revealing the tension within him.

"Mm-hmm," I hummed in agreement, my eyes heavy-lidded. "Since you were late getting here, I'm already on my third. That's a lot of calories. You wouldn't, by any chance, be inclined to help me work off some of those, would you?"

"Three martinis, huh? That's quite the feat."

"Just the right amount," I retorted, a flirty grin dancing on my lips. "I could rattle off the numbers from a hundred in reverse if you'd like. But don't you dare ask me for the alphabet backward—not even when stone-cold sober can I pull that off."

"Are we doing a round three? Is that what you want?" The fire in his eyes gave him away, swirling with anticipation.

"Round three of...?" I played coy, dragging out the suspense.

"Oh, come on," he chuckled. "Don't act like you don't know what I'm talking about."

"Alright," I confessed with a fake pout. "If I said no, I'd be lying through my teeth. And don't be a smartass. You want it, too."

A hint of a smile tugged at his lips. "Have we possibly reached the point where we can make it to an actual bed this time? I mean, I'll always cherish the memories of you in my car and dressing rooms, but the thought of having the room and leisure to explore every inch of your delectable body is incredibly enticing."

Hell yes.

"I'm all for that," I murmured, searching my purse for my wallet.

"I've got it," Cory interjected, silencing my protest with a sharp, commanding look that sent delicious shivers down my spine.

"Thank you," I breathed, sliding off the stool. "Your place or mine?"

He considered it for a moment. "Whichever one's closer?"

His place was just a five-minute drive away, and our enthusiasm trumped any second thoughts. As he swung into the private garage, I tried to steady my breathing as Cory killed the engine, and we climbed out of his car. The short drive had been filled with tension, our hands brushing against each other in the confined space, sending sparks of electricity through me with every accidental touch. Standing outside his apartment, I could feel my heart pounding in my chest.

"Are you sure about this?" Cory asked, his voice low and husky. I nodded, biting my lip as I met his gaze. The uncertainty I'd seen in his eyes earlier was gone, replaced by a smoldering intensity that made my knees go weak.

"I'm sure," I whispered, reaching up to trace his jawline. He leaned into my touch, a soft groan escaping his lips as he pulled me closer. The kiss was slow and deliberate, a promise of what was to come.

We hustled to the elevator, and I'll admit, I was tempted to give in to the urge to get down on my knees and acquaint myself with his taste, cameras be damned. But I somehow managed to keep it together...barely.

His hand tightened around mine, and I glanced over to see his eyes burning with desire. "The idea of shocking my new neighbors is pretty damn tempting," he admitted, his voice a husky rasp in my ears, "but the only thing holding me back from making you scream right here is the thought of security guards getting an eyeful of your ecstasy on camera."

"Damn," I breathed out, squeezing my thighs together so hard I thought I might bruise them. "I was thinking the same thing."

"Patience, my dear," Cory said with a grin that sent chills down my spine.

If his place had been any higher than the third floor, I might have actually given the neighbors a show they'd never forget. But luckily (or unluckily), we reached his door just as I was considering it, and before I knew it, we were practically tripping over each other, stumbling into his apartment.

The door had barely shut before his lips were on mine, eager and ravenous. That elevator ride was like pouring gasoline on our already blazing hormones, in the sexiest way possible. Our tongues were doing the tango like they'd been practicing their whole lives for this very moment. The outside world? Poof, gone. All I could think about was the way his cologne smelled like sin and how good his hands felt on my waist.

His fingers traced a path up my sides, eliciting shivers that danced down my spine as they lightly grazed the undersides of my breasts. I let out a gasp into his mouth, and he seized the opportunity to delve deeper into our kiss, his tongue exploring every nook and cranny of mine. My hands wandered over his broad shoulders, reveling in the firmness of his muscles beneath his shirt. I was hopelessly consumed by him, and it seemed the feeling was mutual.

He pulled away just long enough to growl in my ear, "I've been dying for this all damn week." The warmth of his breath on my skin set off a fresh wave of lust, and I moaned. He must've taken it as a green light because before I knew it, he'd scooped me up like a sack of potatoes and was carrying me towards the bedroom. We collapsed onto the bed in a tangled heap of limbs and lust like two starving animals. His hands were everywhere like he couldn't get enough of me. I was no exception, my own hands roaming over his chest, abs, and then...lower.

He groaned as I reached the waistband of his pants, and I smiled against his lips. "Patience, my dear," I teased, echoing his earlier words. He growled in response, rolling us over so that he was on top. He pinned my hands above my head, his eyes blazing with desire as he looked down at me.

Cory's fingertips danced along my cheekbone, sending shivers down my spine. His deep, gravelly voice rumbled, "Get naked. I want you on my face."

I wasn't one to argue with that. But I enjoyed teasing him a bit. I loved how his confidence sometimes faltered, and it was refreshingly human in a guy like him.

"Mmm, that's a tough one," I purred, pretending to think it over. "What if I'd rather savor the taste of your...cock instead?" I asked, glancing down, a bulge already forming. His cheeks turned as red as a tomato, and I grinned. Cory McCrae, the big, bad CEO of one of the most intimidating finance firms in town, was blushing like a schoolgirl. It was priceless, and I loved it.

Seizing the chance, I purred, "Or, we could always create a little symphony of pleasure, you know, where we... explore each other... at the same time?" I let my voice trail off suggestively. That did the trick. Cory's eyes practically caught fire, and we were both tearing off our clothes in record time.

Cory helped me onto the mattress, my grip on his hand tight as I straddled his head. Normally, I might have felt self-conscious, with my most intimate parts bared for his view, but my focus was solely on the impressive erection jutting from the wiry nest of curls.

Fuck, his cock was every bit as enticing as I remembered.

Time to discover if it tasted as good as it looked. Cory's hands settled on my knees, sending a jolt of electricity up my thighs. He traced a path upward, leaving trails of heat wherever his skin encountered mine. I let a shiver run over me, my body already humming with anticipation.

Leaning in, I cinched my fingers around the root of his stiff cock. Its weight and girth filled my palm, a promising preview of the delight to come. His only response was a subtle tightening of his grip on my ass, but that was enough for me. I knew I'd have him writhing beneath me soon enough.

A sly smile spread across my lips as I pumped him gently, relishing the thrill of withholding the full intensity of my touch. I wanted to toy with him, to stretch out his pleasure until he was desperate for more. I'd barely grazed over him three times when the warm breath that tickled my sensitive skin became a hungry tongue.

My eyelids fluttered as the tip of his tongue moved over my clit, feather-light, exactly the way I was touching him. He was matching my rhythm, stroke for stroke, and it was driving me wild. I could feel myself growing wetter with each pass of his tongue, my body aching for more.

I tightened my grip on his cock, increasing the pressure a little. He groaned in response, the sound sending a thrill through me. I loved knowing I had this effect on him, that I could make him lose control with just a touch.

But I wasn't done teasing him yet. I released his cock and leaned back, giving him a coy smile. "Not so fast," I said, my voice low and husky. "I want to make sure you're nice and wet, too."

With that, I lowered my head and took him into my mouth. He tasted just as good as I hoped, salty and sweet at the same time. I swirled my tongue around the head of his cock, savoring every lick.

Cory's hands tightened on my ass, pulling me closer. I could feel his hips starting to move, thrusting his cock gently into my mouth. I took him deeper, my lips sliding down his shaft until I could feel him hitting the back of my throat.

I inhaled deeply, gearing up for more. I wanted to make this the best damn blowjob of his life, to make him lose it in my mouth. I closed my eyes and pictured him moaning my name as he came, his warmth washing over my tongue. God, that thought alone was enough to send a shiver through me. My own arousal was building, my body trembling with need.

I pulled back, my lips slurping off his engorged cock with a wet pop, and I looked up at him through hooded eyes. "Not so fast," I purred, a devious smile curling my lips. "I've got a new plan."

Cory's answer was a low growl, his hands tightening on my hips. I smiled, feeling a thrill of power run through me. I was in control, and I loved it.

Crawling around him like a sexy panther, I smirked when I saw the hungry look in his eyes. He'd already rolled on a condom and was more than ready for act two. I straddled him, positioning myself above his rock-hard cock. Slowly, I lowered myself down, taking him inch by delicious inch, relishing in the way his eyes rolled back into his head. As I felt him fill me completely, I moaned, my walls clenching around him. I started to move, grinding my hips in circles, teasing him as much as I was teasing myself. I loved the way his breath hitched with each thrust and the way his hands gripped the sheets as if that was the only thing keeping him from exploding right then and there.

It was intense, hot, and completely erotic. I could feel

every inch of him inside me, his cock hitting all the right spots. I closed my eyes, letting myself get lost in the sensation.

Cory's hands were everywhere, touching me, teasing me. He knew exactly what I liked, and he wasn't holding back. I could feel myself getting closer, my body trembling with need.

But I didn't want to come yet. Not until I had him right where I wanted him. I leaned forward, pressing my breasts against his chest. "Come with me," I whispered, my voice barely audible.

Cory's response was immediate. He thrust upward, his cock hitting me deep. Oh fuck, he was big. I could feel him tensing, his body on the edge. I moved with him, my hips rocking back and forth as we raced towards the finish line.

And then it happened. I felt myself coming, my body shaking with the force of it. Cory followed a moment later, his cock pulsing inside me as he came.

We stayed intertwined for a moment, our ragged breaths mingled in the air. The intensity of what just happened still lingered, a delicious warmth that left me craving more. But exhaustion won, and I melted into him, succumbing to sleep.

When I woke up, the room was cloaked in darkness, with only the faint outline of Cory's form visible. His arm was flung carelessly over his face, the sheet clutched at his waist. I knew the contours of his body well already; each muscle was etched into my memory. The temptation to trace those lines with my tongue was overwhelming.

But even after the mind-blowing sex we had, my brain was still a chaotic mess of thoughts. I needed some breathing room and a gulp of fresh air to sort things out. As stealthily as a ninja, I wriggled free from the tangled sheets and scooped up my clothes.

The perk of living in a city? Taxis were always plentiful, eager to whisk me back to the sanctuary of my own place. The dreaded morning-after chat could wait, or maybe it wouldn't even happen. For the time being, all I craved was a little space.

TWENTY-ONE

Cory

I slowly peeled my face off the desk, my eyes still foggy from last night's sleep deprivation. Rylee had made a quiet exit before the sun even showed up. A part of me was grateful she didn't stick around - our tangled connection was already complex enough, and we didn't need any cringe-worthy morning chats. But this tiny voice was in my head, whispering a wistful sigh that she hadn't stuck around for a "one more for the road" before vanishing into the twilight.

I kept revisiting every earth-shattering moment of last night. Never had anyone lit me up like Rylee did. She sparked a blaze inside so fierce the embers were still smoldering. But now, with my head clearing, I just didn't know where things stood between us. Where could we possibly go from here?

If I was being real, things between us were tangled, even before our little misunderstanding. She was my toughest competition - the one person who could single-handedly topple everything Fury and I had painstakingly built up.

I let out a deep sigh and rubbed my temples. It was time to buckle down, focus on work, and stop letting Rylee Palmer take up all the space in my head. But even as I tried to concentrate on the task at hand, my mind kept drifting.

For the fifth time, I squinted at the last sentence of my email, frustration rising. This one stubborn phrase just wouldn't gel, and I was ready to throw in the towel. With a dramatic sigh, I settled for reinforcements.

"Warner," I called out, "I need your eagle eyes for a second."

Moments later, Warner popped in my doorway, curiosity piqued. "What's up, boss man?"

"I've been staring at this blasted email for fifteen minutes and still can't nail the wording. Can you lend me your literary prowess?" I motioned toward my screen and scooted my chair out of the way so he could come around the desk and read it.

As I waited for Warner to work his linguistic magic, I glanced into the hallway and spotted Fury slipping into his office. I squirmed in my seat, realizing I hadn't chatted with my cousin since our last club hangout.

I had a hunch that Fury wouldn't be jumping for joy about Rylee and me hooking up again. Don't get me wrong, Rylee wasn't the big bad wolf I'd thought she was, but she was still on the opposing team. So, yeah, it wasn't exactly the news I was excited to share with my cousin.

"Mission accomplished," Warner declared, stepping away from my computer with a satisfied grin. "What do you think?"

Shoving aside the mental minefield of Rylee, Fury, and potential drama, I scooted my chair back to the screen and scanned Warner's work. "Spot on," I praised. "Thanks, man."

"Need anything else, chief?"

I shook my head. "I'm good for now. You can get back to your stuff."

He split, leaving me staring down a batch of emails that just wouldn't quit. Somehow, they all needed my two cents. I slogged through them for another half hour until Warner buzzed me, saying Nadine was on the line.

I inhaled deeply and told Warner to put her through. Despite my ceasefire with Rylee, I was still dead set on landing this account.

"Good morning, Mrs. Seaworth," I drawled, laying on the charm thick. "How's your day treating you?"

"I'm good," she replied. "I'd like for us to meet today."

"Sure thing," I said, my brain scrambling to keep up with her sudden request. I pulled up my calendar, fingers flying over the keys. "Did you have a time in mind?"

"In an hour, at my place."

Luckily, my schedule looked sparse for the next few hours. I could easily bump around my few appointments if it meant securing Nadine's account.

"You got it," I said.

"Good. I'll be waiting."

And just like that, she was gone. I shook my head, still clutching the phone. Man, if there's one thing I've learned in this biz, it's that the richest folks are also the neediest. Go figure, right?

Over the next thirty minutes, Warner shuffled my appointments like a seasoned pro. Meanwhile, I quickly texted Fury to give him the heads-up about my unexpected meeting with Nadine. Then, I frantically gathered all the necessary paperwork that, fingers crossed, might get signed by the end of the day if luck was on my side. I mean, if Nadine was treating me like her genie and summoning me out of the blue, there was a good chance she was dead serious about signing with Gracen & McCrae. I might as well be prepared, right?

Rolling up to the Seaworth's place, I felt confident, ready to seal the deal with our newest client. But then I spotted a car and had a good idea about who it was.

Uh-oh.

Fuck.

Trying to stay optimistic, I made my way to the front door. But my instinct had been spot on. Rylee was here, too, and things weren't as locked down as I'd thought.

"Hey," she said, beating me to the punch. "I didn't expect to see you here."

"Ditto," I croaked out, my voice sounding weird. I cleared my throat and prayed she didn't notice my flushed cheeks.

"Mrs. Seaworth called me," Rylee added, almost whispering.

A sinking feeling hit my gut. "She called me too."

What the actual hell was Nadine up to?

"Well, isn't this just peachy," I muttered under my breath as the butler led us down a long, dimly lit hallway. The walls were lined with portraits of stern-looking ancestors, their eyes seeming to follow us as we passed. Rylee shot me a sideways glance, but I just shrugged and tried to keep my cool.

The butler stopped in front of a heavy oak door, which creaked open to reveal a cozy sitting room. Mrs. Seaworth was perched on a velvet armchair with a steaming cup of tea.

She looked up as we entered, her eyes twinkling with mischief.

"Ah, there you are," she said, gesturing for us to take a seat. "I hope you don't mind me calling you both here on such short notice."

Rylee and I exchanged a wary glance as we settled onto a plush sofa. The butler discreetly disappeared, leaving us alone with our mysterious hostess.

"So, what's this all about, Mrs. Seaworth?" I asked, trying to sound casual. But my heart was pounding in my chest, and I couldn't shake the feeling that we were being set up for something.

Mrs. Seaworth sipped her tea, her eyes never leaving our faces. "Well, my dears," she said, setting her cup down on a delicate saucer. "I have a proposition for you both. And I think you're going to find it very...interesting."

I had to fight the urge to steal a glance at Rylee. My body buzzed with her presence, but my mind was locked on Nadine and sealing the Seaworth deal.

Nadine turned to face Rylee. "My son and I chatted about you the other night. He told me that you're quite interested in acquiring my business and that you hoped he'd put in a good word."

Rylee squirmed next to me, and I couldn't help but steal a glance.

"No need to worry, Rylee. Can I call you that? I think we should all be on a first-name basis here." Nadine's look was as plain as vanilla. "I don't hold it against you. I like someone who takes initiative. Besides, my son turning against you means you rejected him. Good for you."

A twinge of guilt washed over me as I recalled the not-so-nice thoughts I'd harbored about Rylee - the snarky comments I'd hurled her way about her little rendezvous with Bennett. It turned out he had been plotting against her. It was a classic case of sour grapes, and it served him right for getting rejected.

"Cory, you're not getting off easy either." Nadine swiveled her gaze towards me. "You and your cousin have spoiled me rotten with all this attention. That play is old as dirt. I think we've had our fill of that, don't you? I want to see results, not flattering."

Neither Rylee nor I said a word, but Nadine didn't seem to need us to. It hadn't taken me long to realize that Nadine would've been the queen of any court in another life.

"No doubt about it, you two are the cream of the crop when it comes to personal attention," Nadine remarked, glancing at Rylee. "Your firm may still be wet behind the ears, but word on the street is you're giving the big dogs a run for their money. And let's be real, a woman running the show in a boy's club? That's got some serious charm."

My jaw clenched, but I managed to keep my mouth shut.

Nadine's attention swung my way again. "But, Cory, I can't discount the weight of a name. Gracen and McCrae? Those are some heavy hitters, even individually. Together? They're a powerhouse."

Nadine was like a ping-pong ball zipping back and forth between us. I was clueless about where she was going to settle.

"So, it hit me last night," Nadine said, "if I'm stuck choosing between you two based on numbers and our chats, then I need a game-changer. Something that'll make it crystal clear who's the perfect fit for my needs."

A cold shiver ran down my spine. This wasn't just about revealing her decision or giving us one last shot to plead our cases. Nope, Nadine had something else up her sleeve.

She nudged a folder towards Rylee, then slid one my way. We both eyed them like they might be ticking time bombs.

"Inside those folders," she declared, "you'll find a project I want both your companies to tackle. Make sure you follow the instructions to the letter to keep everything fair and square. One week from now, we'll meet again and see what you've managed to cook up."

Was this some kind of TV reality show? I half-expected a drumroll or a lightning bolt - this had to be a joke, right?

"If you have questions, feel free to reach out," Nadine added, pushing back her chair and standing. "But remember, the best man *or* woman wins."

I slowly opened the folder, my mind racing. What the hell was Nadine playing at with this bizarre competition? Next to me, Rylee also picked up her folder, scanning the contents with furrowed brows. Clearly, she was just as perplexed by this stunt as I was.

"I know it's unconventional," Nadine continued, "but I have complete faith in both of your abilities. Consider this your chance to showcase your skills and wow me."

She glanced between Rylee and me expectantly. I managed a weak smile while Rylee gave a polite nod. Inside, my head was spinning.

Nadine clasped her hands together. "Excellent! I look forward to seeing what ingenious ideas you come up with. The clock starts now, my dears. I'll see you back here in precisely one week."

TWENTY-TWO

Rylee

I stepped through the glass doors into the office lobby, the enticing aromas of freshly baked bread and roasted vegetables wafting from the giant takeout bag clutched in my hand. I had stopped at the cozy little cafe around the corner, my favorite lunch spot in the neighborhood, to pick up an assortment of sandwiches and sides for the team.

As I ambled down the corridor, heads began popping up from their cubicle fortresses, and office doors opened as my coworkers caught wind of the delicious aroma. By the time I shoved open the break room door, nearly everyone had congregated, eyes sparkling with anticipation.

"Good morning, troops!" I greeted them cheerily, slamming the overstuffed bag onto the table. My teammates wasted no time divvying up the edible gold, cooing over the flawless BLTs, the crisp garden salads, and the toasty warm sourdough rolls.

I plopped down at the table, eyeing my employees as they chowed down on the food. They'd been busting their humps, and I figured a little treat would do them good. Plus, after the rollercoaster ride I'd just been on at the Seaworth house, I needed to spread some positive vibes.

Nadine's moves made sense, in a cold, calculating kind of way, but I'd been blindsided by Cory's presence and that proposal she'd dropped in my lap. I'd flipped through it in the car while waiting for my order, my brain whirling like a hamster on a wheel.

Now, here I was, surrounded by happy munching and the low buzz of chatter, weighing my options. Should I go all in, Cory-style, or shake things up with a little creativity? Both approaches had their perks and pitfalls. The old reliables were tried and true for a reason, but sometimes, stepping off the beaten path led to some seriously sweet payoffs. I'd always tried to find a nice balance, especially for the big accounts like Seaworth, which usually gave me more wiggle room. But this little competition with Cory meant we were working on a tighter schedule.

Mallory popped up beside me, looking a bit worried. "How 'bout some protein to go with that lunch?" she asked, giving my neglected plate a not-so-subtle glance.

I grabbed a grape and tossed it in my mouth. "Nah, I'm good, thanks."

She didn't look convinced, but she wasn't the type to push it. We hadn't worked together long enough for her to get all up in my business just yet. She kept a watchful eye on me as I nibbled on a few more things from my plate. Once I'd eaten enough to ease her worries, I got up and waved everyone to continue their lunch.

I had a plan brewing, and I needed Sergio's input to make it happen.

"Sergio, swing by my office when you're done eating," I said, flashing a friendly smile. "There's no rush, just whenever you're ready."

I made a quick exit before anyone could start asking questions. Sergio was my new go-to guy for delicate matters, and I wanted his take on my strategy. Plus, I figured maybe he knew what Cory might be planning.

While I waited for Sergio, I jotted down the idea that had been swirling in my head. As I saw it come to life on paper, my confidence started to build. I wasn't sure if Nadine would approve, but this was exactly what I promised all my clients: a unique approach from a fresh perspective. If she wanted something more traditional, then maybe Gracen & McCrae would be more her speed.

I looked up from my jottings as a knock on my open door brought me back to the present. There, leaning against the doorway like a bored model, was Sergio. I had to resist the urge to chuckle at his effortless pose— the guy could make a stack of dirty dishes look like high fashion.

"Take a load off." I gestured to the chairs opposite my side of the desk.

"Are we having one of those 'hush-hush' chats?" His smirk was almost too much, and I could practically hear the air quotes around his words.

Instead of giving in to an eye roll, I kept my voice even. "Yeah, yeah. Just close the door, will you?"

He obliged and then strolled over, strutting like he was on a catwalk. I intentionally kept my focus on the scattered papers until he took a seat.

"So, I had a little tete-a-tete with Nadine Seaworth this morning," I started, explaining the competition she'd whipped up and the rules and objectives. Once I'd finished dishing out the details, I slid the papers I'd slapped together across the desk. "This is my plan of attack, and I'd love your help on this."

"Well, don't I feel like the chosen one?" Sergio grinned at me, his eyes flickering to my lips for a sizzling second before bouncing back up to meet my gaze. "I'm guessing we'll spend some quality time together under the midnight sun?" I felt the tension in my jaw as I forced myself to unclench my teeth. "Hey, I'm not complaining," he said, palms up. "Sounds like a pretty sweet deal to me."

"Great," I said, gesturing to the papers he was holding. "How about you take those back to your cave and spend the afternoon poring over them? I'm curious to hear your take on what works and what needs a tweak."

He puffed up like a peacock, sitting a little straighter in his chair. "No problem. I'm always down to take a gander at those documents for you."

Unfortunately, his grin had a bit too much mischief dancing in it for my liking.

"In fact, I'd be stoked to give anything of yours a thorough once-over."

I exhaled, trying my best to keep my cool. "Sergio, let's just focus on the job and leave the jokes in your back pocket, alright?" His smirk softened into a more genuine smile, and he raised his hands in a peaceful gesture. "Apologies, ma'am. I didn't mean to ruffle any feathers."

"It's all good, I believe you." Well, I hoped I did. Confidence is key in our line of work, so I had to give Sergio props for that, even if his swagger bordered on cocky. Maybe he was one of those guys who couldn't help but flirt and needed a gentle reminder to tone it down. I added, "And hey, we're up against Gracen & McCrae for this account, so I need to know if there's anything they might consider that I haven't."

Sergio flashed a grin. "Don't worry. I'm one step ahead of them. You see, I have some dirt on Nadine."

I leaned in, eager for details. "So, give me the lowdown on Nadine Seaworth. What's her deal?"

Sergio crossed his leg, propping his ankle on his knee like he was posing for GQ or something. The guy sure knew how to work a pair of patent leather shoes.

"We met at a swanky party my old firm threw a few years back," he said, lost in the memory. "Nadine's got that 007 Bond Girl vibe, you know? Classy and drop-dead gorgeous, especially for her age. And get this...*she* made the first move on me. Can you believe it?"

"Really? She came on to you?"

He smirked, his eyes practically on fire. "Oh, not just that, my dear. We went on a couple of 'dates,'" he said, air quotes dangling from every syllable.

A glimmer of hope flickered in my brain. "You think she'd remember you, I mean... that?"

Sergio looked at me like I just asked if the sky was blue. He arched an eyebrow, and his fingers formed a steeple of arrogance on his knee. "Trust me, once I give a woman my 'extra attention'...well, let's just say I'm hard to forget," he winked, leaving me to fill in the blanks on his 'date' with the cougar.

"This could work," I said, sounding more confident than I felt. "One of my goals in this competition is to show Nadine that Palmer Money Management can compete. Just because we're smaller doesn't mean we can't hold our own against the big players like Gracen & McCrae."

"You got it, boss!" Sergio said with a grin. "We'll prove we can compete with the big dogs like Gracen & McCrae. And don't worry," he added with a wink, "I'll to go the extra mile if you catch my drift. I mean, for the sake of the team, of course." He flashed me a cheeky smile.

Yep, leave it to Sergio to slip in a borderline-inappropriate comment. As much as I tried to brush it off, that pesky voice in my head wouldn't let up. My old man's words kept echoing in my mind, telling me I had no place in this "man's world" if I couldn't handle a little locker room banter. I mean, 'boys will be boys,' right? But why did they have to be such pigs?

But there was no time to dwell on those thoughts now. I had a competition to win and a business to run. I had to remind myself that I could hold my own against Gracen & McCrae.

"Just make sure the 'extra mile' is within the boundaries of our guidelines. But, enough chit-chat," I said, forcing a smile and pushing aside my frustration. "I found more background information about Nadine. We can reconvene in the morning and hash out your ideas then. Maybe even develop a game plan to show Nadine that we're serious about going the extra mile."

Sergio flashed me a grin, his eyes twinkling with mischief. "You got it, boss. I'll make sure to give those papers a *thorough* examination. If you know what I mean."

I groaned inwardly. As long as Sergio was willing to work hard and help Palmer Money Management compete with the big dogs, I could tolerate his lewd comments- for now.

TWENTY-THREE

Cory

The sun had long since dipped below the horizon when I found myself slumped back in my desk chair, massaging my throbbing temples. This little rivalry with Rylee had started to wear on me more than I wanted to acknowledge. I'd been squinting at my computer screen for what felt like an eternity, desperately trying to cook up a proposal for Nadine Seaworth that would knock her socks off. But my brain was as blank as a freshly painted wall and just about as useful.

Fury had offered to take over since he knew my history with Rylee complicated things. And a part of me wanted to hand this off to him. It would certainly be easier. But my pride wouldn't let me quit, especially when I'd already put so much work into getting this account.

At first, I felt confident I could win Nadine over. Fury believed in me and said I had this in the bag. But the more I tried to think of creative ways to impress Nadine and her sophisticated financial tastes, the more I realized my ideas were totally uninspired. Generic. Run-of-the-mill. It was the kind of thing Rylee would top easily.

With a groan, I dropped my head into my hands and racked my brain for a unique strategy. Something tailored specifically to Nadine Seaworth. I thought about her background, her interests, her family history. There had to be an angle I wasn't seeing. A way to appeal to her on a personal level.

I stared blankly at the screen, mentally sifting through every detail I knew about Nadine, when a knock on my door drew my attention. Warner stood there, his jacket draped over his arm.

His sudden appearance snapped me out of my strategy-brainstorming daze. I glanced at the clock, and the time stared back at me accusingly. Yikes, it was super late. Warner had stuck around way past normal work hours, all because I'd been so wrapped up in outsmarting Nadine.

"Sorry about that, Warner," I said, wincing. "I lost track of time again. I didn't mean to make you work the graveyard shift."

Warner flashed me a grin. "Any breakthroughs on that Nadine proposal yet?"

I let out a heavy sigh and rubbed my hand through my hair. "To be honest, man, I'm still in a rut. I keep thinking how Rylee's going to try to one-up us."

Warner rolled his eyes. "Just do your thing, man. Focus on our game plan and forget about what Rylee's planning."

Warner was spot-on, but it wasn't as simple as that. Nadine was no pushover, and the mere thought of disappointing Fury made my stomach somersault. I was determined to prove to him I had the chops to land a big client for our company, like he always did.

Warner seemed to sense my resolve and backed off. "Alright, boss man. I'll let you get back to it."

I smiled, appreciative of his empathy. "Thanks, Warner. And again, sorry for keeping you so late."

"No worries." He replied, turning to leave.

He turned to leave but stopped, turning back with a serious look. "Don't pull an all-nighter, alright? Work's important, but it isn't everything."

His words echoed in my mind as he walked toward the elevator, and my thoughts, again, went to Rylee. Not that they'd ever been far from her in the first place.

I'd barely scribbled a few thoughts when the elevator chimed, making me wonder if Warner had forgotten something or if Fury had returned to check up on me. I glanced up, and lo and behold, an unexpected yet familiar figure emerged. Raising my eyebrows, I got up and headed towards my office door.

"Becky?"

"Hey, neighbor!" she greeted me, sounding cheerful. "Your assistant Warner was kind enough to let me in downstairs. Such a darling, that guy."

For a moment, I felt like I was stuck in some bizarre, out-of-body episode. Becky's curls cascaded around her shoulders, her makeup flawless. Her sundress seemed a tad too chilly for the almost spring temperatures, but she didn't appear cold at all. Perhaps it was because she clutched something warm enough to require pot holders. Something that smelled suspiciously like meatloaf.

"What in the world are you doing here?" I blurted out the

words before I could filter them, but Becky kept beaming at me, unfazed.

"Well, I noticed it was getting late, and you weren't back yet." She closed the distance between us with a determined stride, forcing me to either dodge out of the way or risk being sandwiched between her and the wall.

I opted for the dodge, stepping aside as she breezed past me and into my office, her sundress swirling around her. She set the casserole dish on my desk and turned to face me, leaning back against it with her hands clasped behind her.

"I figured you probably hadn't had dinner since you've been working so hard, so I thought I'd bring over some of my famous meatloaf." She said it like it was the most natural thing in the world to show up unannounced with a hot dish.

I was still processing this information when she added, "If you could just point me to your plates and utensils, I'll get us set up."

"Uh, sure." I rubbed the back of my neck, feeling a little flustered. "They're in the kitchen, in the bottom cabinet to the left of the sink."

"Great, I'll be right back." She scooped up the casserole dish and flashed me a smile before disappearing into the hallway.

Well, color me surprised, and a tad amused as I watched Becky sashay toward the kitchen. That girl was a force to be reckoned with, no doubt about it. And it seemed I was about to become the unsuspecting host of an impromptu dinner party.

I hastily saved my work, more than ready to usher Becky out of my workspace and get back into the world of quiet and tranquility. But who was I kidding? With her infectious energy and that mouthwatering meatloaf, a little company might just be what I needed.

When she returned, she carried two plates, each heaped with a generous portion of meatloaf, mashed potatoes, and green beans. The aroma filled the room, making my stomach growl.

"Go on, dig in," she said, plonking the plates down in front of me. "I hope it's to your liking."

I thanked her as I took a seat and picked up my fork. The meatloaf was just as scrumptious as she'd made it out to be. I had to give it to her; she knew her way around a kitchen.

I shoveled in a few more mouthfuls, eager to finish up and send Becky on her way. I wasn't exactly sure how I would do that, but I knew I couldn't have her hanging around my office forever.

"Well, what's the verdict?" she asked, eyes gleaming with excitement. "Does my meatloaf live up to the hype?"

I almost choked on the morsel of meatloaf in my mouth, scrambling to find the right words. "Uh, it's... it's really good, Becky. You can definitely cook."

"I'm thrilled you think so." She leaned in closer, her breasts nearly spilling out, unrestrained by a bra, the outline of her nipples teasing me. "I've spent years tweaking this recipe, and I think it's finally perfect."

I nodded, my gaze flickering between her face and the tempting sight before me. "It's...it's clear you've put in the effort. It's exquisite."

"I'm delighted you enjoy it," she breathed, her voice dropping to a sultry whisper. "And just so you know, I have an abundance of other things that are just as enticing. Possibly even more so."

Becky's hips swayed hypnotically as she sauntered across the room, the very air molecules seeming to cling to her curves. My heart skipped a beat, and my grip on my fork loosened. She didn't say a word; she simply took my fork, moved the plates aside, and straddled my lap, her body molded against mine.

"Becky," I rasped, my voice hoarse. "You can't just...do this."

She looked at me, her eyes wide and innocent, the picture of temptation. "Can't do what?" she purred, her voice low and seductive.

"This," I managed to say, my voice strained with effort. "You can't just stroll in here and...and..."

"And what?" she challenged, her voice dripping with sultriness. "Kiss you? Touch you? Make you feel like you're on fire?"

I swallowed hard, my heart pounding. "I don't want you to do any of those things," I said, my voice barely above a whisper.

She giggled and nuzzled my neck. "Why not?" she murmured. "We're both single, aren't we?"

I tried to push her off gently, but she was unexpectedly strong. "No, Becky. This isn't right. Besides, I need to finish working."

Her chuckle was like a whisper of seduction, a soft, smoky sound that sent shivers cascading down my spine. "Cory," she whispered, her lips grazing my ear, "you know you want me."

I let out a low groan as Becky molded herself to me, the warmth of her body seeping through my clothes like a cozy blanket on a chilly night. Her hands, sneaky little devils, slipped under my shirt and began tracing patterns on my skin, sending a jolt of electricity through my body that made my toes curl.

"Stop it!" I stammered, finally managing to extricate myself from the fiery furnace that was Becky. "I mean, don't get me wrong, the meatloaf was fantastic, and you're an amazing cook," I said, attempting to smooth things over. "But I'm not really looking for this sort of thing..." I trailed off, gesturing vaguely at the encounter between us. "I really need to get back to work," I stammered.

She sighed, stood up, and reattached her dress. "Fine," she said, her voice laced with disappointment. "I'll go. But just so you know, I'm not giving up."

With that, she turned and left my office, leaving me alone with my thoughts and a growing sense of unease.

I sat there for a long time, staring at the door, trying to process what had just happened. I felt like I'd been caught in a whirlwind and wasn't sure how to escape.

I didn't get it. I'd never flirted with her or done anything to show any sort of interest. But that didn't matter, I supposed. All that mattered was I now had to figure out a way to convince Becky I had no desire for her in that way. And it wasn't because of Rylee either. I wouldn't want to go out with Becky even if I'd never met Rylee.

Dammit. What was it with the crazy women in my life? Rylee. Nadine. Now Becky.

TWENTY-FOUR

Rylee

I'd always been a numbers gal. The simplicity, the logic, the sensibility - as long as you played by the rules, they couldn't be beaten. No hidden agendas, no second-guessing. Even in investments, where human whims and a dash of luck played a part, it was a walk in the park compared to the tangled web of people and their wants. What they were thinking, especially if you'd been dumb enough to tangle with a rival.

I sighed and buried my face in my hands, trying to evict yet another Cory McCrae-shaped thought from my brain. I'd gotten pretty adept at it. Not at keeping them from barging in - that would be too much to ask. But once they appeared, I just needed a minute, a deep breath, and a vivid visualization of cramming that thought into a box and shoving it into a closet labeled 'Deal with this later.' Once I did that, I started counting backward from twenty, letting everything but the numbers slip away until my mind was clear and focused again.

Except this time, I barely made it to thirteen when my door slammed open, smashing into the wall with a bang that had me leaping to my feet before my brain could even catch up.

"You sly little witch!" Bennett Seaworth stormed over to my desk, eyes blazing, his face beet red.

Behind him, Mallory appeared in the doorway, her face pale as she held up her cell phone in a wordless question. I gave an almost imperceptible shake of my head. I'd give Bennett a shot at calming down, but if that failed, I would press the emergency button on my desk phone, and the building's security would step in.

"Hey, Bennett, why don't you sit down and fill me in on what's got you all riled up?" I tried to sound casual, conscious that we might have some eavesdroppers. "Care to clue me in?"

"Clue you in? You've got to be kidding me, Rylee!" He halted at the edge of my desk, eyes narrowing into angry slits. "Are you seriously that dense?"

I had to resist the sudden impulse to put some distance between us, a quick step backward to escape his reach. Man, was he ticked off! But something told me he wouldn't actually try to deck me. Still, I reassured myself that if he did, I could probably dodge him like a pro. At least, that's what I kept repeating in my head.

"Alright, buddy, let's hash this out calmly," I said, trying to keep my cool. "But you gotta dial down the volume and the cussing."

"I'll be as loud as I damn well please!" he snapped. "Everyone in this office deserves to know what a snake you are!"

I cut him off, my tone sharper. "Bennett, you can't just throw around accusations without telling me what's going on."

"Fine," he spat. "I'll play your little game and pretend you're not already aware of what I'm talking about."

I steeled myself, planting my hands firmly on the desk and squaring my shoulders. Man, even when Cory had been ticked off at me, he'd never turned my stomach into a washing machine like Bennett was doing right now.

"Since you couldn't get *me* to go along with your little schemes, you sent that slick associate, Sergio, to sleep with my mother so she'd hire your company to handle her finances."

I let my jaw drop, not because I was stunned but because I wanted Bennett to see that I was clueless about Sergio's moves.

"I did no such thing," I said, my anger starting to simmer. "But I'll fix this. Trust me."

"You'd better fire that punk," Bennett warned. "Or I'll make sure everyone knows how fucking unethical you are."

I gritted my teeth and swallowed the insult, doing my best to remain calm. It was tempting to tell Bennett he was being a tad overdramatic, but I knew I had to own up to my team's actions. If this was true, I was resolved to clear the air about it. It was crucial that our existing and potential clients realized Sergio was a lone wolf and he'd be facing the music.

"Trust me," I said, taking a moment to gather my thoughts, "this is definitely not how Palmer Money Management rolls."

"Oh, please." Bennett's gaze swept over my attire. "That's totally how you roll."

My fingers clenched into tight fists, and I was stuck between a rock and a hard place. On one hand, I was fuming that Bennett assumed I'd lower myself to sleep with him for an account. But on the other hand, I was seething over his insinuation that I should have done just that. It was as if he couldn't comprehend the idea that someone could turn him down. That there was something money couldn't buy him. Seriously, did I need more reasons to loathe this guy?

I sucked in a deep breath, mentally reminding myself to keep it professional before letting it out in a dramatic sigh. "Look, Bennett," I said, trying to keep my voice from sounding too strained, "I turned you down because there just wasn't any chemistry there. I don't sleep with people to get accounts, and I'm offended that you'd even think that's how I do business." I could feel my voice getting tighter, and I tried not to show my frustration. "Sergio wasn't acting under my orders, I swear. I had no idea he'd even talked to your mom."

Bennett let out a derisive snort. "Well, that doesn't exactly instill me with confidence. What kind of company can't keep its employees in line? Not exactly a glowing endorsement for someone handling my money."

I had to bite my tongue to keep from reminding him that he didn't have any money to handle until Nadine kicked the bucket. I had enough on my plate without adding to it because I couldn't let a snide comment go. I'd had plenty of practice swallowing my pride, so I figured I might as well put it to good use.

"Well then, I guess I'll just sit tight and wait for your employee-wrangling update," Bennett said, practically dripping with sarcasm as he gave me a final, scathing look. "Good luck with that."

He huffed out of my office like a storm cloud, and I watched him disappear into the elevator before turning to Mallory. "I need a freaking minute," I said, slamming the door shut before she could even respond. I trudged back to my desk and fell into my chair, feeling like I'd just run a marathon in high heels.

"Ugh, dammit, dammit, dammit!" I groaned, slamming my hands against my desk hard enough to make my palms sting. I was this close to punching something - or better yet, someone. Specifically, Sergio. That guy was really starting to test my patience.

Yikes, I was seething mad. I'm not usually one to go all Hulk-smash, but Sergio had me feeling like a ticking time bomb. I tried to think back to any conversation we'd had since Monday that could've given him the green light for this nonsense.

And then it hit me like a ton of bricks. His comments about Nadine and their little fling from the past. Ugh, why hadn't I stopped that right then and there? I felt a wave of guilt wash over me, and I made a mental note to never let that kind of crap slide again, no matter how talented or easy on the eyes the employee was.

The whole "boys will be boys" mentality was a load of bull, and I was done making excuses for it. I breathed and hit the intercom button. "Mallory," I said, trying to keep my voice steady, "could you please track down Sergio and send him my way?"

As I waited, I grabbed the necessary paperwork, preparing for the upcoming conversation. I'd give Sergio a chance to explain himself, of course. I'm not one to jump to conclusions based on hearsay, especially when it's from someone like Bennett. But my gut told me he hadn't been lying.

The only possible scenario I could think of was that Sergio had charmed Nadine and reminded her about their previous encounter, and honestly, it wouldn't surprise me if it had been a mutual seduction, but that didn't change the fact that I couldn't condone one of my employees getting cozy with a potential client.

A rapid tap on my door was followed by Sergio swaggering in, his posture and that cocky grin plastered on his face, saying he clearly expected a pat on the back. He was in for a rude awakening, though, as he seemed clueless about my earlier visitor.

"Sit down." I didn't bother sugarcoating it with a 'please.' I'd already exhausted my supply of fake niceties on Bennett.

Sergio's strut hiccupped for a sec, but he quickly regained his cocky swagger and sauntered over to my desk. He plopped down, so laid-back that it only fueled my irritation.

"So, I just had a little chat with Bennett Seaworth." I took a beat, waiting to see if Sergio would react, but his expression remained unchanged. "Care to tell me what went down between you and Nadine?"

Sergio puffed out his chest like a peacock, and his smirk morphed into a Cheshire cat grin. "I took one for the team."

His words echoed in my head, bouncing around like a ping-pong ball on steroids. He'd used that same line when we'd first talked about him helping me win the challenge. Ugh. I'd brushed it off as a cheesy, lame boys club joke instead of taking it seriously. Big mistake.

"We had quite the thrilling and, let's say, athletic night," Sergio went on, another smirk playing on his lips.

"I'm not surprised she sent Bennett over to hand us the account."

I stared at him, my eyes wide with disbelief. That's what he thought Bennett had come here to talk about?

He shook his head, a grin spreading across his face like this was some huge, hilarious prank. "You know, because she would probably be walking funny."

"Just stop," I blurted out, my voice laced with exasperation. "Seriously, just stop talking. You're only digging yourself deeper into a hole."

His eyes bulged, and all traces of smugness were wiped clean from his face. "Wait, what? I landed us the Seaworth deal, just like you asked."

"Nope." I shook my head, setting the record straight. "I wanted us to win the challenge Nadine threw our way. Beat Gracen & McCrae fair and square."

"Oh, right." He folded his arms, a sulky tone creeping into his voice. "That's why you brought me on board, not because I had something up my sleeve you didn't. Those Gracen & McCrae boys would've done the same if I hadn't beaten them to it."

I'd reached my limit. More than my limit, actually.

"You're fired."

"I should be...what?" His sentence trailed off as my words sank in, and his attitude did a quick 180. "Whoa, whoa, whoa! You can't be serious."

"You're fired," I repeated, leaving no room for misunderstanding.

"You're kidding, right?" He gaped in disbelief. "I pulled off a win for us!"

"Nope." I got to my feet, beyond exhausted. "Your job

was to collaborate with me and follow my instructions to the letter. It wasn't to have sex with a potential client because you thought that was the best move."

"As if you've never used your looks and sexuality to get your way." His expression morphed into an ugly sneer. "Batted your eyelashes, flaunted your assets. Dropped some not-so-subtle hints about getting into bed if someone just played along."

My cheeks burned but with rage, not shame or guilt. "If you want to avoid a sexual harassment suit, I strongly suggest you stop right there while I'm still feeling generous."

"Generous?" He shot up and gave me the middle finger. "That's what I think of your so-called generosity."

My half-open door swung wider, and in strolled a pair of security guards. "Your assistant mentioned there's a former employee who needs a gentle nudge off the premises," said the older one, his eyes locking on Sergio.

"That's correct," I replied, smoothing my skirt and praying my hands weren't trembling like leaves. "He has ten minutes to empty his desk and hand over his keycard before hitting the road."

Sergio shot me a venomous glare but kept quiet as the guards led him away. Just as they turned the corner, he hollered, "You're a fucking bitch!" The trio had barely disappeared when he shouted, "You're all a bunch of bitches!"

I sauntered over to my door and peeked out. My employees had gathered like a flock of curious birds, watching the spectacle.

Before anyone could pepper me with questions, I retreated to my office, shut the door, and returned to my desk. The weight of the situation pressed down on my shoulders as

I sat and buried my face in my folded arms. All the progress I thought I'd made on the project, the potential of the Seaworth account, and the pride I'd felt in my business vanished, eclipsed by the actions of one arrogant jerk and my own failure to manage my staff.

For the first time since setting foot in Palo Alto with stars in my eyes, I questioned if I'd bitten off more than I could chew and had made a colossal mistake.

TWENTY-FIVE

Cory

The next day, I dragged myself into the office, totally zombie-like and desperately in need of caffeine.

Once I plopped down at my desk, my brain was still buzzing on overdrive from Becky's surprise appearance the previous night. I mean, who does that? She had the gall to waltz into my office with a slab of meatloaf, trying to woo me. The whole situation was beyond bizarre, like something out of a cheesy rom-com.

I gave my head a good rattle, attempting to shake off the annoyance that was fogging my brain. This was going to be a long day.

I palmed my trusty coffee mug, ready to guzzle down some caffeinated goodness, but alas! It was as empty as my social calendar on a Saturday night. Warner, my usual savior, was MIA from his post.

Not one to be deterred, I set off on a quest to the breakroom. I was just a few steps shy of the promised land when Warner's voice wafted towards me.

"You must be kidding me. Hooking up with a prospective client? And not even trying to keep it hush-hush?" I heard Warner say.

I slowed my pace, even as my heart started to race.

"Not exactly the image a new business should be going for," Jules chimed in. "I'm dying to know how many of our ex-clients Palmer Money Management managed to lure in with the same tactics," she added.

My stomach dropped. I didn't have to wonder who they were talking about - it had to be Rylee and Bennett. Anger and jealousy boiled up inside me at the thought of her being intimate with him. After our last night together, I thought we had moved past manipulating each other, but clearly, Rylee was still using her feminine wiles to get ahead.

I clenched my fists, crumpling the papers I was holding. Rylee seemed so sincere when she said we should stop wasting time fighting each other. Had that just been a ploy to throw me off while she went after the Seaworth account by any means necessary? The thought of her with that sleazeball Bennett made me want to puke.

I passed on coffee and trudged back to my office, sinking into my chair. I sucked in a few deep breaths, trying to chill out and shake off the jealousy zapping my brain. Maybe I was just being paranoid, right? Bennett could've been spinning tales to get back at Rylee for turning him down. But that nagging doubt was already sprouting like a weed in my mind.

I had to know the truth, even if my feelings for Rylee had blinded me to her ambition. Until I had some answers, I couldn't have any distractions. I had to stay focused on winning, no matter what. The stakes were sky-high now, and I couldn't afford to lose.

I noticed Warner coming back, and I stormed to his desk. "I need you to find Bennett Seaworth," I said, my voice low and insistent.

Warner nodded and turned to his computer. "I'm on it."

A few minutes later, he looked up from his screen. "Looks like he's out playing golf at the Palo Alto Country Club."

I grimaced. I hated golf, but I was willing to make an exception for this. "Thanks, Warner," I said, already heading for the door.

The drive was a breeze, with barely any traffic to slow me down. I crossed my fingers that the rest of this mission would be just as smooth.

As I rolled up to the country club, my heart was thumping. This place was massive, with green lawns that seemed to go on forever. It was like a golf oasis, but I wasn't here for a round of eighteen holes. Nope, I was on a quest for some answers.

But there was a problem: I wasn't a member, and they wouldn't let me waltz in and start causing a scene. I was, pacing outside the gates like an idiot, trying to devise a plan, when I noticed a delivery truck pulling up to the side entrance, and an idea struck.

I hustled to the truck and tucked myself in, pulling off a covert operation like a pro. As we cruised to the clubhouse, I casually hopped out with a box, acting like I belonged there. The security guard at the front door was more interested in his coffee than me, so he barely batted an eye as I swaggered by with my "package." Once inside, things were eerily quiet. Where the heck were all these golfers? And more pressingly, where was Bennett Seaworth hiding?

I weaved through the clubhouse, peeking out the windows for signs of life on the courses. Like a needle in a haystack, I finally spotted him in the club's restaurant. There was Bennett Seaworth, all suave and smarmy, leaning on the bar and trying to charm a woman who looked like she'd prefer to be at a dental appointment.

I marched over, my annoyance bubbling below the surface. "We need to have a little chat," I grumbled, doing my best Liam Neeson impression minus the Irish accent.

Bennett's smirk was almost comical when he looked up and saw me standing there. "Well, if it isn't one of the infamous Gracen & McCrae duo," he chuckled, trying to brush me off like a pesky gnat. But I wasn't about to be dismissed that easily.

I grabbed his arm and yanked him away from the bar, ignoring the woman who looked at us with wide eyes. "This is about Rylee," I said, my voice low and serious. Bennett's smirk faltered briefly before he recovered, trying to play it cool.

"Oh, Rylee," he drawled, attempting to sound nonchalant. "What about her?"

I narrowed my eyes, not buying his act for a second. "I know the deal you two did." The accusation was dripping from my voice. "I know she slept with you to try and get an edge in the business deal."

Bennett let out a booming laugh, like I'd just shared the punchline to the greatest joke ever. "Oh, you poor fool," he said, shaking his head in mock pity. "You think I'd lower myself to sleep with Rylee? Please, no disrespect intended, but I have standards. But, you see, she's not the only one playing fast and loose in that firm. It turns out her partner in crime, Sergio, has been getting cozy with my mom. Can you believe the audacity? Talk about crossing the line!"

Those words landed like a hammer to glass. I stared at Bennett, trying to process what he was saying. It couldn't be true. Rylee wouldn't make her employees do that. But then, I'd been the genius who thought she was banging this tool right here.

Bennett just shrugged, looking all smug and self-satisfied. "Believe it or not, buddy. I couldn't care less. But if you're feeling brave, ask Sergio about his little rendezvous with my mom. I'm sure he'll gladly spill the beans."

Well, that sucked. I didn't know *what* to believe anymore.

I stood there like a statue, watching Bennett stroll away, leaving me alone with my thoughts. I felt like a complete idiot. I had accused Rylee of something she hadn't done, and now I wasn't sure what was true. I needed to talk to her, to hear her side of the story. But first, I needed to find Sergio. And maybe a strong drink. Or five.

TWENTY-SIX

Rylee

I'd never been so thankful for a week to end in my life. Today had been the worst. Every Tom, Dick, and Harriet called, eager to get the scoop on Sergio's drama. It had gotten so bad that I invited Mallory to join Nat and me for dinner. She deserved a hearty meal and some vino after the week she'd had juggling our client's questions.

"I was this close to calling the cops," Mallory confessed to Nat after I finished recounting my run-in with Sergio and his escort out of the building. "I mean, it was absolute pandemonium, and I've met my fair share of weirdness working customer service in a sex shop during college."

Nat nearly choked on her wine. "Wait, you worked customer service for a *sex* shop?"

Mallory gave a solemn nod. "Yep, it was a small call center, and we handled customer service from stores nationwide. Folks have some pretty out-there questions and complaints, believe me."

Nat's smile grew even wider. "Oh, you've got to share

some of these gems. What was the most bizarre call you ever caught?"

Mallory paused for a second, then burst out laughing. "Okay, here's a good one. It might not be totally bizarre, but it's funny. So, this young guy called during my second week on the job, completely clueless. His girlfriend had bought a vibrator and wanted him to, well, you know, use it on her. But this poor guy was completely lost – he thought it was just for sore muscles! That's what his mom had told him when he stumbled upon hers as a kid."

Nat and I busted out in laughter.

"Well, at least he had the decency to ask," Nat chimed in. "Better than those clueless guys who think they're gods in bed when they're really just causing friction."

Mallory continued, "Oh, and then I had this dude who was absolutely fuming on the phone. He'd gotten an earful from his girlfriend because, apparently, he'd been telling her his 'package' was over nine inches. But when she ordered a nine-inch dildo to, you know, spice up the party between the sheets, she discovered he'd been stretching the truth by a good few inches. The dude tried to blame us, saying we had printed the wrong dimensions!"

Oh man, I was so ready for this after the rollercoaster I'd been on for the past few weeks. Just what the doctor ordered!

"Reminds me of this one guy I dated briefly. He insisted on using extra-large condoms. That was all he would buy. Only, he was about this big," Nat said, holding up her thumb and index finger a mere two inches apart. "I mean, seriously?"

Mallory shrugged it off, not a care in the world. "I've got all sizes stashed in my bag, just in case," she confessed. "Honestly, bigger doesn't always mean better. Sometimes, those guys on the smaller side know a woman's body way better than the ones who think they're God's gift just 'cause they're packing heat."

Nat bobbed her head, a wistful smile playing on her lips. "Sure, but you can't beat a big cock if the guy knows what he's doing. Can I just mention Fury? Oh my god, that man is a freaking revelation, and he's got the goods to back it up."

Mallory's eyes nearly popped out of her head. "Wait, you don't mean Fury Gracen from Gracen & McCrae, do you?" She swiveled her head between Nat and me, her eyes sparkling with curiosity.

Nat's gaze swung to me; one eyebrow arched in suspense. "By the way, you still haven't spilled the beans on how Cory measured up."

Shit.

A hot blush crept up my cheeks as Mallory's wide-eyed stare landed on me.

"Ah, crap, Rylee, Mallory didn't know?" Nat grimaced apologetically. "My bad."

"You hooked up with Cory McCrae?" Mallory's voice dropped to a stunned whisper.

"We've...uh...had a thing going on a couple of times." I fumbled for the right words. "It's a bizarre, convoluted tale."

"Talk about awkward," Mallory chimed in, "having to go up against your...um, hookup buddy for the Seaworth account? Yikes!"

In an instant, the burden settled back on my shoulders. "Yeah, it was kinda weird, but I guess it doesn't matter now. Cory's gonna snag the account no matter how amazing my pitch is. I wouldn't be surprised if Nadine axed the whole competition and signed with Cory immediately. And I couldn't really blame her."

"Come on, what Sergio pulled isn't on you," Nat insisted, her voice unwavering. "And if Nadine can't look past that and give you a fair shot, then she doesn't deserve someone as talented as you in her corner."

"Damn straight!" Mallory echoed, hoisting her wine glass my way before downing the last drops of its rich, burgundy goodness.

We drained our glasses and split the remaining vino between us. As I placed the bottle back on the table, my phone buzzed to life with an incoming call. The urge to ignore it was real - I'd been bombarded with calls since Sergio's shenanigans hit the rumor mill - but it could also be someone crucial, so I grabbed my phone to peek at the screen.

Ugh, Dad.

I winced as his name popped up on my screen. Seriously, of all the times for him to call, but I couldn't ignore it. If I did, he'd unleash a barrage of texts and voicemails that would haunt me for days, followed by a monstrous guilt trip. So, with a heavy sigh, I steeled myself and picked up. "Hey, Dad."

"Well, well," he said, his tone dripping with sarcasm. "I was starting to think I didn't make the cut for your VIP call list."

I rolled my eyes and counted to five, trying to keep my cool. "I'm out with some friends," I explained, hoping he'd get the hint and spare me the lecture.

But of course, he couldn't resist. "Out with friends?" he scoffed. "Shouldn't you be working? Putting in extra hours? I heard you were competing for a big account."

I gritted my teeth and took a deep breath, reminding myself he meant well. "It's my business, Dad," I said calmly. "One of the perks is that I can decide when and how I work. And right now, I'm taking a much-needed break."

Dad let out a sigh that was heavy with disappointment. "I don't know what else to tell you, kiddo? How long do you think it'll take before your little adventure tanks your career prospects back home?" He paused for dramatic effect. "Who'll hire you after you go bankrupt with your own company?"

I felt my stomach twist into a knot, and the delicious meal I'd just had sat like a rock in my gut.

"Stop lecturing me, Dad," I managed to say, trying to sound confident. "I like it here in Palo Alto. I'm not moving back to Sacramento."

I stopped myself from telling him that even if my business went under and I had to move back home, there was no way I would work with those same jerks again. I'd rather work at a chain of sex shops than deal with them.

"Well, I guess there's no convincing you, is there?" Dad sighed, clearly defeated. "Always were a stubborn little thing."

Little thing? Seriously? I was an adult for crying out loud. I could feel myself reverting to my teenage self, desperate to prove I was my own person. But I didn't say anything. I just bit my tongue and chalked it up to Dad being Dad.

"I gotta run, Dad," I said, cutting him off before he could launch into another lecture. "The server's coming with the check."

I ended the call before Dad could start up again and turned to my pals. They were giving me "the look" - the one that says, "We're here for you, girlfriend, but we're not gonna ask unless you want us to."

Finally, Nat raised an eyebrow and asked, "You doing okay, girl?"

I forced a smile and replied, "Oh, just the usual stuff. Dad being his regular charming self." I inhaled deeply and looked around at the group. "You know what? I'm not quite ready to head home yet. What do you say we hit up a club, let our hair down, and forget about reality for a bit?"

Thirty minutes later, we were at Natalie's favorite haunt, lining up tequila shots and surveying the human ocean. We weren't hunting for any dudes tonight. Not after what Sergio had pulled and the week I'd had. Nope, tonight was strictly about getting wasted with my friends, something I hadn't done in forever. In the past, even before I moved here, I always kept my wits about me when I hit the town. But tonight? Screw it. All bets were off.

So, I chugged that shot like it was my job and immediately flagged down the bartender for another. Who cared about the taste? I was good as long as it made the world go fuzzy around the edges. The club's music and lights pulsed in a hypnotic rhythm as a bead of sweat snaked its way down my back. I could only imagine how sweltering it was out on the dance floor, with bodies grinding against each other in a sweaty mess.

"Ever wonder how many people tonight will wake up with a stranger in their bed?" I yelled in Nat's ear, practically breathing my tequila breath on her.

She shrugged, a smug smile on her face. "If we three gals hit the dance floor, we could have any dude we want, just like that." She snapped her fingers for emphasis.

"Not interested," I shot back, downing my drink and waving for another. I was teetering on the edge of tipsy town and about to tumble into drunk city.

"Uh-huh, sure," Nat said, nudging me with her elbow. "That's because you've got the hots for Cory McCrae."

"How many times did you bang him?" Mallory blurted out, then quickly clamped her hand over her mouth, looking like she'd just dropped an F-bomb in church. Her eyes darted to me, wide with fear, as if she'd forgotten I was her boss for a minute.

Lucky for Mallory, I wouldn't have given a hoot even if I was stone-cold sober. "How do you count it if you do it more than once in the same night?" I quipped, eliciting a raised brow from her.

"Seriously, how many times in one night?" she asked, curiosity piqued.

Nat decided to chime in, slamming her shot glass on the bar with a triumphant grin. "Fury and I went three rounds in one night. That man's got the staying power of a marathon runner."

I let out a chuckle and threw in my two cents. "But seriously, the real kicker here is how many times he made you see stars. 'Cause lots of dudes can pop off three times, easy peasy."

Mallory burst into laughter, eyes gleaming with amusement. "Pop off? You, my bossy lady, are tipsy."

I squinted at her. "Did you just call me bossy?"

She nodded, a grin playing on her lips. "Yep, you're my bossy lady."

That little comment sent us into a fit of laughter that had people staring our way. Some of those stares came from hot guys, but I couldn't be bothered. Nat was spot on - Cory was the only guy who could get my engine revving.

Ugh, figures.

I heaved a sigh and downed another shot, feeling a bit unsteady as I swiveled on my barstool. "Last one, I promise," I muttered to myself, not keen on the idea of passing out and leaving my fate in the hands of these two tipsy compatriots.

"You're dodging my question, bossy lady," Mallory piped up, her words slightly slurred. "Spill the beans - how many times did you and Cory, well, you know."

I attempted to tally the times on my fingers, but my brain was as fuzzy as a peach, and I kept losing track. Nat chimed in, insisting that my memory lapse was due to Cory's lackluster performance. But that wasn't it—I could recall every single moment his hands roamed my body, his tongue traced my skin, and his, well, you know, filled me. My entire being still hummed with the memory.

"I'm just gonna ask him," I blurted out, rummaging through my purse like a squirrel hunting for acorns. My friends watched, wide-eyed, as I fished out my phone. It took me a couple of tries to unlock it and even longer to locate his number, but I finally managed to hit the call button. I beamed as it rang. "He's gonna dish the juicy details, and then you're both gonna feel like goons."

I brushed off the tiny voice in my head that whispered this might not be the wisest move. But before I could reconsider, he picked up.

TWENTY-SEVEN

Cory

She said yes!

Carson's text left me reeling as I squinted at the screen, trying to wrap my head around it. I wasn't exactly shocked he had popped the question to Vix or that she'd said yes - they were a match made in heaven despite their totally different backgrounds. Their love was the real deal, and it was obvious to anyone with eyes. No, it was more the gut-punch realization that my twin brother, my ride-or-die since day one, was about to become someone's husband. We might have taken different roads in life and lived on opposite coasts, but we were still twins, joined at the hip since our mom died, and we had to face the world together.

Now, he was going to tie the knot and, before I knew it, start a family. A weird feeling, maybe a little jealousy, twisted in my gut, followed closely by a heavy dose of guilt for even thinking about raining on their parade. They deserved every bit of happiness after everything they'd been through.

Whoa, congrats, bro! You hit the jackpot with Vix - she's one-of-a-kind.

Carson's reply zipped in faster than a cheetah on roller skates.

There's no doubt about it, buddy. She's the real deal. But hey, now it's your turn on the marriage roulette.

Yeah, yeah, keep dreaming. That ship has sailed and sunk, but I'm genuinely stoked for you two.

I placed my phone on the table and grabbed the whisky that had been keeping me company for the last hour. My big brother, Brody, always ensured we had a bottle of Shannon's Reserve. Normally, I saved it for special occasions, but after the week I'd had, I figured a little treat was in order.

And my brother getting engaged *is* a special occasion.

I'd barely managed fifteen minutes of peace when my phone started vibrating with an incoming call. It was late enough to send a jolt of worry through me, and the name on the screen only added to my confusion.

"Rylee?" I answered, turning on the speakerphone and wincing at the burst of laughter that blasted through the speakers.

"Nope!" she giggled. "Not me tonight. I'm someone else entirely."

The thumping music in the background made it hard to hear her, but I had a feeling she'd be shouting even if she was in a library. I'd seen her tipsy before, but this sounded like she was full-on hammered.

"Seriously?" I couldn't resist playfully poking at her, especially since she had the power to dispel the lingering darkness that had been clouding my mind. "So, who are you then?"

"I'm me!" she exclaimed, her voice brimming with joy.

Her response made me chuckle. "Ah, I see. So you're not you, you're me?"

"No, no, no," she corrected, giggling. "You're you, and I'm me."

"Got it," I replied, grinning. "So tomorrow, you'll be you again?"

This conversation was off the charts, like the silliest I'd ever had with anyone, and trust me, I'd been through some doozies. Rylee went quiet, and I could hear two others in the background, so I figured she was with her girlfriends. I knew I had no business prying, but I was relieved not to hear any dudes in the mix.

After a solid minute of cricket chirps on the other end, I piped up, "Uh, Rylee? You there?"

Her voice filtered through, sounding like she'd stuffed a sock in her mouth. "What? My phone's talking. Who's this?"

I bit back a laugh. If only I could record this for later for my own amusement. "It's Cory," I replied, sounding as casual as possible.

"Why'd you call me?" she asked, blissfully unaware of the fact that she was the one who'd dialed my number.

"I didn't," I reminded her, trying to keep the smirk out of my voice. "You called me."

A few seconds of silence passed before she finally said, "Oh! Right, I called 'cause we've got questions."

"We?" I asked, half-dreading another round of "Who's on first."

"Me, Mallory, and Nat," she replied like I should know all her friends on a first-name basis.

Their voices in the background were as loud as a pack of

hyenas, meaning they were probably having the best time ever.

Great. I could picture it now. The three of them perched on barstools, slurring their words and spilling their drinks. Classy.

"Are you guys drinking alone?" I asked, trying to sound like the responsible one for once.

Rylee replied, "Of course not. We're with each other."

I sighed. "I meant..." I bit my tongue before I could say anything else. "Never mind. Just tell me where you are."

"I'm here," she slurred, as if that was at all helpful.

"Rylee!" I used my I-mean-business voice. "What club are you at?"

She stuttered out a name I recognized, and thankfully, it was only a twenty-minute drive away.

"All three of you, stay put at the bar. Don't leave with anyone. I'm coming to get you." Before she could protest, I ended the call, already dreading yet also anticipating the circus I was about to join.

"Oh fuck," I groaned, standing up and checking my drink. Thankfully, I hadn't been chugging it and had some food in my system, so I grabbed my keys and headed for the elevator.

My mind was laser-focused on getting to Rylee and her friends before any shenanigans ensued, and I almost stepped out of the elevator before it was fully open. That's when I bumped into someone soft and petite. My hands shot out instinctively, catching them by the shoulders.

"Cory," the voice registered before anything else, and I knew it was Becky.

"Hi," I gave her a half-hearted smile. "Oops, sorry about that."

"No worries; it's all good." She flashed a bright smile, lingering in my bubble even after I let go of her shoulders. "Actually, I was kind of hoping to run into you so we could chat."

I had to interrupt before she got carried away. "Sorry, Becky. Not now. I've got some friends I need to catch up with, and it's kind of urgent."

I didn't stick around for her response, nothing she said would have changed my mind.

It took every ounce of concentration to keep my eyes on the road as I sped towards the club, my brain tempted to imagine worst-case scenarios of the trio passed out in the bathroom or someone spiking their drinks, or some dudes thinking it was cool to touch–

"Come on, get a grip!" I smacked the steering wheel, scolding myself to snap out of it.

By the time I rolled up to the club, my jaw was clenched so tight I could've cracked walnuts with my teeth. I was nursing a budding headache, but that was the least of my worries. As I hunted for a parking spot, I fired off a voice-to-text message to Rylee.

"Hey, I'm here. Meet me outside, and I'll get you and your friends home safe."

Time crept along, and Rylee still hadn't replied. I tried to tell myself it was just a delayed text alert; there was no need to panic. But my imagination had other ideas, conjuring up all kinds of horror movie scenes playing out inside.

The truth was that losing someone at a young age left a

mark. The fear of losing someone again never truly went away. It was like a constant companion you couldn't shake.

I managed to wriggle into a parking spot, close enough to see the club entrance yet feeling a world apart. I quickly tapped out another message.

"You've got two minutes before I come barging in after you."

I lasted all of ninety seconds before I was out of the car and making a beeline for the entrance. The bouncer gave my cash a quick glance and waved me in. Luckily, the line was short, so there weren't too many people to give me the stink eye. Not that it mattered - I had a mission, and nothing would stand in my way.

Upon stepping in, I blinked a few times, allowing my eyes to adjust to the disco inferno of strobe lights and blinking colors. Once the kaleidoscope faded, I hunted for Rylee's face in the crowd. I spotted a head of dark blonde hair that stood out like a lighthouse among the sea of bobbing heads. I recalled Nat, Rylee's Amazonian friend, and figured I was on the right track. So, I dove into the throng, swimming my way toward Rylee, who was holding court like the queen bee she was.

Engrossed in her lively chatter with friends, Rylee was oblivious to my sneaking up on her, so I gave her arm a gentle tap. She spun around, eyes wide and glassy - a total giveaway. Yep, she was three sheets to the wind, alright. It took her a moment to recognize me, but then her face brightened like a kid on Christmas morning.

"Cory!" she shrieked, practically leaping into my arms.

I caught her instinctively, pulling her close and breathing in the heady mix of alcohol, citrus, and her own unique scent.

It was intoxicating, to say the least, and my body responded accordingly. But I had to keep it together - now was not the time to get carried away.

With as much finesse as I could muster, I eased her back down to solid ground, but she wasn't ready to let go just yet. Instead, she latched onto my arm and used me as her personal leaning post, teetering like a Jenga tower on the brink of collapse. "Hey, y'all!" she bellowed to the entire bar, "Check it out! Cory's here!"

I glanced over at the peanut gallery, spotting two women watching the spectacle with varying degrees of amusement. Nat was all smiles, seemingly getting a kick out of the situation, while the other one – Mallory, I presumed – gawked at me as if struck by a lightning bolt. Once she registered my gaze, her cheeks bloomed into a lovely shade of rose. Yep, just as I'd predicted, all three were drunk, sailing close to the wind.

"Alright, ladies," I announced, raising my voice to be heard over the thumping music and boisterous crowd, "Party's over. Time to hit the road."

"Nooo!" Rylee tugged on my arm. "Drink with us."

I raised an eyebrow. "I think you've had enough."

"Thought you said he was fun," Nat said, folding her arms.

"Not tonight," I said. "None of you are in any shape to drive, so why don't you let me take you home."

"We didn't drive here." Mallory rolled her eyes. "We're not stupid."

"We took a Noober." Nat frowned and tried again as the other two women laughed. "An...Uber."

"Well, that settles it, then," I said, glancing at the burly bartender, who gave me a knowing nod. "Let me get you guys home before things get any crazier."

Rylee shoved me, her glare fierce. "We're not 'guys'! We're women. Look, boobs!" She grabbed her chest and jiggled, causing me to choke on my own spit.

I quickly regained my composure and intercepted her hand before she could lift her shirt and flash the entire bar. "Alright, alright. Point taken. But still, it's time to go."

Nat giggled. "Sorry, Ry, but I think your knight in shining armor's got a point. You're fucking toasted."

Rylee huffed. "Fine, fine. We'll go."

I breathed a sigh of relief, only for it to be cut short by her raised index finger.

"On one condition," she added, eyes gleaming with mischief. "You answer all our questions."

"Whatever it takes. Now, can we leave?" I said and guided them to the exit.

I thought answering their drunken inquiries would be a small price to pay to get them out of there. Boy, was I wrong? It took me all of thirty seconds after getting them buckled into my car to realize just how off the mark I was.

"Nat and I have a little wager going," Rylee announced triumphantly as she finally clicked her seatbelt in place. "Who is the biggest dick? You or Fury?"

I slowly turned to face her, blinking in disbelief. "Uh, come again?"

Nat and Mallory were practically rolling in the back seat with laughter.

"Who *has* the biggest dick," Mallory finally managed to gasp out. "*Has*, not *is*."

"That really doesn't make the question any better," I pointed out, my voice strained.

"Too bad." Rylee grinned at me. "You promised to answer all questions."

I started the car and began to pull out of the parking spot.

Rylee wasn't letting up. "You said you'd answer anything. That was the deal."

I felt my face getting hot. "I'm not discussing the size of my...you know."

"Fury's is eleven inches," Nat said from the back.

I resisted the urge to squeeze my eyes shut in disbelief.

"No way," Rylee shot back. "Cory, spill the beans."

"I have never, and will never, measure my cousin's penis," I said, trying to keep a straight face. "And no, we don't compare sizes."

"But you've seen him naked," Nat pointed out.

"That doesn't mean anything," Mallory said. "Is he a shower or a grower?"

The trio erupted in a fit of giggles, and I just sat there, shaking my head. They were behaving like a bunch of hormonal high schoolers.

Mallory's pad was just a stone's throw away, so I let them continue their wild guesses and giggling fits while I focused on the road. Every now and then, they'd toss a question my way, but it seemed like they'd already forgotten they wanted answers from me. I was more than happy to sit this one out, especially since most of their questions felt like they were trying to size up my skills in the bedroom against Fury's.

I had my work cut out for me, trying to drive with Rylee, playing some kind of twisted game with her trying to see if she could sneak a feel whenever we were at a stoplight. By the time I dropped Nat off at her place and it was just Rylee in the car with me, my poor guy was completely confused – the way she kept manhandling me had me half-hard the whole damn time. But I wasn't about to take advantage of her in her drunken state.

"Where to now, Mr. Driver?" Rylee twisted around in her seat, giving me an eyeful of those endless legs.

I raised an eyebrow. "I'm taking you home, Rylee."

"Perfect." She leaned in close, her fingers brushing my jaw. "Your bed's so cozy."

I shook my head, putting the car back into gear. "No, I meant *your* home."

She grinned, tugging at the hem of her shirt. "Well, I don't have my pajamas. I could borrow one of your shirts."

"Rylee," I sighed, "you're going to your place. You can wear whatever you want."

Her grin widened. "What if I don't want to wear anything?"

I groaned, biting back a few choice words. "It's your call, Rylee. Sleep in whatever you want."

When she didn't respond, I finally asked, "So, why the heavy drinking tonight? Was it some kind of secret celebration?"

Rylee shrugged, a little smile playing on her lips. "Just the opposite. This week was a total dumpster fire."

I could relate, but I wasn't going to delve into the rumor mill.

As we drove, I listened to her talk about her friends. When we pulled up to her building, she invited me to come upstairs. Well, I wasn't sure she could manage getting there on her own, so I said yes.

I let her grab my hand as we stumbled our way to her third-floor apartment. It was the kind of place where you had to drag yourself up three flights of stairs, but hey, at least the rent was probably cheap.

She somehow managed to unlock the door without my help, but she left it wide open as she waltzed inside. I took that as my cue to follow her, but not to join her in bed - just to get her safely tucked in. Given her yawning and eyelids sagging, I doubted she'd even notice I was there.

As I tucked her into bed and brushed her hair out of her face, I realized I would miss her. It didn't make a lick of sense, but then again, nothing about this whole thing between Rylee and me had made much sense. And I had a feeling it wasn't going to get any easier to figure out.

TWENTY-EIGHT

Rylee

I dragged myself out of the murky depths of that weird twilight zone between sleep and consciousness, positive that I had been there for ages. Long enough to sober up, at least. My head was seconds away from a full-blown explosion. I could feel it. Great, just what I needed to make the week perfect- a fucking hangover.

My tongue felt like a puffy, furry creature was taking residence in my mouth, and my lips were stuck together with a layer of grossness. I pried my eyelids open and raised my leaden hand to scrub the gunk from my eyes. The room was bathed in that soft, shadowy light that told me the sun was up, even though I had to squint at the clock on my bedside table to see that it was 9:30 a.m.

As I groaned and pressed my palms to my face, flashes of memories from last night started to play in my mind like a movie. It was a fun girls' night out, with a nice dinner and lots of laughter. Then came the club, where things got a bit blurry. But I could still remember chuckling and downing drinks with Mallory and Nat.

And then, there was the part where I called Cory.

"Oh, crap," I croaked, my voice sounding like I'd gargled with gravel. I fumbled around for the water bottle that lived on my nightstand.

I chugged down the water, desperate to recall what I'd blabbed to Cory, but all I got were fragments. Whatever it was, it must've been good enough for him to swoop in and save us. I vividly remembered that part - him appearing before me like a real Prince.

A real Prince? More like my imaginary Chippendale.

"Son of a biscuit," I muttered, flopping my head back onto the pillow as my cheeks turned into a raging inferno.

Yeah, I'd been all kinds of handsy with him. Touching, flirting, praying for a kiss, or even more. The sting of disappointment still lingered when he said he wouldn't play along. But the knowledge that I'd gotten to him, that I'd turned him on, was hard to ignore.

I owed Cory a massive apology for my antics. And Mallory? I owed her one, too, considering I was her boss, and she shouldn't have had to witness *that* train wreck. Nat, on the other hand, was in for a different conversation. A chat about why, in the name of all things holy, she'd let me call Cory, let alone throw myself at him like a lovesick puppy.

Oh, right. She'd been drunk off her ass, too.

I'd always preached about owning up to our mistakes, and it was high time I practiced what I'd been preaching. Grown-up panties on, it was time to face the music.

Yep, I'd messed up big time.

I could only cross my fingers that my little escapade

hadn't caught the eye of anyone familiar with my face. If it had, well, my wild night might become the main course for social media vultures- just the cherry on top of this disastrous week, right?

For the umpteenth time, I questioned my decision to move here, except now, the doubts weren't just whispers—they were loud and screaming that I'd bungled my life with my choices, and it was time to deal with the fallout.

But first, a shower—a long, hot one—was in order.

I lingered under the hot spray for what felt like ages, letting the water wash away the remnants of my wild night. By the time I emerged from the bathroom, the sports drink and aspirin had worked their magic, and I was starting to resemble a functioning human being. All I needed now was a jolt of caffeine and a little something to calm my rumbling stomach.

My body seemed to be on autopilot as I brewed a pot of coffee and toasted a couple of slices of bread. I collapsed onto the couch with a sigh of relief, grateful for the simple pleasures in life. With each sip of coffee and bite of buttery toast, I felt a little more like myself.

Just as I polished off the last crumb, a knock at the door startled me out of my hangover fog.

Cory's face popped into my mind, and my heart took off like a jackrabbit. I tried telling myself it was wishful thinking and my tequila-infused shenanigans probably ensured I'd never see that handsome face again. But, hey, a girl could hope, right? So, I gave my hair a frantic fluff and cinched my robe extra tight, hoping to avoid the total trainwreck look.

In my hurry, I neglected to peek through the peephole, so

I had no clue the person waiting on the other side was the last person I wanted to see: my dear old dad.

Tall and gangly, Dad sported silver hair and a face so smooth, you'd think he was pushing fifty, not sixty-three. It was beyond me how a guy who perpetually wore a scowl and acted like life was playing a never-ending practical joke on him could look so darn youthful.

"Dad," I blurted, my voice echoing my shock.

He scanned me from my wet hair to my bare toes, his disgust evident as he spoke. "Are you going to let me in, or would you prefer your neighbors speculating about the kind of daughter you are?"

Clamping my tongue between my teeth, I moved aside and motioned for him to enter. My sluggish brain scrambled to figure out my next move, but I was still reeling from his unexpected appearance.

"I'll just go throw some clothes on," I said, shutting the door. "Make yourself comfortable."

I cringed even as the words left my mouth, aware I didn't mean them, but I knew it was what my dad expected. Caught off guard, I'd automatically reverted to old habits. I rushed to my room, praying I'd get there before he said something that required a response. I needed a moment to compose myself before finding out why he'd shown up.

I managed to wriggle into a pair of jeans and a cozy sweatshirt before scurrying back to where he was stationed. Of course, he was smack dab in the center of the room, scanning the place like a hawk, his nose crinkled in clear disapproval. I wasn't sure if it was my humble abode, my quirky decor, or the fact that his little girl was a single, independent woman thriving in a city far from home.

"Can I offer you a drink?" I asked, trying my best to be the hospitable daughter.

"I'm good," he replied curtly. "I'm not here for a chit-chat."

I sighed and crossed my arms, more for my comfort than to show any defiance – though I suspected he wouldn't catch the difference. "I kind of figured that."

"You need to come home," he stated, cutting right to the chase.

Well, if he was going to skip the small talk, so could I. "I am home," I said, gesturing around. "Right here, in this cozy little pad."

He shot me that classic exasperated glance that instantly transported me back to my teenage years when I announced my plans to dive headfirst into a math-heavy high school curriculum instead of sticking to home-ed.

"Sacramento is home," he emphasized as if trying to drill the words into my head. "I know you felt like you needed to distance yourself from everything that happened. But this little escapade has gone on long enough."

I sighed, shaking my head. "Dad, I told you the last time we had this conversation that I wasn't moving back. I needed a fresh start."

He seemed to consider this for a moment, then relented slightly. "I understand you don't want to return to your old job. But there are plenty of other firms in Sacramento where you could work if you really wanted to stay in the field. And if you didn't..."

The unspoken words hung heavy in the air, and I couldn't help but roll my eyes. Even though I'd followed in his footsteps and became a successful money manager – and a damn good one at that – there was still a part of him that wished I'd chosen a different path. Working in a male-dominated field just wasn't his vision for my life.

"I love what I do," I replied softly, hoping he could hear the sincerity in my voice. "And Palmer Money Management is thriving. I've got half a dozen employees, and we're handling some big accounts."

I bit my tongue before blurting out that I'd recently fired an employee for getting too cozy with a potential client. Dad hadn't heard about it yet, so why add fuel to the fire?

With a heavy sigh, Dad shoved his hands into his pockets. "You know I just want the best for you," he began, and I could already predict the coming sermon. "But how can you even consider marriage or starting a family if you're running your own business?" Dad asked, raising an eyebrow. "You're the boss, for crying out loud. How are you going to take maternity leave?"

Typical Dad, I thought, amused. I tell him my business is thriving, and he's worried about me taking maternity leave.

"I'll cross that bridge when I come to it," I said, rubbing my forehead. "Seriously, Dad, did you drive two hours just to ask me about my hypothetical future baby plans?"

Dad looked slightly offended. "Of course not," he said. "You've barely been answering my calls or texts. How else was I supposed to check up on you?"

Guilt washed over me like a tidal wave. Sure, Dad and I didn't always see eye-to-eye, and sometimes I wondered if he was still pining for the son he never had. But deep down, I knew he loved me in his own quirky way. And now that Mom was gone, he was all alone.

"I really am sorry I haven't made more time to catch up,"

I said, sighing as I twisted my hair into a messy bun. "Hey, how about we order some food, and you can fill me in on what's been happening with you lately?"

His forehead was creased in contemplation, his gaze distant, as he mentally debated pushing me for more details about my job and living situation. After a brief pause, he nodded. "Sounds good to me."

TWENTY-NINE

Cory

No matter how this whole shebang wrapped up, I was more than ready for this ridiculous competition for Nadine's account between our firm and Rylee's to be done and dusted. Sure, I wanted to come out on top, but I couldn't say I'd be jumping for joy about how Nadine had gone about things, even if we did score the account. The more time I spent on it, the more agitated I became.

I'd initially presented Nadine with a solid portfolio, and I knew Rylee had done the same. That had always been enough for our other clients. But this? A competition like some TV reality show. I mean, seriously?

There was a moment when I'd nearly picked up the phone to call the whole thing off and tell Nadine that if our usual presentations weren't up to her standards, then she should go ahead and find someone else. But, I'd held back. Most of it was just frustration talking, and getting the account would be worth it.

Now, this meeting wouldn't be a walk in the park. When

Nadine summoned me this lovely morning, she casually mentioned that Rylee would also appear. Just the thought of Rylee being there had my heart doing backflips. We hadn't even texted each other since I bailed on her last Friday night. I'd come this close to reaching out all weekend just to see how she was doing, but every time I started typing, I froze, unsure of what to say or if I should even bother.

I'm usually an overthinker, but Friday night had been anything but typical.

As if things between Rylee and me weren't already weird enough.

Approaching the Seaworth residence, my mind was a whirlpool of questions, and none of them had anything to do with work.

Would Rylee be red-faced and mortified about what had happened, so mortified that she'd rather avoid me altogether?

Could I look her in the eye without flashing back to the way her hands had teased and tormented me?

Should I play it cool and pretend like nothing had happened?

Would that make Rylee think I was trying to keep things professional and respectful, or would she think I was horrified by her actions?

"Come on, Cory, get it together," I muttered, hoping the sound of my voice would somehow yank my brain back to where it needed to be.

I wasn't entirely sure if my head was back in the game, but by the time I parked my car, I'd managed to wrestle at least eighty percent of my focus back to work stuff. Alright, fine, it might have been more like seventy percent, but hey, at least it was the majority.

I was halfway to the door when I heard the crunch of gravel behind me, signaling the arrival of another car. Despite my earlier pep talk, I stopped dead in my tracks and turned around, my heart pounding. Was it Rylee? Of course, it was.

As Rylee climbed out of her car, she smiled at me, but her eyes lacked the usual sparkle. "Morning," I said, hoping my voice didn't sound as shaky as it felt. "Are you ready for this?"

Rylee's gaze flicked briefly in my direction before darting away again. "I should hope so. I've been going over my presentation all weekend." There was a hint of an edge in her voice, and it suddenly dawned on me that she might have taken my question the wrong way. Oh, crap. She thought I was asking if she was ready because of what happened on Friday.

"I sure hope Nadine's grateful for our blood, sweat, and tears on these proposals," I said, trying to lighten the mood as we strolled up to the entrance. We'd be lucky if our relationship, or whatever you'd call it, survived this absurd contest. If we were already feeling this awkward, I doubted we'd ever cross paths again after this.

Despite all the questions swirling in my head about us, one thing was crystal clear: I didn't want us to end.

"You know, if any other client suggests a competition like this in the future, I'm going to have to pass," I chuckled, pressing the doorbell. "Our reputation should do the talking."

The moment the words slipped out, I cringed. I'd completely spaced on the dent Palmer Money Management's reputation had taken last week. Before I could muster an apology, the door swung open, and Nadine's butler ushered us inside.

I let Rylee take the lead and somehow managed to keep

my eyes from straying to her backside - no easy feat, let me tell you. Once we were inside, I shuffled up next to her as we trailed behind the butler, who led us to a new room.

"Mrs. Seaworth, your guests have arrived," he announced, standing guard at the doorway. I peeked over his shoulder, catching a glimpse of the built-in bookshelves in Nadine's office.

"Thank you, Stevens," she replied. "Show them in."

The Nadine Seaworth sitting behind the massive mahogany desk was a far cry from the cheerful and flirtatious woman I'd been chatting with for weeks. Her mouth was pulled tight, and lines around her eyes hadn't been there before.

As her gaze shifted from me to Rylee, it became clear why her mood had soured. I suddenly questioned if I should have insisted on meeting with Nadine alone. If she was planning to ream Rylee out for that jerk employee's actions, I wasn't sure I wanted to stick around - especially since I wasn't entirely clear on what had exactly gone down.

I'd heard Sergio skipped town after getting the boot last week. Had Nadine liked this guy and was genuinely hurt and humiliated after Sergio left?

Whatever the reason, I didn't think it was too far-fetched to assume I would get the Seaworth account. I just had to sit through the rest of this charade so Nadine could get whatever she needed out of it.

And I silently begged that it wouldn't mean embarrassing the woman beside me because I really didn't know how I'd respond if Nadine started tearing into Rylee. Thankfully, the older woman's face softened into a neutral expression, and I hoped it meant we'd at least start off on a friendly note.

"Please, take a seat," Nadine motioned to the chairs before us. "I've been eager to see what you've got for me."

As I settled into my seat, I caught Rylee tensing slightly out of the corner of my eye before she sat beside me. I got why she seemed taken aback. Truthfully, I wondered if Nadine planned to go through with the whole thing. Why not just end it now?

"Ms. Palmer, would you like to begin?"

As Rylee dove into her presentation, I was struck by a healthy dose of awe. Sure, I knew she was good - after all, she'd swiped a solid chunk of our clients with her pitches and charming demeanor. But this? This was the next level.

I stole a glance at Nadine, who watched Rylee with rapt attention, her eyebrows knitted together in a look of genuine interest.

Once Rylee wrapped up, she flashed Nadine a grateful smile before settling back into her chair, ready for whatever came next. That's when Nadine turned to me, and for a moment, I blanked. But then it all came flooding back, and I plastered on my most winning smile, sliding my info packet across the desk towards her.

As with every other presentation I'd ever done, I'd written and memorized everything, so once I flipped that mental switch, it was like second nature. I didn't need to think about what I was saying, and I relaxed into the rhythm of the words and the natural movements that accompanied them.

And just like that, I was done. "Thank you for your consideration," I said, trying out the new phrase for size. It was a bit different from my usual fare, but then again, so was this whole competition thing.

Rylee and I sat there, quiet as church mice, while Nadine took her sweet time comparing our printouts. I'm talking at a snail's pace, folks. It felt like she was just messing with us for fun. The frustration was building up inside me like a pressure cooker, and I could practically see the steam coming out of Rylee's ears.

If Nadine ended up awarding us the account, I made a mental note to let Fury deal with her from here on out, even if she didn't like it.

"Well, kudos to you both for all the hard work," Nadine said, shutting those folders like she was sealing our fates. "I've been racking my brain over this, and honestly, both your firms are neck and neck in so many ways."

I had to swallow a surge of irritation, biting my tongue to keep from telling her to just *spit it out*.

"And after much deliberation..."

She even paused for dramatic effect.

"I'm going with Gracen & McCrae."

I waited for the rush of excitement, or relief, or something. But there was just...nothing. I wasn't thrilled about the opportunity or glad she'd chosen us. It took me a second to remember I needed to respond.

"Thanks," I mumbled, the words bouncing off the walls of my hollow chest. "I think Gracen & McCrae is the perfect fit for you."

I meant it. I really did. But a sneaky little voice in my head made me wonder if things would've been different if Rylee's ex-employee hadn't been a total jerk face. The thought soured my victory, and it felt like my win was tainted. I could only imagine how Rylee was feeling, and I didn't like the taste of it one bit.

THIRTY

RYLEE

I was steaming mad, but not exactly shocked. Cory's presentation was solid, just as I'd figured it would be coming from a big-shot firm like Gracen & McCrae. But mine? Mine was better. And no, I'm not just tooting my own horn here - I can be objective about my work, and even though it wasn't my magnum opus, it was still damn impressive. Better than Cory's by a mile.

Of course, I had a pretty good idea why I hadn't landed the account. I'd known it the second I got the call from Nadine asking to meet with me. Then I saw Cory there, and it all clicked - she didn't just want to hand him the account; she wanted me to watch her do it.

What really got to me was that she'd given me a glimmer of hope during the presentations. But in the end, it was all for nothing. She'd still gone with Gracen & McCrae.

If it'd been a fair competition, I would've been frustrated, but now I just felt like I'd wasted so much time. The thing was, I knew I couldn't even really focus my anger on Nadine either. Yes, she could have cut things off right after everything happened with Sergio, but he was the one responsible for all of this.

I wasn't exactly Ms. Innocent in all this mess, either. I brought him on board and let him skate on thin ice with his sketchy antics. If I'd nipped that in the bud pronto, perhaps he wouldn't have dreamed of hitting the hay with someone we were hoping to sign. Things might've turned out another way.

All those thoughts swirled in my brain like a whirlpool, and before I knew it, Cory was thanking Nadine. Then he had the audacity to say that Gracen & McCrae was the perfect fit, which just added fuel to my simmering anger.

I had to grit my teeth and clench my fists to keep that anger from bursting out like a volcano. Somehow, I managed to slap on a fake grin and mumble congrats to Cory, but there was no way I would stick around for the rest of the happy dance.

"Sorry, gotta run!" I sputtered, bolting upright and dashing out of Nadine's office before anyone could object. I made a beeline for the entrance, my strides long and hurried.

Once I reached my car, I didn't immediately drive off. Instead, I slumped over the steering wheel, my forehead resting on the cool leather. I took a few deep breaths, trying to rein in my emotions. There was no way I could go back to work in this state. One tiny misstep and I'd end up snapping at an unsuspecting coworker.

The sound of a car door slamming shut jolted me out of my thoughts. I raised my head in time to see Cory starting his engine. As he drove away, I caught a fleeting glimpse of what looked like a satisfied smirk.

That was the last straw. Without giving myself a chance to second-guess my actions, I started my car and followed him. I tailed him all the way to downtown Palo Alto and straight into the Gracen & McCrae parking lot.

It took me a hot second to find a parking spot, but who cared? I wasn't going to lose this guy. I knew exactly where he was headed and embarrassing him in front of his employees was the least of my worries. I was in it now; there was no turning back.

Once inside the building, I caught up to Cory as he was about to enter his office, barging past his co-workers without a second thought. "Hey, Cory!" I hollered, surprising him. He looked happy to see me for a split second before realizing I was on a warpath.

"Rylee," he said cautiously.

I got up real close, jabbing his rock-hard chest with my finger. "What the hell was that about back there?!"

"What?" He feigned ignorance, eyes wide.

"Don't play dumb with me," I snapped. "You only won that competition because you were flirting your butt off with Nadine."

His expression hardened. "Are you seriously accusing me of cheating to get the Seaworth account?"

"If the shoe fits," I shot back, practically vibrating with anger. "Who knows what kind of insider info you got while cozying up to Nadine."

Cory stiffened, his eyes turning to ice. "Be careful with unfounded accusations, Rylee. None of my employees got the boot for unethical behavior."

The words hit me like a blow, and I took an involuntary step back, hating him for saying it and myself more for it being true. I forced the words out: "That wasn't me. And I didn't sanction what Sergio did. And yes, you're right, I fired him for it!"

"Why are you even telling me–"

Before I could interrupt, a large body stepped between the two of us, and Cory stopped mid-sentence.

"I think you need to leave, Ms. Palmer." The deep voice was calm, even ... and firm. There was no arguing with the owner of that voice.

I tilted my head back to look up at the imposing figure of Fury Gracen looming over me. I wasn't intimidated...but suddenly realized that I was making a scene in the middle of a rival company's office where all the employees could see and hear me.

Dammit.

This was so much worse than drinking too much at a bar and drunk dialing a booty call. Worse than pretty much any embarrassing thing I'd ever done in my entire life.

Without saying another word, I turned around and walked away, taking the stairs so I didn't have to linger by the elevators. My face burned, and I could feel tears forming in my eyes, clouding my vision. By the time I reached the front doors, the angry tears had spilled over, and I was wiping them from my cheeks. As I stepped out into the cool April morning, I was vaguely aware of bumping into someone – a woman – and I mumbled an apology that I wasn't sure she heard. I didn't care, though. I just needed to get out of there.

In fact, I didn't ever want to see Gracen & McCrae again. Especially *that* McCrae.

THIRTY-ONE

Cory

My head spun as Rylee stalked away. Of all the weird things that happened today, Rylee's confrontation was the weirdest. I understood she was upset about losing the account, but her accusations made no fucking sense.

"What was that all about?" Fury asked as he turned toward me, concern on his face.

"We got the Seaworth account," I said.

Understanding showed on my cousin's face. "She's pissed because that idiot who worked for her screwed everything up by screwing Nadine."

I shrugged with a grin. "Wouldn't you be?"

Before Fury could even reply, a familiar voice drifted from behind him.

"Cory?"

My brows knitted together as Fury moved aside, and there stood Becky, a look of uncertainty etched on her face.

"Becky? What's the deal? You're just popping up here again?" I blurted out, sounding more abrupt than I'd intended. The day's chaos had left me frazzled, and my manners were clearly taking the hit.

"I brought you lunch." She raised a small cooler, her lips quivering ever so slightly. "Unless you've already got plans..."

I suppressed a sigh and the urge to massage my temples. "Becky, I'm swamped today. Sorry, there is no time for a midday feast. And seriously, stop bringing me food. It's starting to feel a bit...odd."

"Oh." A single tear welled up in her vivid green eyes.

Great. Just what I needed. What is it with the women in my life today? Has everyone lost their minds?

"How about I walk you to your car?" I suggested, trying to be the gentleman.

"I took a cab," she sniffled.

I really didn't need a weeping woman causing a scene in the office, so I did the only thing I could think of.

"Alright, let me drive you home."

"Really?" A glimmer of hope sparked in her eyes.

"Yep, no worries." I glanced at Fury, who was grinning like a loon. "I'll be back soon."

He just bobbed his head, watching me intently as I waved for Becky to head towards the elevators.

"Are we really unable to find a secluded spot for a quick meal?" Becky inquired softly, her voice quivering with uncertainty.

"I apologize." I gave her a brief glance before quickly refocusing my gaze on the gleaming doors in front of me. "We just landed a major account, and I need to review some details with Fury."

Another sob escaped her. "I understand."

Great. Just what I needed. More sniffles.

"I genuinely appreciate your understanding," I managed to say.

"Of course." She flashed me a warm smile. "You're an important man who deserves to be looked after."

I was completely clueless about how to react to that, but fortunately, the doors swung open before I could bumble my way through a response. Instead, I opted to change the subject.

"My car is just over here." I guided her to my parking spot and swung open the passenger door with a flourish. Sure, I might've stumbled over my words around women, but I could still pull off a gentlemanly move or two.

"Thanks, Cory. You're a real sweetheart." Her smile was radiant.

I slid into the driver's seat, and that's when it hit me: Becky's voice had totally changed. No more teary-eyed tone, not even a hint of the mess she'd been minutes ago. I glanced over at her; her eyes were dry like a desert highway, and there were zero signs of the waterworks from 30 seconds ago. I didn't wanna be a jerk and bring it up, so I just cranked the engine and started driving us home. At least I knew where I was headed since we lived in the same building.

"You know, Cory, we never really get to chat," Becky mused as she placed the cooler on the floor. "Every time I see you, you're zooming off somewhere. And if you're always working and too busy to eat, when do you find time to hang out?"

I gave a half-hearted shrug. "I'm just not big on the whole social scene."

Becky nodded knowingly like a sage bestowing ancient wisdom. "Now, that's where you're going wrong. You just haven't met the right woman to share your time with. Swapping stories about your day and all the work drama? It's one of life's treasures, I tell ya. Or maybe you *have* met the right person but just not realized it yet."

I let out a vague "hmph" as Becky's words got me pondering the early days with Rylee when we barely exchanged two words. It made me curious about the kind of banter we could've had if our first encounter hadn't been so...well, let's just say unusual.

But then again, who knows if I'd met Rylee under different circumstances? Without that mask, I might've been too bashful to even ask her to dance, which could've meant today would've never happened.

No rivalry with Nadine. No reason for Rylee to be mad at me. No awkward showdown in front of my whole team.

Becky was still chatting away, but I was only half-listening, her words barely registering.

"...surprises are great, but maybe planning it out would be better..."

No matter how ticked off I was at Rylee for lashing out at me, the hurt cut deeper. I thought we'd moved past all that drama.

"...a coffee break every now and then would be nice..."

I had genuinely believed that once the competition was behind us, Rylee and I could start untangling the mess that was our relationship. I was under the impression that's what she wanted, too. But now, it looked like she'd rather throw me into a pit of fire than spend another minute with me, let alone be in a relationship.

"You're a really good listener."

I glanced over at Becky to find her smiling fondly at me.

Then, her words registered, and I felt a stab of guilt for not paying attention. It didn't, however, stop me from lying. Sort of.

"Thank you," I said. "You are, too."

"You're sweet." Becky chuckled. "But I haven't had much to listen to. You don't talk very much, do you?"

I shrugged, not knowing what to say.

"How do you even get to know people if you don't talk to them?" she asked, genuinely curious.

I was tempted to tell her that I didn't care to get to know anyone, but my parents had drilled manners into me, and Becky seemed harmless enough. Besides, she was just being friendly.

Becky's hand grazed mine as we pulled into the parking lot, lingering for a moment before she pulled away. Okay, maybe she was being a little *too* friendly, but I was almost off the hook. I'd walk her to her door to be polite and then head back to the car, back to work, and try to forget my crappy morning. No need to debate a goodnight kiss or worry about her inviting me in. I'd just ensure she got inside her apartment safely and then be on my way.

"This was fun," Becky chirped as we approached the staircase. "We should do it again, you know."

Great, because I love nothing more than awkward conversations with a neighbor who seems to be catching feelings.

"Not the whole 'you driving me home after I bring you lunch' thing," she giggled. "I mean the hanging out part."

The door opened to her floor, and I ushered her ahead with a sweep of my hand.

"I'll have to check my schedule and let you know when I'm free," she joked.

When we finally reached her door, I could barely contain my sigh of relief. "Thanks again for bringing me lunch," I managed to say as she fumbled with her keys.

But before I could make my escape, she leaned in, and her lips were on mine. It took me a solid three seconds to register what was happening.

Oh, crap!

"Whoa, hey!" I blurted out, grabbing her shoulders and pulling back. "Sorry, Becky, but I thought I made it clear the other night. I'm not interested in you like that."

I tried my best to keep my voice soft and non-confrontational, but as her expression morphed into anger, I realized I messed up big time. She was done taking no for an answer. I quickly dropped my hands and took a step back, giving her some space.

"I'm really sorry if I gave you the wrong idea," I said, trying to explain myself. "I was just trying to be nice since you went out of your way to make me lunch and bring it all the way to my office."

"*Nice?!*" she practically spat at me. "You think it's *nice* to lead me on, bring me home, and then reject me out of the blue? I thought we were having a great time together, and you were just doing it out of pity?"

I stood there, dumbfounded, trying to process her words. From my perspective, her kiss had come out of nowhere, not my actions.

"I'm sorry," I apologized again, unsure of what else to say.

"Oh, you'll be fucking sorry," she hissed, her face turning red with anger. "You'll regret this."

Before I could respond, she chucked the cooler at me. I managed to catch it out of reflex, more surprised than anything else. The door slammed shut behind her, making me wince and glance around at the other doors in the hallway. Thankfully, no one came out to see what was going on.

After standing there for another minute, I set the cooler down and walked away, still trying to wrap my head around what had just happened.

THIRTY-TWO

Rylee

The entire ride back to work, my brain was stuck on repeat, playing two tunes in an endless loop.

I really fucked up this time, and *maybe Dad's been right all along.*

Neither of those thoughts made me smile, but I pulled myself together enough to fix my makeup before heading inside. My eyes were still red, but I planned to lock myself in my office and only talk to Mallory. That meant I just had to make it to my door without being spotted.

Well, for once, the cosmos decided to throw me a bone, and I managed to sneak all the way without being detected. No sooner had I plopped down in my chair when *rat-a-tat-tat* – someone was knocking on my door, and Mallory's voice came floating through.

"Come in," I said, trying to sound as nonchalant as possible.

Mallory's gaze zeroed in on my face, and she hastily closed the door, scurrying over with concern etched in her eyes. "I'm gonna take a wild guess here and say that the universe just handed you a big, fat lemon."

I let out a sigh, my voice low. "You're my assistant, Mallory, but right now, I really need a friend."

She dropped into the chair opposite me, setting aside her ever-present tablet. A warm smile spread across her face. "You're an amazing boss, but I've gotta say, I like being your friend even more." Crossing her legs, she flashed me a look that said she was all ears. "Alright, lay it on me. What's the scoop?"

I swallowed hard, a rush of gratitude. Not everyone from my old firm had been a total sleaze, but I'd never called any of them friends. The few who saw me as a colleague were tolerable, but there wasn't much common ground for friendship, no shared love of tacos or bad reality TV. The rest either brushed me off or saw me as nothing more than a set of boobs with a half-baked brain on the side.

"My dad popped by my place on Saturday morning."

I breathed and recounted the whole messy saga with my dad and his unexpected cameo at my place. Then, I dove into the epic disaster that was the "ceremony" at Nadine's mansion and how I'd gone full drama queen showdown on Cory in his office. As I shared my story, it was as if a weight was slowly lifting off my shoulders. I was still upset, but it no longer felt like it was suffocating me. By the time I wrapped up my tale, it felt like I'd scrubbed away some sort of gunk clogging up my soul.

Breathing easier than I had in days, I leaned back in my chair and braced myself for Mallory's take on the whole soap opera.

"Uh, no offense or anything, but your dad's kind of a

jerk." Mallory scrunched up her face. "I mean, come on! You're incredible. Smart, dedicated, and genuinely caring. You've built this whole firm from the ground up and even managed to snatch clients from established firms. Heck, you've given 'em a run for their money!"

Mallory's words were like a fierce, protective mama bear defending her cub. They soothed the sting I'd carried around all weekend like a balm for my battered ego.

"And let's not forget about Nadine Seaworth." Mallory's scowl deepened, and she shook her head. "She's the one missing out here. Sergio crossed a line, sure, but that's not on you. Not only did you not ask him to do it, but you also gave him the boot for his actions. If Nadine can't see past that, then she doesn't deserve what you bring to the table."

"You're buttering me up now, aren't you?" I teased, nudging her gently. "Aren't you even a tiny bit curious if Cory's presentation outshone mine?"

Mallory just shook her head, a smirk playing on her lips. "Nah, not really. I mean, Gracen and McCrae are no slouches, and I'm sure it was a nail-biter. But you, my friend, put in some serious elbow grease on that project. There'd be no way Cory's PowerPoint slideshows could compete with your masterpiece."

Even though our friendship was still in its early stages, it was already crystal clear that Mallory was a straight shooter, never one to beat around the bush.

"And let me tell you," Mallory continued, her dark eyes sparkling with determination. "If Nadine or her son ever show their faces around here again, I'll make sure they know exactly what a colossal mistake they made by not choosing you."

"I appreciate that," I replied, my voice barely above a whisper, but the sincerity was palpable.

"I'll tell Cory McCrae, your dad, or anyone else who'll listen the same thing." Mallory leaned in closer, her gaze intense. "Don't you dare let what happened last week make you doubt yourself or think you're not at the top of your game. You deserve everything you've worked your butt off for."

"Thanks," I managed a hoarse whisper, my eyes welling up.

"You know what really grinds my gears? Cory's role in this whole deal," she grumbled, shaking her head. "He ought to be backing you up just like he did when he strutted into the club the other night, playing Uber driver for the three of us." She briefly paused before throwing a curveball my way, "Oh, and now is the time to spill all. Did anything go down between you and Cory after he gave all of us a lift home?"

I shook my head, "Cory's not the type to take advantage. He's too much of a stand-up guy." I blushed, remembering how I'd basically thrown myself at him. Mallory might be onto something about work, but she didn't know the half of it when it came to Cory. She had no clue how much of a gentleman he'd been, especially when I'd been a total jerk, accusing him of being shady when all he'd done was being straight with me.

And there I was, going off on him today, even though I knew he was a stand-up guy. I accused him of things when I knew full well how decent he'd been with me. He could've taken me up on my not-so-subtle offers, and I wouldn't have batted an eye. I wanted him then, and if I let myself think about it, I'd have to admit I still wanted him.

Self-loathing flooded me, pushing away all the good feelings Mallory's support had brought.

"Don't do it," she said, her tone sharp.

"Don't do what?"

She looked at me. "Don't start beating yourself up again over whatever you were thinking about just now."

I wanted to ask her what to do if I messed up and hurt someone who didn't deserve it. But her next words reminded me of what my priorities should be.

"You're a strong person, Rylee. Show everyone just how strong you are. Show them what they're missing, how wrong they are."

I nodded, pushing other thoughts aside and focusing on work.

"You're right," I said. "Thank you."

She stood and picked up her tablet. "You're welcome. Now, I'm going to get back to work. Shout if you need me."

"I will," I said. "And I think I'll be working late, so let me know before you leave."

"Will do, boss," she said with a grin.

I flashed her a grin, probably exactly what she hoped for with her little pep talk. Then I took a big old breath and got down to business. I had my own groove when it came to work and was determined to find it again. So, I dove headfirst into my email, tackling each one like a boss.

But as the minutes turned into hours, my self-assurance faded. When Mallory popped by to see if I needed anything else before she left, all I could muster was a weak smile and a mumbled, "I'm good."

The truth was, I wasn't good. Not even close.

And things only went downhill from there. Every time I

looked at one of my accounts, all I could see were the mistakes and opportunities I'd missed. Any success I'd had felt like a fluke, a lucky break in a game where luck played a big part. The only thing I could acknowledge was how someone else - Cory - would've done a better job.

The weight that had lifted from my shoulders earlier came crashing back down, sapping me of all my energy and willpower until I felt utterly exhausted. I lost track of time as I trudged through endless pages of data and read through my employees' notes and suggestions.

I couldn't do this.

I slumped back in my chair, feeling completely defeated. I was going to fail, and it wouldn't just be me who went down. I'd drag everyone else with me, everyone who'd put their faith in me. They all believed I knew what I was doing, and here I was, questioning everything.

My arrogance was going to screw us all six ways from Sunday.

Who did I think I was, thinking I had what it took to run my own business? And then, I had the nerve to rope in other folks, convincing them to trust me and my big, bold vision. Sure, I never bought into what my old company was doing, but maybe Dad was right about my inability to pull this off. Not because I was a woman but just because I wasn't cut out for it.

I rubbed my hands over my eyes as tears streamed down my cheeks.

I was clueless about what to do next and couldn't ask anyone for help. I'd started this venture alone and had to face the music alone. My brilliant plan to move to a new city where I barely knew anyone was coming back to haunt me.

But let's be real, I didn't have much support back in Sacramento either. Dad would just tell me I'd made my bed, and now I had to sleep in it. Mom wasn't around anymore. And I'd never made the time to make close friends, a habit I'd tried hard not to carry over into my new life.

But, if Palmer Money Management tanked, even the people who liked me now would jump ship, and I couldn't blame them. I'd understand if Mallory didn't want to be around me anymore.

I'd be jobless, friendless, and completely hopeless. Not the brightest future, that's for sure.

I didn't know—

"Rylee?"

A man's voice made me look up, and for a second, I thought I was losing it because there was no way Cory McCrae was standing in my office doorway after how I'd treated him.

But there he was, walking towards me, concern etched on his face. And that was his voice asking if I was okay.

The genuine care I heard in his question was what finally shattered my fragile façade. Unable to hold it together any longer, I buried my face in my hands and let the tears flow.

THIRTY-THREE

CORY

After finally shaking off Becky for what I hoped was the last time, I zombie-drove back to the office, barely noticing the world whizzing by. This day had been a wild ride, a jumble of emotions that hit me faster than I could process them. The current one? Complete bafflement.

Could I have predicted Becky's latest attempt to cozy up to me? In hindsight, maybe. But let's face it; I've never quite grasped the female mind, their motivations, and games.

This also clarified why I'd been so clueless about Rylee.

Sure, I got that she was ticked off, and I understood why. But why follow me back to the office and unleash that anger on me? I'd merely done what I was supposed to do, no funny business involved. I wanted the account, yeah, but I hadn't pulled any dirty tricks or used underhanded tactics, no matter what she accused me of.

Those were all the things I told myself as I made my way back to my office. Once there, the only person I saw was

Warner, who raised an eyebrow to silently ask if I needed anything. When I shook my head, he simply nodded and went back to what he'd been doing.

It took me a hot second to collect my thoughts enough to dive into the Seaworth account, but those pesky thoughts just wouldn't scram. The more time ticked by and the more files I sifted through, the louder one nagging thought grew.

Rylee should've scored this gig.

It wasn't because she'd knocked her presentation out of the park—although let's be real, she totally had. No, it was more about her nailing what Nadine was after in a money manager. I hated to admit it, but Palmer Money Management was the better fit for Nadine, and I knew she was savvy enough to have clued in.

This meant that she had only given us the account because of what Rylee's employee had done, which wasn't fair to Rylee. If Rylee had condoned it or hadn't fired him, I could see holding it against the entire company – or even Rylee personally – but Rylee hadn't done anything unethical. She deserved to be the one handling this account.

Dammit.

I sighed and leaned back in my chair. I couldn't let this go. It wasn't right.

My phone said it was late, but my gut whispered that Rylee was still burning the midnight oil at her office. I decided to swing by, and if she wasn't there, I'd try again tomorrow. I wasn't exactly sure what I'd say to her, given that a part of me was still nursing a bruised ego from her accusations earlier. But I needed to talk to her and tell her face-to-face that the way the whole Nadine thing went down wasn't right.

I couldn't just waltz in and hand over the account, even if I had a hankering to. Legally, it was a no-go without running it by Fury first. And even if Fury gave the green light, it was ultimately Nadine's call. If we turned her down, she might cozy up to some other third-party schmuck instead of Rylee.

By the time I rolled up to Palmer Money Management, I still hadn't come up with a surefire plan. But when I caught sight of Rylee's car nestled in the parking lot, I let out a relieved sigh. I couldn't fathom waiting another minute to hash things out. I knew darn well I wouldn't catch a wink of sleep tonight with this mess looming over me.

I finally made it to the entrance, only to realize I might've hit a roadblock. The lobby was half-lit, and, of course, the doors were locked. I mumbled a colorful phrase under my breath, reconsidering my options. Just as I was about to turn tail, I spotted movement inside. A security guard was heading my way, likely wondering why this guy was loitering outside his building.

I flashed him a friendly smile and kept my hands visible, trying to look as non-threatening as possible. Granted, I wasn't the biggest McCrae, but my size could still be intimidating to some folks.

"I'm here to see Rylee Palmer," I said once he was close enough.

"We're closed," he replied, stone-faced.

"Ah, right. I'm Cory McCrae from Gracen & McCrae. Mind if I show you my business card?" I asked, pulling out my wallet. Along with the card, I slipped out a crisp fifty-dollar bill and presented both to him, hoping he'd be open to a little rule-bending.

The guard hesitated for a moment before accepting my

card and the cash, then peered at the card as he slid the money into his pocket.

"You have business with Ms. Palmer?" he asked, giving me the stink-eye.

"I do," I confirmed, returning his gaze with a confident one of my own.

He sized me up as if trying to read my mind or something. Whatever he saw – or thought he saw – must've satisfied him because he eventually swung the door open and let me in.

"Thank you," I said, genuinely grateful.

"If you cause any trouble, I'll call the cops, and then I'll come after you myself," he warned.

Considering he was probably a good twenty-five years older than me, I wasn't exactly intimidated, but I respected his position and the fact that he'd put himself in harm's way to protect Rylee.

"Understood," I said seriously.

A couple of minutes later, I entered Rylee's office. My heart did a somersault as I watched the tears cascade down her cheeks.

"Rylee?" I ventured, inching closer without waiting for an invitation. "You alright?"

She buried her face in her palms and let out a sob. I hurried over, suddenly worried that my mere question had triggered this. I knelt beside her, my plans and thoughts about our chat evaporating in an instant. All that mattered was her pain.

"What's up?" I asked, placing a hand on her shoulder. "Spill it, Ry."

To my astonishment, she turned towards me, pressing her tear-streaked face into my shoulder as she hugged my neck. Without thinking, I embraced her, pulling her from her chair and onto my lap. As she nestled in, the word 'fragile' popped into my mind for the first time since we'd met. She felt delicate like a single misstep could shatter her completely.

"It's okay," I whispered, unsure of what else to say. I stroked her hair. "Whatever it is, we'll figure it out."

It was bizarre. Despite not knowing the right words or actions, I felt no awkwardness, only a strange urge to soothe her, to mend whatever was broken.

"No," she croaked, her voice trembling. "I don't think we can."

"Talk to me," I commanded instead of pleading.

For a second, I half-expected her to tell me to hit the road, that her life's drama wasn't my cue to swoop in and play the hero. But instead, she let out this heart-wrenching sigh, and the floodgates opened.

It turned out that some of her rants were exactly what I'd anticipated. She was still reeling from the Sergio-Nadine fiasco and had lashed out at me, even though deep down, she knew I was innocent.

But there was more to her story, things that took me completely by surprise.

Like how she'd been bending over backward trying to win her dad's approval her entire life. The disappointment she felt when her old workplace brushed off her harassment claims. The gut punch of her father's response. How she'd moved here to start fresh, only to feel like it was all crumbling around her, just as everyone had predicted. And then, there was her dad's recent visit – not to cheer her on, but to convince her she'd screwed up and needed to return home to be the "good little woman" and do whatever it was she was "supposed" to do.

"What a misogynistic fucker," I grumbled, barely containing my irritation.

She let out a strangled laugh. "He's really not that bad, you know."

I gently lifted her chin until we locked eyes. "Don't you defend him," I said, my voice hard. "Not when he didn't even bother defending you. His own daughter." My words surprised me with their intensity.

Her wide-eyed expression told me they surprised her, too.

"They were all wrong," I went on, feeling an overwhelming urge to make her understand. "That sleaze who thought he could touch you without permission. Your company for not supporting you. Your father. Bennett. Nadine. Me..." I bit out the last word.

"Cory." She placed her hand on my cheek, kneeling in front of me.

I shook my head, still gripping her arms. "I was wrong, too. I should have told Nadine she was losing the best thing that ever happened to her just because she let herself be fooled by someone who made her feel young and beautiful. That she was being a total witch for taking it out on you."

I'm not sure how much longer I would have kept ranting if she hadn't pressed her lips against mine, effectively shutting me up.

I don't know how I ended up on my feet or how I pulled her up with me, but the next thing I knew, I had her on her desk, and our tongues were tangled together. I bit her bottom lip, and she let out this delicious groan as she tugged at my shirt. Reluctantly, I broke away to get rid of it, and then her shirt was off, too. I cupped her breasts over her cotton bra, feeling the hard peaks of her nipples poking through the fabric.

"I need you," she gasped against my lips, her hands fumbling with my belt.

More clothes hit the floor, and then my palms were sliding over her hot, bare skin. I ran a hand up her spine and buried it in her hair, using it as an anchor to keep her in place as I took control of the situation. I could feel it the moment she let go and let me take care of her.

Keeping my grip on her hair, I pulled back just enough to meet her slightly dazed gaze and dropped my free hand between her legs. My cock had been rubbing against the inside of her thigh, driving me wild, but I needed to be inside her, and I could tell she needed it too.

My fingertips brushed over her damp curls before dipping inside her to find her hot, wet, and ready.

"Cory," she groaned, her hands on my hips, her nails digging into my flesh.

"Condom?" I made it a question because I knew what I wanted. I'd pause and grab one if she said the word, but I hoped she craved the same thing I did.

"I'm clean and on the pill," she said, her expression eager.

"Me too." One corner of my mouth quirked up. "You know what I mean."

She nodded. "I do." Her eyes gleamed as she wrapped her fingers around my cock and stroked me from base to tip.

My cock was throbbing, and I couldn't hold back a moan

as she guided me inside her. She was so wet and tight, and I had to take a moment to adjust before I could start thrusting. But once I did, there was no stopping me. Her nails dug into my hips as she met my every thrust with equal force, and our moans filled the room. "Fuck," I groaned, losing myself in the feeling of her hot, slick walls around me. "You're so fucking tight." She gasped at my words and bucked her hips against mine, driving me deeper inside her. "Harder," she begged, her eyes locked on mine as she pulled me down for a kiss.

Her lips parted against mine, and I slipped my tongue inside. I traced the lines of her teeth as I tangled our tongues together, both of us moaning at the intensity of the feeling. When we finally broke apart, our heavy pants filling the space between us, I ran my hands over her bare skin. It felt so soft and smooth against my palms, and I couldn't resist the urge to lick a trail between her breasts.

The sweet taste of her skin exploded over my tongue, and I felt her body shiver beneath me.

"Oh," she cried out as I dragged my lips up to suck on the side of her neck. "Don't stop."

As if I could even if I wanted to.

Her heels pressed against my ass as she wrapped her legs around me and forced me closer. The change in angle drove me crazy, and I grunted against her throat as my control started to slip. My strokes were faster now, almost frantic, and I knew it wouldn't be long before I came.

"Touch yourself," I ordered, leaning back enough to watch as her hand dipped between us, and her fingers found her clit.

Her breathing grew ragged as she rubbed herself, and I

dropped one hand between her legs to push her fingers aside. I swirled my own thumb over her slick nub and felt her pussy grip me even harder than before.

"Cory," she moaned. "I'm gonna...oh! I'm going to come!"

A low groan rumbled through my chest as I watched her eyes slide closed.

She was absolutely beautiful when she came. Her whole face relaxed as pleasure washed over her, her pussy throbbing around my cock until I couldn't hold back another second.

"Rylee," I rasped, giving her one last powerful thrust before letting myself go, filling her up with my release. She looked absolutely stunning in that moment - her hair all messy, her cheeks flushed pink, and wearing nothing but a satisfied grin on her face.

For a moment, I let myself believe that she was mine.

But reality came crashing down all too soon.

My phone buzzed on the floor, snapping me back to the present. I was in her office, and I had just had sex with Rylee on her desk. I took a few deep breaths, propping myself up on one arm next to her head, before reluctantly pulling out of her with a sigh.

I stepped back and reached for my shirt, but as I turned around, I caught sight of her lying naked on the desk, and any thoughts of getting dressed flew out the window. I wasn't quite done with her yet.

She let out a tiny gasp of surprise as I tugged her down, her ass teetering on the edge. Without hesitation, I dropped to my knees, spreading her thighs wide open. She didn't resist; instead, she welcomed my eager mouth as it buried itself between her legs. And she certainly didn't protest when

I ate her pussy with an eagerness I hadn't known since the last time I had her.

It was the only thing that mattered. Licking her again.

And again.

Until she was trembling, begging me to fill her again.

So I did. And it was like coming home.

THIRTY-FOUR

Rylee

After a night without much sleep, I lazily extended my arms above my head, sighing as I settled into my desk chair. The Palmer Money Management employee handbook was spread out in front of me, and it was clear that some serious revisions were in order. After the Sergio fiasco last week, we desperately needed more explicit guidelines about appropriate behavior towards clients.

As I started revising the document, adding some crystal-clear language that forbids romantic or sexual entanglements with clients *and* potential clients, my thoughts kept wandering back to last night with Cory. It was like my brain couldn't let go of the memory of his crooked smile and how his eyes lit up when he laughed. Oh well, at least it was a pleasant distraction from the task at hand.

When he'd shown up at my office, I was a mess; tears had streamed down my face as I'd tried to make sense of everything that had happened with Sergio and the Seaworth account. But Cory, he was there for me. He hadn't judged me or told me I was overreacting. Instead, he'd listened. He'd let me vent and cry and scream into the void. And then, when I was out of words, he held me in his arms.

I don't know what came over me. Maybe it was the past week's stress, or maybe it was simply how Cory looked at me with those warm, understanding eyes. But before I knew it, we were kissing. And then, well, things got a little heated.

One minute, I'm drowning in paperwork, and the next, Cory and I are going at it on my office desk. Papers and folders flew everywhere as we lost ourselves in a whirlwind of passion. It was raw and intense, just what the doctor ordered after the Sergio debacle.

We didn't stop there, either. We took our little love fest to the couch and may or may not have christened the photocopier.

Then he followed me home, and after hours of non-stop fun, I knew it was time to send Cory packing. I needed some alone time to process everything and figure out what it all meant for me and my business.

So I told him to go, even though every fiber of my being wanted to beg him to stay. I watched as he walked to his car, my heart aching with every step he took. And then I was alone, left to wonder if I had just made the biggest mistake of my life.

But no matter what, last night changed things between us. The animosity seems to have dissolved, replaced by a simmering mutual desire and caring that thrills and scares me. I didn't know where this unexpected connection would lead, but I was excited to find out.

My reminiscing was interrupted by a knock at my door. I quickly minimized the policy document, calling out, "Come in!" and turned to greet Mallory, unable to keep a giddy grin off my face.

Mallory practically fell through the doorway, white as a ghost. "Crap, what's wrong?" I asked, dread pooling in my stomach.

She set a tablet on my desk, her hands shaking so badly I thought she'd drop it. "Cory..."

A hand clenched around my heart. "Tell me," I said, my voice shaky.

"He's...he's been arrested." Mallory looked like she' could puke any second.

"For *rape*."

It was like all the air had been sucked out of the room. My lungs burned with their need for oxygen, but there wasn't any for me to give them. Mallory's lips were moving, but I could only hear the blood rushing in my ears. That, and a single word echoing in my head.

Rape.

Cory, the guy who'd turned me down when I'd been hammered and practically throwing myself at him. The guy who always double-checked that we were both on the same wavelength before any kind of physical contact.

Now he's being charged with rape.

My brain short-circuited. It was like trying to solve a Rubik's cube while wearing boxing gloves - just not happening. There was no universe, no alternate reality, where Cory McCrae would ever force himself on anyone.

As a woman, I knew I should side with the alleged victim and give her the benefit of the doubt. But I also knew Cory. I knew the kind of guy he was. And despite my unwavering loyalty to my fellow ladies, I couldn't bring myself to believe this of Cory.

Not *my* Cory.

"Rylee!"

Mallory's voice snapped me out of my daze, but it wasn't until she gave me a good shake that I really came to. "Whoa, there. What's up?" I croaked, blinking my eyes and trying to focus.

"Oh, thank God." Mallory let out a relieved sigh. "I was about to resort to desperate measures. I was this close to smacking you, but I didn't think HR would appreciate that."

I shook my head, trying to clear the cobwebs. "Sorry, I'm here now. So, what do we know?"

Mallory hesitated for a moment before straightening up. "It's not much, just rumors, really."

"I'll take anything at this point. I need a place to start."

Mallory took a moment to gather herself before telling all. "Apparently, Cory was minding his own business at work when two beefy cops barged in, slammed him against the wall, and slapped the cuffs on him. They accused him of sexually assaulting and raping some woman named Becky." She scrunched up her face. "Then they hauled him out of the office while he was hollering and cussing up a storm, directed at the cops and women in general."

I furrowed my brow. "That doesn't sound like Cory. I can't imagine him doing something like that, and the screaming and cursing part? That is just straight-up strange."

"I know what you mean," Mallory chimed in. "I don't know him as well as you do, but from what I've heard around the office and how he was at the bar with us, it just doesn't add up."

"No," I murmured, shaking my head. "It doesn't."

Mallory's gaze locked onto mine, and a sense of tranquility seemed to wash over her. "I'll hold down the fort here. You go find out what the hell is going on."

I should start with Fury. He must know something. Halfway to the door, I stopped and glanced back at her. "I owe you one."

A half-smile tugged at her lips. "Anytime, boss."

Plopping into my car, I suddenly realized I had no idea where Fury might be. The police station? Home? I was at a loss for a hot second, feeling like a dog chasing its tail. I took a deep breath and asked myself, "Alright, where's the best place to start?"

Now, Fury was no dummy. He'd want to help his cousin but also know that showing up at the station wouldn't do squat since he wasn't a lawyer. But he could make some calls, and he'd soon figure out that going home to make those calls would just be a waste of time.

So, that led me to the most logical conclusion: He was at work.

With that in mind, I pointed my car towards Gracen & McCrae.

I couldn't shake the déjà vu feeling as I made my way over. Hadn't I done this before? But no, it was to wrangle Cory last time, not to keep him out of harm's way.

As I pulled up and spotted four squad cars outside, a shiver ran down my spine. It wasn't exactly a cop convention, but it still gave me the creeps.

Trying my best to blend in and not draw attention – which is trickier than you'd think for someone like me – I slipped into the lobby and headed for the elevators. Somehow, I managed to sidestep a pair of chatty uniformed officers deep in conversation with the security guards. I wasn't sure if I'd even make it to the Gracen & McCrae floor, let alone get a warm welcome.

Luck must've been on my side because when the elevator doors opened, no one seemed to notice me. Everyone was too busy huddling in little groups, some chatting with the officers, all wearing expressions like someone had just run over their puppy.

Well, crap.

I'd really been hoping the rumors were way off base. I'd show up here, and everyone would look at me like I'd lost my mind because everything was just peachy.

Clearly, that wasn't the case.

"I've covered all your bases, buddy." The voice next to me sounded familiar, and I swiveled my head to see Fury.

"You call that cooperating?" A gray-haired man, who was clearly a cop despite his lack of uniform, glared up at Fury. "All you've done is insist we're on a wild goose chase."

Fury gave a nonchalant shrug. "What can I say? You are barking up the wrong tree." He caught sight of me approaching, and his eyes narrowed, but something in my expression seemed to clue him in that I wasn't here to add fuel to the fire.

Without a backward glance at the cop, Fury announced, "I've got a meeting," and marched towards me, grabbing my arm and hauling me through the nearest door and into the ladies' room. Once inside, he released me with a scowl. "What's the deal, honey, showing up here?"

"What the fuck's going on?" I asked, trying to ignore the flush rising in my cheeks. "My assistant told me Cory got arrested. I want the facts, not just hearsay."

Fury let out a sigh and raked his fingers through his hair. "They're claiming Cory broke into his neighbor's apartment downstairs, roughed her up, and...you know."

I shook my head emphatically. "No way. He's not that kind of guy."

Fury's eyes softened, and something resembling relief flickered in them. "No, he's not."

"So, does Cory even know this neighbor?" I asked, curiosity piqued.

Fury nodded a hint of incredulity in his eyes. "Get this - she was here yesterday, right after you took off."

"Wait a sec," I interjected, trying to connect the dots.

He waved his hand dismissively. "Look, I don't give a damn about what you have to say. Not unless you're on Cory's side."

"But I *am*," I confirmed. "But when exactly did this so-called attack happen? Because if she came here yesterday..."

"Last night," Fury said, his voice heavy with concern.

A spark of hope ignited within me. "Alright, hit me with the exact timeline."

It looked like Fury was going to argue for a moment, but his shoulders sagged in defeat. "When she was here, she said she didn't have a ride home, so Cory gave her a lift back to their building, dropped her off, and hightailed it back here. He was still here when I left at seven-thirty."

Seven thirty. That was still over half an hour before he arrived at my office. I felt a knot in my stomach as Fury continued.

"Detective Jerkface out there said Becky claims she was watching the early news when Cory knocked on her door, forced his way inside, and..." Fury trailed off, unable to finish the sentence.

I didn't blame him; I didn't want to think about it either. But it was alright that he couldn't bring himself to say it because I had something that was going to turn everything on its head.

"After Cory stopped by my office around eight last night, we spent a lot of time together there. He didn't leave my side until around two thirty this morning." I could see the hope in Fury's eyes, and it tugged at my heartstrings. "And we were... wide fuckin' awake the entire time. He's got a solid-as-a-rock alibi."

THIRTY-FIVE

Cory

I was so lost in my head that I hardly noticed the room's chill or the cuffs' bite on my wrists. My brain was in replay mode, reliving every moment of what had gone down.

Just a little over an hour ago, I was parked at my desk, working on a letter to Nadine explaining why Gracen & McCrae couldn't represent her anymore. But really, my mind was wandering back to last night with Rylee - her on her desk, me on my knees pleasuring her with my tongue, the whole nine yards.

My guy downstairs felt a bit tender from all the action, but was it worth it? There was not a single second of regret.

Yikes, suddenly, the door slammed open with a bang. There was no warning, no nothing. And in walked two cops, looking like they were about to go full dragon on me.

I didn't even have time to worry about the poor door. Nope, my full attention was on the two officers as they demanded my name and told me to turn around and put my hands on the wall. It wasn't until one of them started patting me down that I heard the words "sexual battery" and "rape" and realized I was in deep trouble.

I was so stunned that it took me a second to even register the name they were throwing around. Becky Scheinberg, my downstairs neighbor.

I'd been in a daze since the cops slapped the cuffs on me, accusing me of something I'd never even considered as a possibility. Rape? Seriously? And Becky, my nice neighbor, was pointing the finger at me.

But as I mulled it over, I realized that "nice" wasn't exactly the right word. She'd been friendly, sure, but when I'd turned down her advances, she'd been livid. She told me I'd regret it. I just never thought she'd go this far. Who would?

Anger was slowly replacing the shock that had been my constant companion since the cops slapped the cuffs on me. I mean, really? Becky had actually filed a police report? It was beyond belief.

I kept looking at the door like a puppy waiting for its owner to come home. Come on, someone had to come and sort out this mess, right? I mean, I hadn't even laid a finger on her, apart from a polite handshake or a friendly pat on the back. She was the one who'd made a move on me, and I'd turned her down. No harm, no foul, right?

All I needed was someone to listen to my side of the story. This whole thing was just a massive misunderstanding, and I was more than ready to clear the air.

So there I was, all alone and clueless about the time, with my hands cuffed and butt glued to a chair in this ice-cold, concrete room. Had someone played a practical joke on me but forgotten to tell me the punchline?

I knew the drill with these interrogation rooms - they

wanted to mess with your head and make you feel uneasy. But the longer I sat there, waiting for someone to take my statement or ask me questions, the more irritated I became.

Finally, a stocky guy in a not-so-flattering suit walked in. I was tempted to request a lawyer to give them a taste of their own medicine for keeping me waiting, but I held my tongue. When he offered to remove the cuffs, I simply extended my wrists and waited for him to say something more.

"Where were you last night? Specifically, what time did you leave your office, and where did you go after that?" he asked.

Well, crap. I genuinely hoped Rylee wouldn't be mad at me, but I wasn't going to lie to the cops. Not when it was going to be a 'he said / she said' situation and honesty was crucial.

"Yeah, I walked out of the office around 7:45 last night and I went to Palmer Money Management. Rolled up to the place around 8:10 or so."

"So, what was the deal with your visit?"

"We had some unfinished business about a shared project," I told him. "The place was locked up tighter than a bank vault, but I sweet-talked the security guard into letting me in."

"Just like that, he let you stroll right in?" The detective sounded intrigued, not suspicious.

"Well, I might have sweetened the deal with a fifty-spot," I confessed with a smirk. "Rylee and I had a little tiff that morning about the project, and I wanted to make nice. So, he buzzed me in, and I headed up to Rylee's office." I considered how much to reveal and decided honesty was the way to go without getting too detailed. "One thing led to another, and I trailed her home around eleven. I stuck around until about 2:30 in the morning, then drove back to my pad and crashed. I slept alone until my alarm went off at 5:30. I rolled into work by 6:30." I took a breath before adding, "And, well, you guys know the rest of the story."

"And Ms. Palmer will back up your story?" the detective inquired.

I was hoping Rylee's story jived with mine because I was telling it straight. I rubbed the back of my neck, feeling the knots there. "You can check the security footage in my building to see when I swung by and took off. The GPS in my car and the location data on my phone should seal the deal, too. But hey, I'm not here to tell you how to do your job."

The detective gave me a long, hard stare before hauling himself up from his chair and tossing an envelope onto the desk. "Ms. Palmer's already talked and corroborated your story. We'll double-check everything just to ensure it's all on the up and up, but for now, you're free to hit the road."

I figured I'd be doing a happy dance once I was back on my feet, but instead, I just felt a slow burn of frustration. I really hoped Becky would get her comeuppance for her little stunt. It wasn't just about the headache it gave me, but all the time that could've been spent chasing down actual bad guys.

With my stuff back in my hands, I followed the detective, making our way out of the room and down the hall toward the lobby. I figured I'd either have to flag down a cab or wait for Fury to appear. But as luck would have it, there was Rylee, looking all anxious and worried, pacing back and forth in the lobby like a caged animal. As soon as she caught sight of me, relief washed over her face, and she practically sprinted towards me.

"I was terrified you'd pull that dumb noble crap and not tell them you were with me because you thought I'd be embarrassed or something," she rambled, the words tumbling out of her mouth like a waterfall.

I didn't let her finish; instead, I pulled her into a hug, effectively silencing her. She melted into me, her arms snaking around my waist.

"I was so worried about you," she murmured into my chest.

"I'm alright," I reassured her, planting a kiss on her head. I didn't give a hoot about who might be watching or what they might think. "Can we get the heck out of here?"

"So, where to now?" she asked, pulling back from our hug.

Leaving the police station, I half-expected a swarm of journalists with cameras, but the place was deserted. "Hmm, no reporters."

"Fury must've pulled some strings and sent the vultures on a wild goose chase," she chuckled, although I could still see the worry etched in her eyes.

It struck me then how much she'd been fretting over me. And as much as I hated causing her distress, a tiny part of me was thrilled. It meant she cared, really cared, and that was something.

Yeah, I was a jerk for thinking that way.

"Back to the office?" she queried as we slid into her car.

I shook my head. "Home. I'm not up for the whole 'what happened' interrogation." Or the pitying looks, but I kept that to myself. She shot me a glance that told me she'd caught my drift.

We drove in silence until she pulled into my parking spot.

"Listen, would you come up? I think it's high time we discussed this thing. We've danced around it long enough," I said.

She offered me a gentle smile. "I'd love to, but only if you're feeling up to it."

Reaching over, I gave her hand a reassuring squeeze. "Right now, you're the only thing keeping me from losing it."

The raw honesty of my words hit me like a truck. I'd been dodging this conversation for way too long, scared she'd shove me away or burst into laughter at the thought of being with a socially awkward mess like me. Not because I thought she was heartless but because I saw myself as weak in that department.

But spending last night with her had changed something within me. It showed me I could be the rock she needed, and I didn't want to let that slip away. I couldn't lose her, not after those cops showed up and especially not after she stood up for me today.

I'd promised her last night that I'd have her back, and today, she'd proven she'd do the same for me. Now, it was time to find out if her feelings for me were as strong and genuine as mine were for her. If she was ready to put in the work to make this thing between us real.

No more stalling. No more running. Time to face the music.

THIRTY-SIX

Rylee

Cory and I had been through all sorts of encounters, both of the sexy and non-sexy variety. But the moment he wrapped his arms around me in the middle of the police station to hold me, it felt like we'd reached a new level of closeness. It was reminiscent of last night in my office when he'd comforted me before we'd gotten down to business. This time, the roles were reversed, and I was the one offering the support.

I was dying to ask him what it all meant. What had happened last night? Did this change things between us? But I knew better than to bring it up now. He was just released from jail after having been accused of rape. It was not exactly the ideal moment for a deep and meaningful chat.

When we arrived at his place, he gave me a little nudge to come upstairs with him for a chat. My stomach did a happy flip as our fingers intertwined in the elevator. You know how "we need to talk" convos usually spell disaster? But his hand-holding technique made me feel all warm and fuzzy like there was nothing to worry about.

We stayed silent during the ride, but that was cool with me. I'd already decided what I wanted, and his sudden appearance last night, followed by the arrest drama, only cemented it further. I was ready to roll the dice and see if we could make this thing between us real. We had our bumpy moments, but he'd earned my trust more than once.

As we reached his apartment, he gave my hand a reassuring squeeze before letting go to unlock the door. He was about to usher me in when he suddenly froze, his eyes glued to something inside. I followed his gaze and immediately understood his shock on a gut level, even before my brain had time to process the scene.

A petite, curvy redhead, who seemed oddly familiar, stood inside Cory's apartment... and she was brandishing a gun at us.

"Becky?" Cory blurted out.

Just as the gears in my brain started turning, connecting Becky to that dreadful rape accusation against Cory, she swung the barrel of her gun to the side and let out a shot. The sound pierced my eardrums, leaving a high-pitched ringing in their wake. It was like my fear had a flavor, a metallic tang that coated my tongue. Cory, ever the shield, took a calculated step and positioned himself between me and the wild-eyed Becky.

"You really need to lower that," Cory's voice was a picture of calm, though it sounded a bit fuzzy to my still-ringing ears.

Becky re-aimed the gun at us, her grip steady. "Get your

butts in here. Both of you. Now!" she commanded, her tone leaving no room for argument.

Cory tried another approach, gesturing with his arms spread wide, making himself a larger target. "Someone heard that shot, you know. The cops will be on their way any minute now," he reasoned, his voice steady as a rock.

Becky's response was a bloodcurdling scream. "Get in here, already!" she shrieked, making Cory flinch. I hadn't known Becky long enough to say whether she was usually the loud, emotional type, but Cory's reaction to her outburst made me think this was a far cry from the girl he used to know.

"I'll fucking shoot her," she snapped. "Shoot that little whore you've been screwing around with."

I could feel Cory's reluctance, but he begrudgingly stepped inside, and I followed suit. At least in here, we didn't have to fret about some poor neighbor getting caught in the crossfire.

"Close it," Becky barked, nodding at the door.

I obliged and then cautiously tailed Cory into his apartment.

"I can't even believe this," Becky muttered, her head shaking in disbelief. "If you'd just given me that kiss, none of this would've happened. We'd be an item, and you wouldn't have seen the inside of a jail cell."

A nagging question popped into my head about how she'd gotten wind of Cory's release, but the wild look in her eyes told me this wasn't the time for a Q&A session. Instead, it seemed like smoothing things over and keeping everyone in one piece was the more pressing issue. Because as ticked off as I was about what she did to Cory and her current antics, it was becoming increasingly clear that something was seriously amiss with her.

"When that cop called, asking if I was absolutely positive about what went down since you had an alibi..." She shook her head, her features twisting into something ugly. "I knew there was only one way to make you pay. One surefire way to guarantee that we'd be together for all eternity."

I tiptoed forward, trying to play human shield for Cory, who was doing the same dance with me. It was like a bizarre game of chicken, and in another world, our little awkward shuffle might've been hilarious.

"You need to be with me!" Becky spun around, her eyes blazing like green infernos. "He's mine! You can't just waltz in here and steal him!"

"Becky." Cory attempted to step in, saying her name in a slow, careful voice. It was a classic move straight out of the Protective Idiot Handbook.

"No!" Becky shot him a scathing look. "You said you didn't want me, but if I can't have you, nobody can! You're mine! Even if this is the only way I can keep you." She waved the gun around like a conductor gone rogue.

The whole 'if I can't have you, nobody can' argument was older than dirt, but that didn't make it any less deadly.

"You're not getting your claws into him, either!" Becky spat at me, venom practically dripping from her words. "Miss Flirt-a-lot, always throwing herself at every guy in sight."

Whoa, talk about low blows. Cory attempted to interject, "Becky..."

"It's cool," I murmured softly, waving him off. No need to add fuel to the fire.

"Don't you dare tell him what to do, you bitch!" Becky

lunged towards me, the gun in her hand shaking like a leaf in a hurricane.

Most people don't realize that holding a gun steady is a real pain, especially for extended periods, and even more so when you're trying to manage it with one hand. The longer we kept her ranting, the more her arm would tire out, and hopefully, that would give us a chance to disarm her.

If she didn't pull the trigger first, that was.

Her face twisted up suddenly, eyes bugging out like a cartoon character. "Wait a minute, did you...did you put a spell on him, you freaking witch?"

I had to bite my tongue to keep from laughing. But then I saw she was dead serious.

"Nope," I replied, keeping my cool. "I didn't do a thing to him."

"Liar!" she snapped, practically baring her teeth. "You used some hocus pocus to make him notice you, to make him want you."

Cory tried to pipe up, "She didn't –" but Becky cut him off with a glare that could have melted steel.

Becky steamrolled right over him, her eyes wild and crazy. "It all fits together now. I couldn't figure out how he could go from being all sweet and caring, wanting to spend time with me and be with me, to saying he didn't want me."

Oh boy, she was really going down the rabbit hole now.

"You did something to him," she continued, "to make him attracted to you instead, lured him into your clutches, made him want to be with you." The gun in her hand steadied as she took aim right at me. "And the best way to break the spell is to off the witch who cast it."

THIRTY-SEVEN

Cory

With adrenaline pumping like crazy, my brain should've been a well-oiled machine, firing on all cylinders. But the moment I saw that gun aimed at Rylee, there was only one mantra bouncing around in my head.

Protect Rylee.

Ironically, Rylee seemed to be doing the same, trying to be the hero and get herself in the line of fire.

Then Becky went off on this bizarre tangent about witchcraft, and I realized things had gone from bad to bat-shit crazy. When she mentioned the only way she could have me was by breaking the supposed spell Rylee had cast on me - by killing Rylee, it was the wake-up call that finally cleared the cobwebs from my brain.

"Becky." I made my voice as sharp as a tack to grab her attention, then softened it. "Look at me, would ya?"

She gave me a quick glance, but her gaze slid right back to Rylee, a glint in her eyes that I didn't like one bit.

"Becky, hon." I took a tiny step closer, angling myself to block Rylee from Becky's view without being too obvious.

Her gaze swung my way; the gun was still trained on Rylee, but at least she was looking at me now. It was time to play the game and make her think I was on her side.

"You were right, Becky." I kept my tone gentle and soothing like I was coaxing a skittish kitten. "I fucked up, big time."

"So why'd you push me away?" Her eyes squinted, suspicion written all over her face. "Was it her doing?"

"No, not at all. I don't want her. She's my competitor." I shook my head quickly, hands up in a placating gesture. "I'm the idiot who screwed up here."

"Then what's the deal?" Becky asked, eyeing me cautiously.

"I was spooked, to be honest." A dash of truth always makes a lie more palatable, so I threw in some genuine feelings from the past few weeks - just none that directly involved Becky. "I've never been a smooth talker around women, unless I've got a few drinks in me. I'm all thumbs and awkwardness."

"You? Awkward? No. You just have a hard time flirting."

I shrugged, attempting a bashful smirk. "Yeah, I do. I was a late bloomer. Didn't lose my V-card till I was twenty, and that's only 'cause my brother Carson played wingman."

"Not wanting casual flings is perfectly okay," Becky said. "You're after something real. Like what we've got."

"Yes, exactly," I said. "But as you say, it's tough for me to fess up when I'm after someone like you. I kind of choke. Which is what happened yesterday when..."

I trailed off, giving her a chance to fill in the blanks.

"That's why you did an about-face when I kissed you?" she asked.

Deceiving her like this, seeing the hope in her eyes might've made me feel guilty if she hadn't been trying to off the woman I'd fallen in love with.

Fallen in love.

Damn.

"Yeah, freaking out is my default when a beautiful woman makes a move on me," I said, trying to be calm. "Fury even told you that."

I could feel Rylee's gaze on me and wondered if she knew how much of this was true.

Becky took a step closer. "But you don't have to freak out. I love you, Cory. I mean, I tried being subtle, but doesn't the fact that I kissed you mean you shouldn't be nervous."

"It does," I said. "Everything you did showed me how you felt...all those meals and stuff. It really meant a lot. No one's ever gone to such lengths just to get my attention."

The words felt wrong in my mouth, but I forced them out anyway.

"That's exactly what I'm hoping for," she replied, her grin growing wider and the gun slowly drifting downward, but still aimed at Rylee. "I knew we were on the same page. You always flash me that heart-melting smile when you see me, and don't even get me started on your chivalrous door-holding ways."

I resisted the urge to glance at Rylee, knowing it could spell disaster. I had to focus on Becky, keeping her gaze locked on mine.

"I'm sorry about the whole police charade," Becky went on. "But honestly, it's partially your own fault. You could've clued me in that you wanted me to take charge. Then I wouldn't have had to go to such insane lengths to show you we're meant to be."

"It's all water under the bridge," I said, hoping my face wasn't broadcasting my insincerity. "Everything's worked out in the end."

"Let's never go through that again," she said. "It was agonizing to say those awful things about you."

I could practically feel the steam coming out of Rylee's ears, and I silently prayed she'd keep her cool. I was just about to suggest that Becky send Rylee packing so we could have some alone time when everything went sideways.

"Let's ditch the dead weight so the witch can't meddle anymore," Becky growled.

Time seemed to slow down, and every little detail became painfully clear against the encroaching darkness.

Becky's face hardened, her eyes turning to ice, as she swung the gun upward, pointing directly at Rylee.

I reacted instinctually, launching myself sideways as I saw Becky's finger tighten on the trigger. It was a pure reflex move without thinking about it, and I hoped it would be enough.

There was a thud that felt like I'd been hit by a freight train, followed by screaming and then…nothingness.

THIRTY-EIGHT

Rylee

It happened so fast I didn't even move when Becky pointed the gun at me. Because one second it was aimed at me, and the next there was a loud boom and Cory was there and he was falling falling falling...

"No!" I screamed as he hit the floor, but it was like my body knew what to do before my brain could catch up. I lunged at Becky, every self-defense tip I'd ever read flashing through my mind in a split second.

In a swift motion, I pushed the gun to the side with one hand, ignoring the searing pain of the hard metal against my wrist. With the other hand, I landed a solid punch to Becky's cheek. She let out a shrill scream, but I didn't let it throw me off. I was laser-focused on getting that gun away from her.

The gun went off again, but I didn't worry about where the bullet went. As long as it wasn't heading in Cory's direction.

"You bitch!" Becky snarled, reaching for me. But I was ready for her. I grabbed her wrist, holding her at bay.

We struggled for a minute before I twisted her arm behind her back, tightening my grip until the gun fell to the floor. Ignoring the litany of filth pouring from her mouth, I used the leverage to force her to the floor and jammed my knee in her back.

"Let me go, you bitch! He's mine! You can't have him!"

When she turned her head and tried to bite me, I reacted on instinct and slammed her head into the floor. Her body went limp, and I might've felt guilty about it if I hadn't realized that Cory was still lying on the floor, not moving, not making a sound.

"Cory!" I hurried over to him, fear turning my blood to ice.

The floor beneath Cory was turning a gruesome shade of crimson, and I felt the wetness seeping through my pants as I crouched down beside him. My eyes started to sting as I gently rolled him onto his back. His shirt was drenched in blood - way too much for my liking. I could feel my chest tightening as I frantically tried to locate the source of the bleeding. And when I finally spotted the gaping hole in his shoulder, I quickly pressed my hands against it, leaning in closer to his face.

"Hey, buddy, getting shot doesn't give you a free pass to skip out on our chat," I whispered, putting on a brave face. "We've got some serious unfinished business to settle, and this is not how this story ends."

Before I could continue my one-sided conversation, a loud shout echoed from the hallway.

"Police!"

"Come in!" I hollered, tears streaming down my face. "Please, just get in here!"

"Is anyone armed?"

"No, the gun is on the floor, and someone's shot, so hurry up and get in here."

The door burst open before I could finish my sentence. Cops rushed in, guns drawn, and the room erupted into chaos. One of them had to physically pull me away from Cory, promising that medics were there and they'd get him to a hospital. My hands trembled as the officer knelt before me, his eyes filled with concern.

"Ma'am, are you okay? Are you hurt?" He squeezed my hands, trying to get my attention. "Ma'am?" The voice jolted me back to reality.

"I'm okay," I told the cop, my gaze fixed on Cory. "But is he gonna be okay?"

"We'll take care of him," the cop replied, gesturing towards the door. "You need to get checked out, too."

"No, I'm fine," I said, waving him off. "This blood isn't mine. Well, except for maybe a few drops on my knuckles from when I decked Becky and some scratches from our scuffle, but I'm not the one who got shot."

The cop raised an eyebrow. "I'm gonna need you to slow down a bit."

My eyes followed Cory as they wheeled him out on a stretcher, an oxygen mask over his face.

"Alright, let's take a seat," the cop suggested, guiding me to a table nearby.

I trailed after the cop, doing my best to avoid the splotches on the floor. There was the massive puddle where Cory had gone down and the scattered droplets from Becky's bloody nose. I secretly hoped I'd broken her schnoz. The thought was harsh, but she'd been acting like a complete lunatic, and it was obvious she was dealing with some heavy-duty mental health stuff. Still, it wasn't her crazy rants or her unhealthy fixation on Cory that pushed me over the edge. No, it was the fact she'd hurt him. Badly.

"Let's kick this off with the simple stuff," the officer said, pulling out a notepad from his pocket. "Name, please?"

Spilling the beans about what went down came naturally, mostly thanks to the cop's no-nonsense questions. It still hurt to go over the whole mess again, especially that god-awful moment when Cory took a bullet on my behalf. But somehow, Officer Truham's unflappable cool helped me keep my shit together.

And before I knew it, we were wrapping up.

"It looks like that's it for now," Officer Truham said, tucking away his notepad. "We'll give you a call if we need anything else."

I nodded, my hands pressing into the table as I pushed myself up. But then I saw the dried blood caked on my skin, and my heart started racing. It was like I couldn't catch my breath.

"You can use the bathroom to clean up," Officer Truham offered.

"Right. Thanks." I nodded again, but I couldn't seem to move.

"You still need to get checked out, so I'll take you to the hospital when you're ready to go."

Another nod from me, then a mumbled "thanks" as I made a beeline for the bathroom. I scrubbed my hands until they were red and raw, but no amount of soap could wash away the feeling of being stained. But it didn't matter. My main mission was getting to Cory, pronto.

Once my hands were as dry as they were going to get, I hightailed it back to Officer Truham. With the help of some ear-splitting sirens and blinding flashing lights, we pulled into the hospital parking lot fifteen minutes later. I thanked him before sprinting inside like my life depended on it.

I hurried to the front desk, asking about Cory McCrae. The woman there was in the middle of telling me she couldn't share information when I heard a gravelly voice behind me.

"Rylee?"

I turned to see Fury approaching, his face etched with worry. "How...?" I couldn't finish the question. I wasn't sure I wanted to know the answer.

"He's in surgery," Fury said, his voice as rugged as his appearance. "We just have to wait."

"Shit. I suck at waiting."

Fury nodded. "Me too." He gestured toward the elevators. "But at least we can suck at it together."

I looked up at him, his worry mirroring my own. "After you."

THIRTY-NINE

Cory

Beep. Beep. Beep. Beep.

The beeping noise was like a persistent mosquito, slowly pulling me from my dreamless slumber. I was groggy and disoriented, my mouth as dry as the Sahara and my eyelids heavy as lead.

I tried to swallow, but it felt like I was gargling with broken glass. Had I been sick? Why couldn't I remember? The questions should have sent me into a panic, but I just felt detached. My thoughts were like those of a curious bystander, observing the situation without getting emotionally involved.

It was then that the puzzle pieces started to click together. Well, some of them. Enough for me to realize that I had drugs in my system. And since I'd never been one to experiment with recreational substances, that meant I'd been to the doctor for something.

Doctor.

Beeping.

Hospital!

I was in the hospital, but not because I was sick. My throat was hurting for another reason. Probably the same reason I hadn't opened my eyes yet. Something had happened. I could feel it in my bones. But what? And how had that led to me being in the hospital? Had I been in a car accident? Fallen down the stairs?

Yes, I'd fallen. I remembered that now. I was hitting the ground- no, the floor- in my apartment.

But the fall hadn't put me here.

Something had hurt me.

A bright flash.

Not something. Some*one*.

Fuck.

Everything came rushing back all at once. Asking Rylee to come up to my apartment. Becky being there. With a gun. Trying to distract her from Rylee. Jumping to protect the woman I loved. Becky pulling the trigger.

Pain.

And that was it.

The beeping sped up as adrenaline flooded my system. I struggled to breathe as my chest tightened.

"Cory?" A voice I'd know anywhere. "Cory, babe, you're good. It's all good. I'm right here. You're good. Just open those eyes, and you'll see."

Rylee. That was her voice, but I had to see her, make sure Becky hadn't hurt her. I tried to pry open my eyelids- just for a second at first, long enough to catch a glimpse of those worried amber eyes locked on me. And that was all the motivation I needed to give it another shot. And another until I could keep my eyes open and focus on the face that had become my everything.

"Cory." Rylee practically choked on my name as she pressed my hand to her forehead. "I was freaking out."

"You said everything was cool." My voice was barely a whisper. I cleared my throat and winced.

"Let me grab you some water." She hopped up, wiping her cheeks with the back of her hands. "You had a ventilator during surgery, so your throat's gotta be killing you. I should've thought of that sooner."

I wanted to reassure her that my throat was the least of my worries, that her well-being was what truly mattered. But dang, the pain was a stubborn beast. So, I settled for watching her as she headed towards the pitcher of water, trying to decipher her body language for any hints of discomfort. Luckily, she seemed to be moving without any trouble, and I couldn't see any bruises. The relief that washed over me was more potent than any painkiller, and I released a small sigh of relief.

"Here." She held the cup to my lips, giving me a look that dared me to argue. I wasn't used to being bossed around, but I obeyed, sipping water from the straw until the burn in my throat subsided. I leaned back against the pillow, completely wiped out from that tiny effort. It was then that I noticed the scrapes on her knuckles.

"What happened?" I reached for her, but the IV in my hand tugged at my skin, stopping me short.

Rylee blushed, taking my hand and letting me inspect her knuckles. "I may have broken Becky's nose," she said.

"You did what?" I tried to sit up, but the pain shooting through me made me think better of it.

"Sit back," she said, something like panic in her eyes. "You got shot, and you're worried about my hand?"

"Of course I'm freaking out about your hand," I said, squeezing it gently. "Don't you see I'm so head-over-heels in love with you that worrying about you was the one thing that dragged me out of the abyss?"

Her breath hitched as she absorbed my words, and I could feel my heart racing. The monitor next to me beeped wildly in response, betraying my nerves. Rylee locked eyes with me and leaned in, brushing her lips against mine in a soft kiss.

"And I'm so crazy, wildly, ridiculously in love with you that seeing you on the floor, bleeding and unconscious, was like being sucker-punched by life itself. I mean, seriously, you getting shot was the most terrifying moment of my entire existence."

I raised my free hand and rested it on her cheek, giving her a weak smile. "I just couldn't let that psycho hurt you, you know?"

Rylee nuzzled her face into my palm, pressing a tender kiss on the center. "Well, you didn't, my prince," she replied with a teasing grin.

"You sure you're okay?" I gently swept my thumb over her scraped knuckles. "She didn't...you know?"

Rylee flashed me a cheeky grin. "Nope, not even close." She recounted the story with a gleam in her eyes. "I clocked her one right in the nose, snatched the gun, and then sent her crashing to the floor."

My heart skipped a beat. "Wait, you...seriously?!"

Before I could press Rylee for more details, the door to my hospital room swung open, and a man in a white coat and green scrubs walked in. Rylee took a step back and started making her way toward the door.

"Whoa, hey, don't go just like that!" I blurted out, my voice laced with panic.

Rylee flashed me a smile. "Fury and your folks went to grab some coffee. They're gonna want to know you're back in the land of the living. I'll go give 'em the good news."

"Yeah, yeah, but you gotta promise me you'll come right back," I pleaded, not even trying to hide the desperation in my voice. I was done pretending she wasn't the center of my universe.

Taking a bullet tends to have that effect on a person.

"I promise," Rylee whispered, her voice as soft as a summer breeze. "I'll be back before you know it."

"Mr. McCrae," the doctor said, drawing my attention to him as Rylee vanished from sight. "How's my patient?"

With Rylee's antics playing on repeat in my head, I barely managed to answer the doctor's questions and digest the details of my injury. By the time he finished his spiel, a knock echoed through the room.

The doc's lips curled into a half-smile. "I'm guessing that's your anxious parents and the lovely lady who's been your shadow since she was allowed in. I'll go let them in."

I gave a nod, fidgeting to find a comfortable position that didn't make me feel like, well, a guy who'd been shot in the shoulder. Moments later, the door swung open, and my stepmom, Theresa, darted to my side, her dark eyes brimming with concern.

"Hey, Mom," I greeted her, watching as her eyes sparkled with the same warmth they always did when I called her that. She never expected any of us McCrae boys to do it, just like my dad never expected the Carideo kids to call him Da. But it always made them grin from ear to ear when we did.

"Out of all you lads," Da said, stepping up beside her and shaking his head in disbelief. "You were the last one I thought I'd have to worry about getting shot." He reached down to give my hand a reassuring squeeze. "Let's none of you try to give me a heart attack for at least a year, aye?"

"Aye," I replied smiling, trying to lighten the mood. Carson and I had been so young when we left Scotland that we hadn't retained much of the accent or lingo, but occasionally, we'd throw it in just to make our family chuckle. And after all the worry this had caused them, it was a good way to let them know I was going to be okay.

"You're an idiot." Fury nudged my foot as he stopped at the end of the bed. "How can you not recognize psycho pussy when you see one?"

"Fury." Theresa shot him a warning look. "He just got out of surgery."

He shrugged. "At least I'm not punching him in his shoulder. I think that counts as restraint."

"Don't worry, Cory," Rylee chimed in as she came around to the far side of the bed. "I've got your back."

"I'd take that anytime," I said, reaching for her hand. "Word on the street is my woman broke Becky's nose and then body-slammed her to the floor."

"You bet." Rylee brushed some hair back from my face. "Anyone messes with you, they're gonna have to deal with me."

"Right back at ya," I said, giving her hand a squeeze. "We've got each other's backs."

For a moment, it was just Rylee and me in the world. I

forgot where we were and that we had an audience. Then Fury cleared his throat, and when I looked at him, he shot a pointed glance at our parents.

Oh right.

"You've met my parents?" I asked.

"Sort of," Rylee said, her smile becoming shy. "I wasn't actually sure how to introduce myself."

I intertwined my fingers with hers and turned toward my parents, watching the exchange with amused smiles.

"Mom, Dad, this is Rylee Palmer. My, uh, girlfriend." I might've been presumptuous, and Rylee's raised eyebrow suggested I'd hear about it later, but she didn't disagree.

"Rylee, these are my folks, Patrick and Theresa."

"Nice to meet you," Theresa said, her eyes gleaming. "And thank you for what you did for Cory."

"He kinda took a bullet for me," Rylee pointed out.

"But you ensured that woman couldn't hurt him even more," Theresa countered. "Thank you."

Before we could continue our conversation, the door swung open, and a nurse announced it was time for my visitors to leave so I could rest. I wanted to argue, but I could feel my energy waning, and she was right. I needed to sleep.

Rylee gave my hand a little tug, but I held on for dear life. "Hey, how 'bout you hang out for a bit?" I asked my voice just a hair above a murmur. "Maybe until I doze off?"

She hesitated for a moment, then scooted closer and planted a soft kiss on my forehead. "Alright, deal."

The knowledge that she'd be there when I opened my eyes again made me throw in the towel. Her face was the last thing I saw before I let sleep sweep me away.

FORTY

Rylee

Cory McCrae was hellbent on giving me a heart attack. Instead of bouncing back quickly and heading home the day after his surgery, he contracted an infection and extended his stay several days, hooked up to an IV of antibiotics. To say I'd been a little preoccupied would be an understatement - I'd barely set foot in the office all week, and my apartment had seen me even less.

Cory had tried hard to shoo me home for some shut-eye, but I'd seen the conflict lurking in his eyes, so I stayed as long as I could.

Fast forward to Friday afternoon, and Cory finally got the green light from the doctor to be discharged. I hightailed it home to quickly sweep the place while Cory waited for the paperwork. I knew he'd want to leave as soon as he was allowed - he'd been trying to talk his way out of there since the day before, but the doctors weren't budging. They wanted to make sure that everything healed correctly before they let him loose.

I was certain that the doc's persistence in keeping Cory in the hospital had a little something to do with Fury's not-so-subtle threat of suing if Cory wasn't in tip-top shape when they released him. Not that I'd breathed a word of this to Cory. He'd be seeing red, and let's be real, Fury was just being an overprotective pain in the ass.

So, I sweet-talked the docs into letting Cory out if he had someone to keep an eye on him. I promised them he could stay at my place for a couple of days. His apartment was still a crime scene, and neither of us was in a hurry to deal with those memories. Thankfully, Fury had hired a professional cleaning crew to scrub the place down, and he swore there'd be no reminders left once they were done.

I wasn't sure if I could ever set foot in Cory's apartment again after what happened, but if he felt the need to move back, I'd find a way to deal with it. For now, we were crashing at my place.

I picked up Cory that same afternoon. He was still a bit on the pasty side, but a definite improvement from earlier. Once I tucked him into my car and we rolled out of the hospital parking lot, I could finally relax a bit.

"So, uh, I did some thrilling stuff while you were still stuck in the hospital bed all day," I said, glancing over at Cory in the passenger seat. He raised an eyebrow, a small smile playing on his lips. "Yeah, like filling out hospital paperwork and picking up your prescription. You know, the usual rock-star lifestyle."

Cory chuckled, wincing slightly as he shifted in his seat. "Sounds like a wild time. I'm glad I missed it."

I rolled my eyes, grinning. "Oh, you have no idea."

We lapsed into a comfortable silence for a few minutes,

the only sound the hum of the car engine. I glanced over at Cory again, noticing how his eyes kept drifting closed. He looked exhausted, and I couldn't blame him.

"Hey, if you want to take a nap or something, it's okay," I said, keeping my voice low. "We're still a ways from my place."

Cory shook his head, forcing his eyes open. "Nah, I'm good. I don't want to miss out on any more of your riveting conversation."

I snorted. "Yeah, yeah. Keep it up, and I might have to start charging admission."

Cory grinned, his eyes drifting closed once more. "Just promise me one thing."

"What's that?"

"No more hospital paperwork," he mumbled, his voice barely above a whisper.

I laughed, shaking my head. "Deal."

By the time I got him home and settled on my couch, I was all set to propose a chill evening of take-out and classic flicks. But it seemed Cory had ideas of his own.

Grabbing my wrist, he pressed his lips to the back of my hand, sending a shiver down my spine, an exquisite tremor of delight. My body ached for him, craving his touch; it had been merely a week since we last had sex, yet my desire felt insatiable. Our kisses at the hospital had been chaste, stolen moments tainted by the sterile air and the ever-present hum of monitors.

"Cory..." I tried to sound stern, a feeble warning, but my hand willingly lingered in his grasp.

"Come here, Ry." His voice morphed into an authoritative growl, instantly dampening my panties. "I need a taste."

Raising a skeptical eyebrow, I leaned in, granting him a fleeting peck on the lips. Before I could retreat, his other hand snaked around my neck, keeping me close as he intensified the kiss. His tongue traced my lips, coaxing them open, and I released a faint, desperate whimper as I yielded to him. As he explored my mouth, the tender pressure on my neck and hand gradually pulled me onto his lap, my legs instinctively parting to straddle him, my knees hugging his thighs.

At last, I broke the kiss, my breath ragged as I struggled to regain control. The mere thought of his lips on mine sent a shiver through me, and I craved him with a ferocity I'd never known. I let out a frustrated moan and closed my eyes, resting my forehead against his.

"You're still recovering."

"Being inside you will make me heal faster." His hands caressed my hips, his fingers digging into my skin.

My eyes flew open, and I laughed, but it was a breathless sound that betrayed the intensity of my desire. My stomach fluttered with each sensation he evoked, both physical and emotional.

"I had a chat with the doc before heading out," he murmured, his hands gliding down my thighs, tracing the edge of my dress where it pooled around my knees. The skilled touch of his fingers on the exposed skin below sent a tremor rippling through me. "Apparently, sex is good to go, as long as I don't get too... ambitious."

"Ambitious?" I shivered, my breaths shallow.

"Guess I won't be pinning you against a mirror in a dressing room anytime soon," he joked, his voice husky with restrained desire.

I ran my fingers through his hair even as his hands

slipped beneath my dress, hot palms skimming over my flesh. Maybe lust was overpowering my reason, but I knew he wouldn't lie to me about this. I rocked against the bulge pressing against me, smiling at the groan I elicited.

"So, if I were to, y'know, slip my hand down there and pull out Mr. Happy, then tug my panties to the side and, uh, lower myself onto that impressive package," I emphasized my point by grinding against him, "that'd be A-OK by Doc's standards?"

He chuckled, but it was laced with an edge of raw, untamed lust. It rolled over me like a wave, heating me up from the inside.

"Yeah, it would," he managed to say, his fingers inching higher until he hooked onto my panties.

My hand gave him a little squeeze through his pants, effectively silencing him. "If it hurts, even a little, you tell me. Deal?"

He nodded, his green eyes blazing with desire.

With eyes locked in a sultry gaze, I executed my plan, hoisting myself up and freeing his rock-hard cock from its confines. I didn't bother removing his clothes; I just grasped him firmly and pulled him out, reveling in the velvet feel of his throbbing length against my palm.

A deep groan escaped his lips as his hands dug into my hips, holding me close.

Using my newfound freedom, I moved one hand to the damp cotton barrier between us. I tugged it aside and positioned myself above him, taking just an inch of him inside me. Our moans harmonized as I paused, allowing my body to adjust to his size. We hadn't warmed up much, and he filled me completely. Despite the initial discomfort, I continued to lower myself on his cock, inch by exquisite inch, each pinch and stretch sending shockwaves through my overloaded nerves.

Once fully seated on his lap, I placed my hands on his chest, and he reached under my dress to cup my breasts. His skilled fingers rolled my nipples in a slow, deliberate rhythm, setting the tempo for our lovemaking. I mirrored his movements, grinding my hips in a hypnotic dance that was as much about pressure as it was friction. I clenched around him, finding the perfect angle to rub against my clit with every motion.

As the pleasure built to an intense, uncontainable crescendo, his mouth captured mine, pulling me tight against his chest. I danced my tongue along his, careful to avoid his still-healing wound. When his hips bucked beneath me, I feared I might have hurt him, but then I felt his breath hitch, and I knew he was close. So was I, the tension of the past week bubbling to the surface, demanding release.

His mouth tore away from mine, a strangled cry escaping his lips as he lost control. The primal sound sent me over the edge, and I screamed his name, careful not to clutch his injured shoulder. I clung to him, my body shuddering as he filled me with his cum, our connection raw and intimate.

He smoothed my hair and pressed a tender kiss to the top of my head. Then he whispered the words I longed to hear.

"I love you."

I shifted slightly, eliciting a groan, and replied, "I love you, too."

Soon, we would pull apart and move on with our evening, but for now, this was exactly where I wanted to be, and he was exactly who I wanted to be with.

EPILOGUE

Cory

High sixties and a touch of sunshine? That's practically a dream come true for a Seattle May wedding, and today was my brother Alec's big day. I was more than grateful for the weather and even more so for the woman on my arm. With my extensive family tree, weddings could get a tad complicated, but Alec and his lovely bride Lumen had made it simple by only having her adopted daughter Soleil and his own daughter Evanne as their wedding party. So there I was, sitting cozy next to Rylee throughout the ceremony and now leading her into the colossal reception space Alec had rented.

"You know," Rylee mused as we entered, "it's one thing to hear about your sibling count, but it's a whole other ballgame to see it in person."

"Don't worry. We won't quiz you." My older brother Brody flashed a grin at Rylee. "Hey, I'm Brody."

"Hi." Rylee's smile was radiant. "And your wife is Freedom, right?"

"That's her." His eyes gleamed with love as he glanced at

his very pregnant wife. "Her sister, Aline, is over there with our brother Eoin."

It was hard not to smile at the sight of that couple. Eoin's war injuries had almost wrecked him, but then he'd fallen head over heels for Aline, and he'd truly started to heal.

A stirring behind us caught our attention. My sister Maggie and her husband Drake both had wounds that could've left them broken, but instead, they'd found strength together. Their twins were due soon, and my sister had never looked more stunning despite the exhaustion.

Carson, my twin brother, popped up out of nowhere. "Hey, bro. Vix and I saved you guys a spot." He nodded towards the table where Fury was already seated with Rome and Paris. "They're probably concocting some wild drinking game as we speak."

I rolled my eyes, looking over at Rylee. "That could be trouble."

She grinned mischievously. "Sounds like a blast, actually. It's been weeks since I've let my hair down."

Memories of her drunk and groping me sent blood rushing south. "Let me get you a glass of champagne, dear." I winked at her as I flagged down a waiter.

Forty minutes had flown by, and there I was, kicking back in my chair, totally entranced by Rylee. She was playfully ribbing Fury about a golden opportunity he'd missed that had scored Palmer Money Management a chunk of change for their clients. Smart cookie that she was, she steered clear of the whole Natalie debacle, which had crashed and burned after Fury got a little too chummy with some other woman. But hey, Fury hadn't been cheating or anything, just being his usual perceptive self, or so he said. Me? I was happy admiring one woman for the long haul.

From the get-go, Rylee was like a refreshing gust of wind compared to the usual ladies I'd cross paths with. Most would've been intimidated by my family, feeling like a fish out of water, but not Rylee. She slid into our tribe as smoothly as a dolphin diving into the ocean waves without needing a bottle of "liquid courage" to steady her nerves. The two glasses of champagne she'd downed only added to her unfiltered charm, which had everyone but Fury and me in hysterics. Because most of her stories? They were all about the two of us.

Carson gave me a nod that could only mean one thing - I had nailed it. I glanced at his stunning fiancée and echoed his gesture. We were two lucky dudes, for sure.

"How's the shoulder holding up?" Paris chimed in, her eyes filled with worry. "I wanted to swing by the hospital, but Mom said it was best to give you some space since we'd all be together at the wedding."

"It's on the mend," I assured her, shifting my focus from Rylee to my elder stepsister. "The infection threw a wrench in things, but I've been keeping up with physical therapy and following the doctor's orders, and it's coming along."

"You back in your pad yet?" Rome piped up, my stepbrother. "Or have you been crashing at hotels all week?"

"He's been bunking with me," Rylee said, joining the conversation. "But I'll have to show him the door soon. He's a very inconsiderate houseguest."

"What? No way!" Vix seemed taken aback, likely missing the twinkle in Rylee's eyes.

"Oh yeah." Rylee flashed a grin. "I hardly get a wink of sleep."

Vix's cheeks flushed pink, and she glanced at my brother. "Guess twins really do share a lot in common."

The table exploded in chuckles as Carson and I did our best to keep our grins in check. We finished our meal, and just as I was about to lean back, Rylee's hand found mine under the table. She gave it a quick, secret squeeze before standing up.

With a polite smile, she announced, "If you'll excuse me, I'm just gonna duck out for a second before the happy couple slices into that cake."

I might've missed that sly little wink she threw my way if I hadn't been so hyper-aware of her every move. What a sneak! Was she suggesting a little private time during the wedding? Here?

Oh, man. That mischievous minx. I couldn't get enough of her.

With the cake-cutting commotion starting, I discreetly trailed after Rylee, my gut telling me she wasn't just seeking a breath of fresh air. Sure enough, she'd tucked herself into a hidden nook of the garden, her eyes gleaming with a wicked glint.

"Well, well, well," she purred, a sly grin playing on her lips. "Fancy meeting you here."

"Just can't resist your charm, can I?" I shot back, my heart hammering in my chest. The air between us crackled with electricity, and I could barely contain my anticipation.

"I suppose I'll have to take your word for it," she replied coyly. "But first, I need a little...proof."

Without a moment's hesitation, Rylee's mouth crashed

into mine, her lips hungry and insistent. I eagerly reciprocated, yanking her flush against me, and in a swift motion, pinned her against the stone wall. Our kiss intensified, each passing second more urgent than the last as if we were trying to consume each other whole.

A primal craving surged within me.

With ragged breaths, I finally tore myself away, yearning to witness the naked desire smoldering in her eyes. "Cory!" she cried out as I hiked up her dress and delved my fingers into the slick heat of her panties.

"I'm dying to see you come undone," I said, my voice rough and gravelly. "I need to hear you shouting my name at the top of your lungs while I send you tumbling headfirst into pure bliss."

With every word, I teased her swollen clit, relishing the way her body trembled beneath my touch. She writhed and squirmed as if trying to escape my grasp, but we both knew that wasn't an option. She was along for the wild, orgasmic ride.

As I continued to explore her slick folds, Rylee's breath hitched, and her eyes fluttered closed. "Cory, please," she begged, her voice barely above a whisper. "I need more."

And with that, I plunged two fingers deep inside her, curling them to hit that sweet spot that never failed to make her see stars. She cried out, her body bucking against my hand as I mercilessly drove her closer and closer to the edge.

"That's it, baby," I murmured, my lips brushing against her ear. "Let go. Let me take care of you."

And with one final, shuddering gasp, Rylee did just that, her body convulsing around my fingers as she surrendered to the intense wave of pleasure that washed over her. As she rode out the last of her orgasm, I gently withdrew my hand, pressing a tender kiss to her lips.

"I think it's safe to say," I whispered, a smug grin spreading across my face, "that I've proved my point."

Rylee chuckled breathlessly, her eyes shining with satisfaction. "I'd say you've more than proved it," she agreed, her voice still tinged with desire. "But remember, Cory – I always pay my debts."

And with that, she pushed me back, her eyes gleaming with mischief as she dropped to her knees before me. Her fingers, nimble and deft, worked at my belt with an expertise that left me breathless. The sound of the leather sliding through the loops seemed to echo in the stillness, a tantalizing promise of what was to come.

Rylee's amber eyes never left mine as she slowly unzipped my pants, the anticipation building with each passing second. The air around us seemed to crackle with electricity, and I could feel my heart pounding in my chest. I looked around, my gaze darting from one end of the garden to the other, and luckily, no one seemed to have spotted us. The thought of being caught only added to the thrill, and I felt a shiver run down my spine.

Oh, yeah, Rylee was definitely trouble – and I wouldn't have it any other way. From the very beginning, something about her fiery spirit and competitive nature drew me in and captivated me. She's a force to be reckoned with, and I knew that life with her would never be dull.

As she pulled my pants down, her fingers brushing against my skin, I bit my lip, trying to contain the moan that threatened to escape, but it was no use. Rylee's touch was like a drug, and I was already addicted.

"Now," she purred, her voice low and sultry, "it's your turn to see stars."

And with that, she leaned forward, her lips closing around me, and I knew that I was in for the ride of my life.

THE END

The Scottish Billionaires continues with Fury's story, coming soon. Until then, turn the page to see a description of all the books available in the series:

THE SCOTTISH BILLIONAIRES SERIES

Alec & Lumen:
When Alec mistakes a young woman's salon for a "happy ending" massage parlor, things get more complicated than he prefers. Especially when their lives become entwined in ways never imagined.

Prequel
1. *Off Limits*
2. *Breaking Rules*
3. *Mending Fate*

Eoin & Aline:
After Aline Mercier, a young American teacher, is taken hostage in Iran, Eoin McCrae is tasked with getting her out at all cost. He never imagined falling for her.

1. *Strangers in Love*
2. *Dangers of Love*

Brody & Freedom:
At his distillery, Brody McCrae crafts the finest Scottish

THE SCOTTISH BILLIONAIRES SERIES

whiskey, while Freedom Mercier is finishing her Master's degree with big plans to change the world. When the two of them are brought together at a holiday party, things heat up more than anyone could predict.

1. *Single Malt*
2. *Perfect Blend*

Baylen & Harlee:
After Baylen McFann discovers that his fiancée has left him, he escapes Scotland to find advice from his friend across the pond, Alec McCrae. As Alec presents his newest statistical analyst, Harlee Sumpter, Baylen's already smitten.

Business or Pleasure

Drake & Maggie:
When Drake Mac Gilleain lays eyes on Maggie McCrae, he believes he's seeing the ghost of his late wife and decides to follow her.

At First Sight

Carson & Vix:
When Carson McCrae, the hottest designer in Manhattan, asked me to model a new bra in a fashion show, I knew it was a line. I'm anything but a runway model. I got more curves than Kim Kardashian.
It was definitely a line. So why did I say yes?

A Dress for Curves

Spencer & London
Spencer York, a dashing and distinguished British theater

THE SCOTTISH BILLIONAIRES SERIES

producer, arrives in Manhattan with the exciting prospects of bringing his production to Broadway's illustrious stages. Destiny steers him to a cozy, intimate pub where he encounters London McCrae, a fiery and ambitious actress with dreams of conquering Broadway's greatest stages.
A Play for Love

Blaze & Trisha
Airport closed and stranded by a Christmas storm, Blaze and Trisha embark on a cross-country road trip from Chicago to San Francisco, discovering laughter, chemistry, and challenges that test their pact to remain just travel buddies.
Mistletoe Detour

Cory & Rylee
Cory McCrae, a charming hunk yet socially awkward finance guru, clashes with Rylee Palmer, a brilliant rival, sparking an intense, steamy romance amid a fierce rivalry and a scandal that threatens their passionate connection.
Rival Desires